Fiona Farrell is one of New Zealand's leading writers. Born in Oamaru and educated at the universities of Otago and Toronto, she has published volumes of poetry, collections of short stories, non-fiction works, and many novels.

In 2007 she received the Prime Minister's Award for Fiction, and in 2012 was appointed an Officer of the New Zealand Order of Merit for services to literature.

The Broken Book, a book of essays relating to the Christchurch earthquakes, was shortlisted for the non-fiction award in the 2012 Book Awards and critically greeted as the 'first major artwork' to emerge from the event. *The Villa at the Edge of the Empire* was also shortlisted for this award in 2016.

Her work, which *The New Zealand Herald* has praised for its 'richness — of both theme and language', has been published around the world, including in the US, France and the UK.

THE DECK
FIONA FARRELL

VINTAGE

VINTAGE

UK | USA | Canada | Ireland | Australia
India | New Zealand | South Africa | China

Vintage is an imprint of the Penguin Random House group of companies, whose addresses can be found at global.penguinrandomhouse.com.

First published by Penguin Random House New Zealand, 2023

10 9 8 7 6 5 4 3 2 1

Text © Fiona Farrell, 2023

The moral right of the author has been asserted.

All rights reserved. Without limiting the rights under copyright reserved above, no part of this publication may be reproduced, stored in or introduced into a retrieval system, or transmitted, in any form or by any means (electronic, mechanical, photocopying, recording or otherwise), without the prior written permission of both the copyright owner and the above publisher of this book.

Design by Gemma Parmentier © Penguin Random House New Zealand
Frame art by iStock.com/akbars
Author photograph by Caroline Davies
Prepress by Soar Communications Group
Printed and bound in Australia by Griffin Press, an Accredited ISO AS/NZS 14001 Environmental Management Systems Printer

A catalogue record for this book is available from the National Library of New Zealand.

ISBN 978-1-77695-000-3
eISBN 978-1-77695-377-6

The assistance of Creative New Zealand towards the production of this book is gratefully acknowledged by the publisher.

penguin.co.nz

For Eleni, Huia, Alseia and Ngaio

The things of this world have no stability, but are ever undergoing change.

The Decameron by Giovanni Boccaccio

CONTENTS

10   The Frame

36   The Novel

    37   The First Day
    50   The Second Day
    65   The Second Night
    92   The Third Day
   127   The Third Night
   161   The Fourth Day
   193   The Fourth Night
   221   The Fifth Day
   248   The Fifth Night
   273   The Sixth Day

284   The Author's Conclusion

THE FRAME

Here you are: a novel. From my fingers to your hand, from my eye to your eye, from the crevices of my crumpled brain to the crevices of yours.

The novelist is making a novel.

She is making it on an Apple Mac in a small room overlooking a small city on an island in the southern corner of a vast ocean.

Midsummer.

Sunlight glints on a harbour and a breeze bellies the curtains at an open window. An undifferentiated hum of traffic and machinery rises from the city. Someone is drilling something in the old Edwardian villa next door and across the road the children at the day-care centre are banging away on the big xylophone they bring outside on sunny days. Overlying the hum is a cheerful gamelan bing bang bong.

Beyond the harbour stretches the ocean, bordered as usual at the horizon by the mass of cloud that could be hills or snow-capped mountains. Air and vapour only but so seemingly solid that Captain Cook, sailing down this coast on his first voyage, detoured many miles to the east over three days in order to satisfy his lieutenant that this was no great continent. 'In search of Mr Gore's imaginary land,' he wrote grumpily in his journal. He himself was 'very certain we saw only clouds'.

The imaginary land has always been present. The novelist remembers it from earliest childhood when she sat crammed with her sister in the back seat of the Austin Standard on Sunday afternoons, her family parked up at Friendly Bay eating ice-creams and looking out to sea, as islanders do. The cool lick of Raspberry Ripple and the cloudy mountains that were the place called Overseas. People sometimes flew there and when they returned they brought pictures to project on the sitting-room wall of palm trees and palaces and skyscrapers and places where the streets were made of water and places where people rode on camels and elephants. Overseas. The bright colours of the cloud land overlaid the beige stripes of the sitting-room wallpaper.

But today the pictures are not so pretty. A plague is raging and the pictures of Overseas are the deserted boulevard, the crowded hospital ICU, the army trucks queuing in the piazza to collect the coffins, the city park crisscrossed with burial trenches. It is months now since the novelist looked up a place called 'Wuhan' and its dubious 'wet market'. Months since she looked up 'pangolins', such sweet little vectors of catastrophe with their coats of armour-plating and their long snuffly noses. Months since she looked up a virus that appeared online as a soft little ball ornamented all over with tassels of red or blue. This past Christmas a woman in the novelist's city crocheted Covid-shaped tree decorations. A dark joke but it proved popular. The novelist bought a few to hang among the tinsel.

Deadly viruses do not necessarily declare themselves by looking repellent. Tuberculosis, for example. When the microbiologist Robert Koch back in 1882 first discovered the tiny silvery rods of *Mycobacterium tuberculosis,* killer of millions for millennia, he thought them 'beautiful'.

For months now, the news has been of global death and infection, the numbers reported daily like some hideous league table that implicitly pits nation against nation, leader against leader, health system against health system, political structure against political structure. Within the past 24 hours the novelist knows this plague has caused 563 deaths in the UK, 1807 in the US, 469 in Brazil, 361 in Italy and on and on, each death its own little individual horror of breathlessness, the lungs choking on dead cells, clots clumping in the blood vessels of the brain, confusion, seizure, stroke, liver failure, kidney collapse. Each number is a woman, a man, who was born into their own world of light and lived there until the virus and the moment where they lay face down on the gurney, going out naked into the dark, profoundly alone.

Today on the league table, the novelist's country has scored zero. For months it has scored zero.

First there was the silence. The country shut down and silence fell. The CBDs emptied as workers retreated to work from home. The motorways emptied, and the airports where planes had roared in, bringing the tourists to see the tree in the lake, the chapel in the carpark, the casino with the pokies, the hotel room with the view of the mountains, and the bridge where it was possible to catch a curated glimpse of your own death from the end of a rubber bungy. The ports emptied where

The Deck

cruise ships had disgorged thousands onto the streets to buy jade carved into the shapes of kiwi and koru. They had bought woollen socks and were taken on the buses to see a sheep being shorn and a cathedral that had fallen down in an earthquake and a vineyard where they could buy pinot noir and sauvignon.

Then the silence. Tourist hotels were repurposed as quarantine facilities as the country threw up defences at speed, using whatever came to hand, like people tearing up the paving stones to erect barricades across a city street. Thirty-two hotels in five cities, Crown Plaza and Holiday Inn, Novotel and Chateau on the Park, with their dimly lit bars and luxury spas, their Superior Rooms and Business Centres, speedily adapted to accommodate a new trade. Wire cordons surrounded their perimeter at street level.

The novelist has looked up at the concrete cliff as she walked past. She's no scientist. She imagines a kind of burr, like a miniature biddy-bid, waiting up there, prepared to attach itself to any unwary passer-by. She imagines a tiny sequin floating on the air between strangers. She has read that it is not even properly alive, being unable to generate ATP, adenosine triphosphate, the fundamental source of the energy of life. Incapable of reproduction, except within a living host. She imagines it up there in the hotel, being sapped of its strange parasitic power in isolation in a room equipped with a super-king bed, Netflix on demand and a view of the CBD.

On this sunny day, the quarantine hotels have become familiar. Like face masks, and the 1pm press briefings where the prime minister stands at one podium and the director-general of health stands at the other and the sign-language interpreter stands between. On either side, the calm recital in the new language of detection, containment, contact tracing, genome sequencing, all of it translated at the centre into a dazzling flurry of flying hands and mobile face. The reports deliver reassurance and a graph of mortality that remains a flat line, while beyond the cloud barrier in the world of Overseas the graphs are jagged mountain ranges of spikes and sharp ascents.

The novelist receives messages from beyond the barrier. A friend in Italy has spent weeks in confinement in a city apartment, busying herself preparing radio programmes but unable to attend the concerts she loves, unable even to visit her son who lives nearby. 'Is this to be my old age?' she writes. 'Is this how I will have to spend the rest of my life?' A friend in New York writes that her father has died of the virus and her mother, too, is terribly ill and cannot be visited. 'We are here in our apartment across town, feeling helpless and grief-stricken and trying to keep calm.' The novelist hears from friends confined with rambunctious children in a small English terrace house. 'We are going mad!' they say. Their voices reach her like the cries of seabirds, plaintive and far away. Unbearably sad. She finds herself replying carefully, omitting mention of the family camping trip at Christmas, the concert in a crowded auditorium, cheerful ordinary things. She does not want to make friends for whom such things are impossible feel more unhappy.

Her room in the house is a sunlit citadel defended by thousands. Battalions of nurses and cleaners and cooks and drivers and security staff are holding the front line at the quarantine hotels. Scientists and laboratory technicians are tracking and tracing with a speed and precision that to the novelist seems completely miraculous. Battalions of IT experts, data analysts, designers of public information campaigns, the civil servants staffing government departments, the ministers and members of Parliament who volunteered for office and found themselves administering a crisis. The director-general of health. The prime minister, the gifted and remarkable Jacinda, the Joan of Arc who leads it all from the front, encouraging, cajoling, choosing the strategic direction.

It's a citizens' army, the greatest peacetime mobilisation in this country's history. This calm sunny day, the children at their day-care centre, the flat line on the graph are its dazzling achievements. They should be celebrated, these cleaners and nurses and laboratory technicians and the rest. The novelist's country has sent men off to do battle in some pointless war-to-end-all-wars with greater fanfare, and hailed them more effusively on their return with medals, trumpets and drums. Historians have pored over the most minute details of their engagements. Poets have lauded their courage, their readiness for self-sacrifice. And it is right of course that they should have done so.

But this force, engaged with an infinitely more potent invisible enemy, has remained largely unsung. Its slightest mishap has been greeted by howls of outrage from the parliamentary opposition — it's politics, after all — and reported in the press in a barrage of alliteration: BORDER BUNGLE! BORDER BOTCHUP! TOTAL SYSTEMIC FAILURE! A SHAMBLES! CHAOS!

But right here, right now on this sunlit morning, it is not a shambles. It is not chaos. Bing bang bong go the children on their xylophone. The city hums happily to itself as it goes about its customary business. It is a fragile calm, of course — the calm of a sunlit savannah in some wildlife documentary where animals peaceably browse, though their ears flicker. They

The Frame

are alert to the slightest rustling in the long grass, when they will rise as one, take flight, stampede from the predator that is seeking out their weakest members. The old, the infirm, the very young. They will scatter and run.

This day is like that. Its sunny calm could shatter in a second. The novelist in her room, the city below, all the people who live on these islands in this corner of the ocean are no more than a breath away from disaster, death, economic collapse. They are only a heartbeat away from a complete revisioning of their existence.

The novelist knows this.

And how does she know it?

Because it has happened before.

She has read about it.

Two small volumes, hardback in faded red cloth, lie beside the Apple Mac. *The Decameron* by the fourteenth-century Florentine scholar Giovanni Boccaccio. This edition is small and shabby, with lots of underlinings and scribbled notes in the margins, the kind of thing that makes a second-hand book so much better than a pristine reprint. It was published in 1930 as one of the one thousand classics the publisher Joseph Dent intended for the edification of Everyman, and presumably, though she is, as usual, not mentioned, Everywoman.

> *I say, then, that the years of beatific incarnation*
> *of the Son of God had reached one thousand three*
> *hundred and forty eight when in the illustrious*
> *city of Florence, the fairest of all the cities of Italy,*

The Deck

> *there made its appearance that deadly pestilence which, whether disseminated by the influence of celestial bodies, or sent upon us mortals by God in His just wrath by way of retribution for our iniquities, had had its origin some years before in the East, where after destroying an innumerable multitude of living beings, it had propagated itself without respite from place to place, and so, calamitously had spread into the West . . .*

This is how it starts, with a prologue by the author, factual and autobiographical, to a collection of one hundred tales told by ten young Florentines — seven women and three men — who have fled to the country to escape the bubonic plague that is devastating their city. One hundred tales told over ten days in the leafy grounds of a villa beyond the city limits. Each afternoon, after dining on dainties and fine wines, the ten recline in the shade entertaining one another with music and dancing and by telling tales to a theme chosen by whomever they have nominated to be queen or king for that day. One hundred tales of love and adventure and a grunty sexual comedy so ribald that prudish English translators have traditionally left one whole section, the tenth tale on the third day, in its original Italian. (It's a story about a naïve young nun being instructed by a randy old hermit on how best to serve God and restrain the Devil by trapping him in the 'little hell' that exists between her legs.)

The novelist has read the tales with their cast of lusty young wives and rampant young men, their randy monks and roaming merchants with their ships and fluctuating fortunes, their princesses in disguise, their weird and brutal sexual politics. But in this era of contact tracing and genome sequencing, quarantine facilities and graphs of mortality, it is not the fiction that absorbs her, but the prologue.

Italians refer to it simply as *la cornice*. The frame. The background of calamity and pestilence that lends these tales their power, the darkness that makes their inventiveness shine all the more brilliantly, that transforms these stories into an assertion of creativity, generative instinct, human inventiveness in the face of death and decay. *La cornice* is short. No more than eight pages from a total of 643 in the novelist's Everyman edition, but it is magnificent in its depiction of a plague in an era before vaccination, genome tracing and all those scientific miracles so calmly reported at the 1pm press briefing. This is an organism in its full rampant glory, surging unchecked through cities and nations, across borders and oceans, killing millions with a savage, simple intent.

It is a curious experience to read *la cornice* on this summer day. Much about it seems distant: the assumption that God and his wrath were the cause, for example, or the influence of some celestial body. It would be several centuries before another source was identified: those 'small stocky spindles with rounded ends' that a Swiss-born bacteriologist, Alexandre Yersin, first discovered when working in a laboratory in Yunnan in China in 1894. It was named *Yersinia pestis*, the bubonic plague that passed to human hosts via the bite of infected fleas.

The bacteria and the fleas are still with us. They infest rats and a wide range of small furry animals all over the globe. Those stocky spindles live on among squirrels in Colorado, gerbils in Kazakhstan, cats, rabbits and hares in India, Africa and Europe.

The Deck

In 2020 two herdsmen in Mongolia died after contracting *Yersinia pestis* by eating raw marmot. Each year, over a thousand cases of bubonic plague worldwide are reported by the World Health Organization. But Boccaccio's dreaded *la pestilenza* has lost much of its terror since 1943, when American scientists derived an antibiotic, Streptomycin, from a microorganism discovered in the throat of a chicken. Streptomycin has driven back bubonic plague and sapped the strength of other scourges, including Robert Koch's beautiful silvery *Mycobacterium tuberculosis*.

The novelist is old enough to remember queuing up with the other children at school to receive the vaccination that would keep her safe from tuberculosis. Her uncle had had the disease. It had crept into his brain and left the shambling wreckage of the man who had been their mother's beautiful little brother, the boy in the photos who played the violin and was the first in the family to go to university, where he was going to become a lawyer. Sometimes they went to visit their mother's brother at the Home. He would lurch to his feet in the sunroom where all the strange damaged men rocked and mumbled in the sunshine, and the air smelled powerfully of disinfectant and pee.

But then all the children at all the schools were lined up to receive their vaccination and no one else she has ever known has had tuberculosis. The sunrooms emptied, sanatoria shut down and became apartments and holiday villages. Truly, we live in an age of miracles.

In the summer of 1348, Florence's governors were not so fortunate. Vaccinations were hundreds of years away. They lacked knowledge of cause, but they did understand the fundamentals of control. They understood that filth contributed to the spread of the disease. In *la cornice* Boccaccio describes how they appointed special officials to cleanse the city streets of 'impurities'. They understood too the effectiveness of isolation, imposing border controls around the city and 'refusing entrance to all sick folk'.

Their efforts proved ineffectual. The spindles had already established a strong footing, having arrived in the guts of fleas carried by rats on the ships of Genoese merchants. The merchants had been engaged in a stoush with a Mongolian army at Kaffa (now Feodosia) in the Crimea, hostilities sparked by religious differences and competition for trade. Italian Christians versus Muslims, for many in the Mongolian army had converted to Islam on their way west. Also at issue was competition for the highly lucrative trade in slaves destined for sale to owners in the Ottoman Empire.

Ten-year-old, pale-skinned Circassian girls evidently fetched a premium, but castrated boys and tall men suitable for impressive entourages were also valuable items. Kaffa was the capital of the trade, a centre where the Spanish traveller Pero Tafur reported 'they sold more slaves, male and female than anywhere else in the world'. He himself snapped up three for a very reasonable price on his visit in 1435.

The Genoese merchants had been under siege inside the city for months. But thanks be to God, plague broke out in the Mongolian army. In the devastation and confusion that ensued, the attackers lost their appetite for fight. They abandoned the siege and, as they withdrew, they catapulted hundreds of their dead over the walls. 'A mountain of bodies' lay in the streets, according to an Italian account.

The Genoese also headed for home, carrying in the holds

of their ships not only the profits of trade, but rats and their seething cargo of bacteria.

By the time the disease reached Florence, it had mutated on its long journey from the East. Boccaccio records that in Kaffa 'an issue of blood from the nose was a manifest sign of inevitable death', but in Italy, 'in men and women alike it first betrayed itself by the emergence of certain tumours' the size of an apple or an egg in the groin and armpit, the 'bubos' that gave the disease its name, and a ring-a-rosy rash on arms and thighs.

As bubonic plague took hold, the bonds of social cohesion fell away.

> *Citizen avoided citizen . . . among neighbours was scarce any that shewed fellow-feeling for another . . . kinsfolk held aloof . . . brother forsaken by brother . . . husband by wife . . . and what is more and scarcely to be believed, fathers and mothers were found to abandon their own children, untended, unvisited, to their fate, as if they had been strangers.*

Bodies littered the streets or were buried hurriedly in huge trenches, 'hundreds at a time as merchandise is stowed in the hold of a ship, tier upon tier, each covered with a little earth until the trench could hold no more'. In the countryside, 'poor hapless husbandmen and their families perished day and night not as men but rather as beasts'. The fields were left unharvested and the livestock let loose by their dying owners to roam at large. The fabric of civilised society unravelled at shocking speed.

It is the responses to this disaster recorded by Boccaccio

that most interest the novelist. Seven hundred years and a whole catalogue of scientific and social advancements separate medieval Florence from this little buzzing city and the 1pm briefing, but the reactions of the citizens have a familiar ring.

Some Florentines adopted a form of self-isolation. This was nothing new. For centuries, ships carrying passengers infected with fever had stood out to sea for a time before entering port, sometimes for a month, the *trentina*, but by the mid-fourteenth century it was more usual to wait 40 days, the *quarantina*. Forty days had a powerful resonance. In classical Greek medicine, Hippocrates and Galen nominated the fortieth day as one of the critical days in the development of a disease. In the Bible, 40 days were also significant as the time it took for the rain to exterminate all living things save those sailing securely on Noah's ark. Forty days was the number of days Jesus spent fasting in the wilderness, and by extension it became the number of days Christians fasted during Lent.

Some Florentines adopted moderation, dietary changes, attention to mental health, 'thinking to live temperately and avoid all excess would count for much as a preservative'.

> *Some banded together and formed communities in houses where there were no sick, living a separate and secluded life which they regulated with the utmost care, avoiding every kind of luxury, eating and drinking very moderately, holding converse with none but one another lest tidings of sickness or death should reach them, and diverting their minds with music and such other delights as they could devise.*

The Deck

Others took the opposite approach, indulging in reckless denial, maintaining 'that to drink freely, frequent places of public resort and take their pleasure with song and revel, sparing to satisfy no appetite . . . was the sovereign remedy for so great an evil'. They roamed the city, occupied abandoned houses, stealing and observing 'no laws, human or divine . . . every man was free to do what was right in his own eyes'.

Others opted for outright flight.

> *This multitude of men and women, negligent of all but themselves, deserted their city, their houses, their estates, their kinsfolk . . . and migrated to the country parts as if God in visiting men with the pestilence would not pursue them with his wrath wherever they might be.*

But whatever approach they tried, writes Boccaccio, all found themselves equally vulnerable while the plague raged through Florence in the five months of that summer. It is not known how many died. He estimates more than 100,000. Later historians think 80,000 is more likely. The precise daily tallies of the 1pm press briefing, the online league tables listing global rates of infection and death belong to the twenty-first century, not the era of *The Decameron*. The number of deaths across Europe, Asia and Africa is equally a guess. Estimates range from 75 million to over 200 million.

It was apocalyptic, widely regarded across Christian Europe as the first of the seven vials God's angels would empty upon the Earth in the last days, as foreseen in The Book of Revelation.

The first vial would deliver 'a noisome and grievous sore

upon the men which had the mark of the beast'.

The second vial would be poured out upon the sea, so it became 'as the blood of a dead man and every living soul died in the sea'.

The third angel would pour his vial 'upon the rivers and fountains of water and they became as blood'. The fourth would pour his vial upon the sun 'and power was given unto him to scorch men with fire', and so it would go, horror piling on horror, darkness covering the Earth. There would be earthquakes and storms of 60-kilogram hailstones dropping from the sky until, eventually, the reason for all this devastation would appear, and it would be, of course, a woman. The successor to Eve, whose disobedience had started it all in the first place and driven humanity out of Eden, flawed and imperfect and consumed by sin. The Whore of Babylon would make her grand entrance at last, clad in red and purple and riding upon the beast, the great whore, the mother of harlots.

These are the images that for over 2000 years have compelled the imagination of millions. This is the story that reaches its conclusion in a climactic battle and the delivery of God's judgement from which will emerge a new heaven and a new Earth.

Boccaccio does not mention the angels, nor the Great Whore, in his catalogue of responses to plague, but bands of men who were convinced of this biblical vision roamed across Europe at this time, whipping themselves to a bloody pulp in public places and preaching hysterical atonement. The Flagellants incited widespread violence against Jews and posed such a threat to public order that in October 1349 the Pope himself was forced to intervene and threaten their excommunication.

The Deck

In *la cornice*, however, there are hints of a new kind of understanding. When Boccaccio writes that the rituals accompanying burial fell away confronted by the deluge of bodies, that women no longer wailed over the dead but indulged in a kind of hilarity, 'the laugh, the jest, the festal gathering' as they laid out yet another body, or when he writes that the women of Florence had abandoned their previous modesty and permitted men to care for them when they became ill, 'with no more shame than if he had been a woman', the creaking of old restraints is clearly audible.

'Practices contrary to the former habits of the citizens,' he writes, *'could hardly fail to grow up among the survivors.'*

And there you have it in a single sentence: the tiny shoots of the future.

New ideas, new modes of behaviour, independent thought, a freeing of the individual from customs, beliefs and notions that had held them previously in check are coming into being. These are the seeds of a profound reassessment of how people should be and how they should live. That one sentence contains the seeds of Renaissance, Reformation, Enlightenment, Revolution, Emancipation, Women's Liberation — the great movements of thought and behaviour that are still working their way through populations worldwide. The qualities of the modern era germinated and took root in those trenches stacked with putrefaction.

In the three and a half thousand words of *la cornice*, Boccaccio conveys the facts of devastation and annihilation. He hints at the cracks opening in the old order and the shoots of a new order. And then, abruptly, the tone switches. He is tired of fact. Its miseries are 'irksome'. He turns instead to fiction.

The Frame

'. . . on a Tuesday morning after Divine Service in the venerable church of Santa Maria Novella' seven young women and three young men, all relatives or friends, meet by chance and plan their escape to the country, where the storytelling begins.

One hundred tales told beneath trees in the heat of the day. Tales of 'those who after divers misfortunes attain unexpected felicity'. Tales of 'those whose loves have had a disastrous close'. Tales of 'those who painfully acquire some much coveted thing, or having lost, recover it'.

The style of storytelling is rapid and highly coloured.

A merchant in a strange land encounters three men who rob, strip and abandon him. He is rescued by a beautiful widow who hears him singing outside her house. She brings him in, offers a bath, fresh clothing and dinner. That night they make love many times and, in the morning, he goes happily on his way.

Or: a merchant of Ravello buys a ship and fills it with goods he hopes to sell in Cyprus, only to find when he arrives that other ships are stocked with the same goods so his own are rendered valueless. Determined not to return home penniless, he sells the ship and buys a smaller, nimbler corsair, arms it and turns to a career of piracy with considerable success. Then he himself is attacked by other pirates, shipwrecked and flung into the ocean. He floats ashore in Corfu on a chest and is rescued by a good woman who happens to be on the beach 'scrubbing her kitchen ware with sand and salt water to make it shine'. When he is recovered, he opens the chest to find it full of precious stones. He rewards the woman and returns to Ravello, wealthier than when he left.

Or: three young Florentines inherit great wealth from their father but squander it. So they go to London where, by living

The Deck

carefully and lending money at exorbitant rates, they amass a second fortune. They return to Florence, leaving their business in the hands of a capable young nephew, Alessandro. Civil war breaks out in England and Alessandro is forced to leave, bankrupted, for Italy. On the way he falls in with an English abbot travelling with a large entourage. The abbot is much taken with the courteous conduct and handsome appearance of the young man. One night at a crowded inn, Alessandro can find nowhere to sleep but on corn sacks spread on the floor of the abbot's chamber. The abbot, to Alessandro's amazement, persuades him to share his bed, where 'laying his hand upon the abbot's bosom . . . he encountered two little teats, round, firm and delicate as they had been of ivory'. This is no abbot but the King of England's daughter in disguise. She sits up in bed, places a ring on Alessandro's finger and 'espouses him before a tiny picture of Our Lord'. They make love all night and, in a few months' time when the civil war has ended, return to England, where Alessandro becomes an earl and directs the re-conquest of Scotland.

Ten days. Ten tales told each day. A simple architecture barely interrupted by comment or detailed characterisation. There is no quirky Wife of Bath in this company, with her gappy teeth and sexual appetite, no con-artist of a Pardoner with his lank, greasy hair. Here, the characters are like paper dolls, like the figures in some medieval miniature, the women with high pale foreheads and slender sloping shoulders, delicate as porcelain, the men in pointed shoes and big round hats. The women are all simply described as beautiful, the men are gallant, the villa is handsome, the food is delicious, the days are hot, the garden is exquisite.

The Frame

The sequence is broken only at the midpoint when, on the sixth day, a couple of servants erupt into a loud argument. The young man, Tindaro, believes that women are virtuous, but the old woman, Licisca, knows better. There is not a woman in her neighbourhood, she insists, who was a virgin when she married, and they continue to play around afterward, but 'this booby would fain teach me to know women as if I were but born yesterday'.

The argument is loud and crude and funny, but in the afternoon of that same day it is balanced by another digression as delicate as a miniature painting. The women leave the villa and its garden and walk to a nearby vale, where fir trees shade grass studded with flowers and a stream emerges from a gorge to form a little lake. Its waters are so clear that stones might be counted on the bottom, and the women strip off in the heat of this long summer afternoon then swim in the cool water and try to catch in their hands the shoals of little fish that dart about.

There is nothing decorous, however, about their stories. Tale after tale is inventive, daft, filled with a kind of wild physical sexual energy that seems consequent on great disaster. To read them is to feel the uninhibited mood of the 1920s after the deaths and mutilation in the mud of Flanders. The frenetic dancing, the explicit sexuality of the clothing of women who cast aside upholstery for silk slips of dresses, cut to the knee, the freedom of the female body. Or, during the Blitz, the heightened sexuality Graham Greene defined as the 'love charm of bombs'.

Moreover, these tales are written not in Latin, the language their author used for his scholarly work, but in the everyday speech of his city, Florence. They are written in the language of the women jesting as they lay out another body in that terrible dark hilarity that can take over a funeral. The speech of the child crying for help that does not come as they lie dying in an upstairs room. The words a man uses as he unlatches the gate, the rash already spreading on his arm, to let his cow out to forage where she can. It's the language to use when writing about a lively wife and her young lover, a grubby hermit and a beautiful but gormless young nun.

Boccaccio defends himself in an epilogue to the collection against charges of unseemliness. Yes, he is a scholar but in these tales he uses the language of everyday speech because it is authentic, it can be widely understood, it is how people actually speak. Like any novelist since, he blames any crudity on his characters. They made him do it: '. . . men and women at large in their converse make use of such terms as *hole*, and *pin*, and *mortar*, and *sausage*, and *polony*, and plenty more besides of a like sort.' He is not only a serious scholar. In this book he has revealed a different persona. 'I am not grave,' he writes. 'I am so light that I float upon the surface of the water.'

It's all so contemporary, so meta. The author teasing the reader. The play of light and laughter against the surrounding dark.

It's the sound of modern fiction taking root in the trenches of 1348.

The novelist sits in her room, planning her novel. The children play bing bang bong on their xylophone, the city buzzes, the statistics fly in from beyond the cloud barrier on the horizon.

A plague is raging.

It has surged out like Boccaccio's plague from the East or,

more accurately on these islands, from the north. From China, from Wuhan and that wet market and the pangolins, or from bats in a cave or, rumour persists, from a research laboratory adjacent to the market.

A team of experts has been dispatched by the World Health Organization to determine the exact point of origin. They are skilled at detection. One expert has previously detected Covid in minks farmed for their fur in Denmark, another detected Ebola among fruit bats nesting in a hollow tree in a village in Guinea, and a third member of the team is president of a New York-based non-profit organisation called the Eco Health Alliance, which has for years funded research into bat viruses at the Wuhan Institute of Virology. His presence has aroused comment in the media. Is he compromised by this connection? Is this story of expert scientific detection a tale instead of concealment and compromise, the kind of real-life story that forms the basis for lightly fictionalised Netflix movies and Amazon bestsellers about corrupt companies or bureaucratic spin and manipulation? Story swirls about this virus and it is not always easy to separate fact from fiction, truth from propaganda.

What is certain is that the organism emerged and has passed person to person, breath to breath, not via a hostile army catapulting dead bodies over city walls, nor along trade routes engaged in the sale of Circassian ten-year-olds. It has passed instead along contemporary routes of trade. Not on the bodies of the dead but on the bodies of the living, crammed into economy class and flung through the air at marvellous speed to land in the cities of the world. It has been carried across oceans on giant cruise ships with their cargoes of 4000 tourists or more, stowed like so much merchandise, deck above deck, balcony above balcony.

It has made its way here and been restrained in the big grey hotels that are the successors to the harbour islands that once offered quarantine to ships flying the yellow flag of contagion: Kamau Taurua, Te Motu-a-Ihenga, Matiu and Ōtamahua became isolation wards dedicated to the control of diseases that were wreaking havoc across the wide blue Te Moana-nui-a-Kiwa. Measles, smallpox, tuberculosis, scarlet fever and syphilis unleashed plagues every bit as devastating as Boccaccio's. Figures vary, but some historians — Kirch and Rallu, for example, in their *Growth and Collapse of Pacific Island Societies* (2007) — estimate that within a few years of the arrival of European ships with their disease-bearing crews, as many as 95 per cent of the inhabitants of Easter Island/Rapa Nui died, 95 per cent of the inhabitants of the Marquesas, 93 per cent of the people on Tahiti, 83 per cent of the people on Hawai`i, 70 per cent of the people in Rarotonga, and 60 per cent of Māori in Aotearoa.

The foundations of the quarantine hospitals are lumpy now under long grass. People visit at weekends. They walk about and picnic on the highest point, they plant seedlings of trees that once grew there in abundance, they photograph the chimney stack pointing aloft like an admonitory finger. 'Take note!' says the chimney stack. 'This is what a virus can do!'

And, when it strikes, this is the way humans respond. They try to isolate. They avoid contact. The scientific technologies of detection and control have changed radically, but the fundamental instinctive responses remain similar to those listed by Boccaccio.

The Frame

A plague is raging, and in the novelist's country some respond by living with restraint. They live moderate lives, with calm optimism and faith in good science. They draw their families close, follow the Health Department's instructions, and wait for the vaccines.

Some are restless. They press for the borders to be opened to admit tourists or kitchen staff or fishing crews or businesspeople, or because they themselves want a way out. They agitate for certainty in uncertain times. Like fractious children confined to the back seat during a long journey through uncharted country, they wail, 'Are we there yet?' 'When will we be there?' 'When *exactly* will we be there?' They are frantic to get out and back to some place they call 'normal'.

There are those whose instinct is to deny the power of the microbe and live recklessly, packing out the bars and clubs, impatient with rules and regulation.

There are those in whom fear of contagion has translated into semi-mystical hysteria. They roam across the open borders of the internet with their posts and tweets inciting hatred of that old enemy, the Jews, alongside a bizarre cabal of Hollywood celebrities, politicians and billionaires in the QAnon mashup of political conspiracy, comic-book evil, paedophilia, blood libel, lizard people, star seeds and aliens emerging from a mountain in a kind of rapture that will usher in a new heaven, a new Earth.

The novelist adjusts the screen for glare. She looks out the window. Is what she sees out there just a pause before the resumption of normal service?

Or is this indeed an ending? Is she witnessing an apocalypse minus God and angels, but not so far, as metaphors go, from the actuality of poisoned oceans, searing heat, a turbulent climate and rivers so toxic they kill livestock and might as well run with blood?

Is it the final chapter of the version of history she learned as a child that began with humans walking out of Africa, then decorating French caves with images of cows and lions and after that, a steady curve called Progress that rose upward via Egypt, Greece, Rome and across Europe to North America and Asia and on to touch all the peoples of the globe, to some initial discomfort, it had to be admitted. The small print mentioned genocide, war, land seizure, a plague or two (*95 per cent, 93 per cent, 60 per cent*), all most regrettable of course, but ultimately, the story went, Progress was to the benefit of all.

Is this the endpoint of that flawed narrative? Have humans in their relentless encroachment on the wilderness, their successful breeding, their sheer force of numbers, created the ideal conditions for the spread of disease, in the same way that they have created the conditions for the extinction of species, catastrophic climate change and planetary destruction? Will this plague be followed by another and another, each with some surprising new adaptation to take advantage of human susceptibilities? Each increasing in virulence and transported at greater and greater speed about a shrinking planet? Is this another step towards human annihilation?

And if that's the case, what is the point of writing fiction? What's the point of starting on a novel? Why try to imagine something when reality eclipses it so conclusively? Is fiction no more than a brief solace, a distraction on the way to our own extinction, like the Strauss waltzes played on the deck of the liner as it slips stern first beneath the icy waves?

The screen is in front of her, waiting. A bare white rectangle.

The Frame

The novelist is about to step out onto the unknown ground that is every new book. She will make up characters and a setting and a plot and walk about in the imaginary land that always lies just offshore, alongside reality. She has no idea if her story will work. It's always a bit of a gamble. Maybe making things up will feel ridiculous, irrelevant before the online deluge of fact. Maybe she'll lose her nerve. Maybe her imagination will fail her, her characters will dwindle to dots. Maybe she will be unable to settle to the daily grind at the computer, distracted by the news reports and their insistence on failure, collapse, shambles.

Maybe she will head off into the crevices of her crumpled brain and lose her way completely.

She writes very slowly. Months, sometimes years, to complete a novel. Anything could happen. Some new mutation of the virus could spot a gap and surge ashore, and the calm could shatter. The sick and dying will fill the hospital wards, the bodies will fill the mortuaries, they will pile up in the streets. (*95 per cent, 93 per cent, 60 per cent* . . .) Fiction could seem completely pointless.

But she has managed to sketch a frame and colour in the background. It's a start. She ties back her hair, puts on her glasses and raises her hands to the keyboard.

'Well, here we go,' she says.

From my fingers to your hand, from my eye to your eye, from the crevices of my crumpled brain to the crevices of yours . . .

THE NOVEL

THE FIRST DAY

Ten o'clock on a Thursday morning in a year that is not this year, not the year when the writer writes, nor the year when the reader reads. It is another year made up of other numbers entirely. Sun, moon and stars in calm alignment and, on Earth, a supermarket.

Temple of commerce. Proof, if any were needed, of global reach, the supremacy of choice and an abiding faith in the doctrine of supply and demand. Seas have been stripped to produce fifteen varieties of flavoured tuna. Rivers have dried to dustbowls to produce milk, cream, a dozen kinds of butter and sixty kinds of cheese. Primeval jungle has been cleared to make way for soybean, rice and palm oil.

And here it is, Earth's bounty, gathered along aisles of polished concrete. Blessed with eternal life, it lines the shelves in cartons, tins and jars, each marked with one of ten billion possible variations of light and dark, line and space. By the

The Deck

farthest wall stands the tomb of the unknown battery fowl, the hormonally enhanced cattle beast, the blessed pig who spent her anchorite's life in a steel crate. Behold the bread, croissant and iced bun, sandwich loaf and ciabatta roll. Behold the pinot noir and sauvignon, shiraz and chardonnay. Beneath the arching roof, behold the apogee of human invention, the culmination of the narrative that began with the dawdle out of Africa.

The waves of want have receded. Plagues have swept across the face of the Earth, and storm and war, and the shelves of the supermarket were stripped. The aisles became bare-boned and bereft. And then the waves receded, the planes began to fly again, the ships began to sail, the trucks rolled back into the loading bays and the shelves were restocked.

There are gaps if you look closely: no tinned sardines, no canned tomatoes, no maple syrup, no cashew nuts this morning. There have been many such disappearances: flour has vanished on occasion, as have coffee beans and Basmati rice and cocoa, but this morning the shelves seem full. The illusion is almost perfect. The old faith has been restored. There are summer flowers by the sliding doors in buckets and posies. There are fresh fruit and vegetables, imported and local, organic and inorganic, and overhead the sound system plays those old, slow, familiar songs that repeated studies have proved comfort the customers and persuade them to tarry a little longer in the cheese section. To spend thirty-eight per cent more than they would if the music were fast or unfamiliar.

At this moment on this Thursday morning it's 'Harvest Moon'. The trolleys trundle placidly down Aisle 1 past the bread and the deli, up Aisle 2 past the wine and confectionery. Up, turn, down, turn, up, turn, down, at the sweet bovine pace of an ox dragging a plough across a field.

A man is surveying the biscuit section. His trolley is parked awkwardly across the width of the aisle. Philippa is forced to stop. He does not notice, engrossed as he is in reading the label on a packet of Tim Tams.

'Excuse me,' she says, because she also wants to buy biscuits. Crackers, sesame or rye, to have with cheese or some pâté from the deli.

The man peers more closely at the packet. His lips move, muttering. What on earth does anyone need to know in such detail about a Tim Tam? It's a biscuit, for god's sake. A chocolate biscuit. That's it.

He's one of those withered men, legs like dry kindling, polo shirt tucked into the waistband of knee-length shorts, hair scraped in damp strands over a pink scalp. Mainstay of the bowling club. Treasurer of the local branch of Rotary. A tidy man who amputates the branches from trees on the boundary fence and mows his lawn with savage intent as if every blade might fight back. A man who has raised two terrorised kids and kept a lifetime grip on a dim, compliant wife.

Philippa knows this within seconds of their encounter because she has known his kind all her life, from the time when the teachers inexplicably picked him, every time, to hand out the reading books and bring in the milk, warm and stale, from the school gate.

And here he is again, blocking everyone's way, and despite Neil and the harvest moon she feels an irrational anger rise, a temptation to ram his bloody trolley into the back of his scrawny legs. Of course she does not do that. She is nice. A nice woman with grey hair nicely cut and a nice little car in old lady blue in the

The Deck

carpark. And she has seen enough in her professional life to know what happens when people give way to irrational urges. They pick up the kitchen knife and plunge it home. They ram the new girlfriend's car, that bitch, when they find it parked in the driveway, they king-punch the fucker in the bar who looked at them funny, they drive one afternoon straight over the cliff with the three-year-old strapped in his car seat, *the wheels on the bus go round and round* . . .

She should have known better than to shop on a Thursday morning, which is Seniors Discount when all the minibuses turn up from the retirement homes with the ambulatory and minimally confused. They roam the aisles with the smallest trolleys, choosing from the global harvest the toothpaste and shampoo to which they gave their branded hearts many years ago. They select the card on which they will be able to write, yet again, *Thinking of you, Deepest Sympathy*. A card with some pallid thing on the front, a lily say, or a cross for those who still think there might be some point to all that, still believe in reunion in the sweet by-and-by rather than rot and putrefaction. But how can you write about rot on a card with a lily? About the howling of the bereft, muffled by the midnight pillow? The desolation of the wall clock stepping closer, tick, tick, tick? The giddy terror at the very edge of the precipice, the wheels on the bus going round and round and round and round and . . . ?

The seniors push their trolleys though the valley of the shadow, and its walls are lined with breakfast cereals and taco kits. They make their selection, for it is necessary still that the teeth within the skull are clean and white and that the hair should gleam. They choose a little treat, a bit of fudge to have with a cup of tea while watching the kind of death that happens somewhere

The First Day

beautiful and very far away, in Venice among the canals, or in Denmark where it snows, or in an English village with a vicar and wisteria. The kind of death that can be neatly resolved because someone caused this death and they can be discovered and brought to justice. This death has an explanation. It is not the random purposeless horror they know from the times when it was their turn to stand in the black dress or the funeral suit newly pressed from the dry cleaners, nodding thank you thank you as the doomed with their white teeth formed an orderly queue for kiss kiss and some banality about loss and love and that terrible lie about remembering.

No. Philippa should not have come to the supermarket on a Thursday morning. It always leaves her feeling irritable. It reminds her that she too is a senior, a super-annuitant, elderly, geriatric, with a limited selection of styles to choose from. What will she be? Crone? Wise woman? Sweet pink apple-pie blob of vacuity? The little old lady of the jokes, forgetful and driving at 30kph on the open road? Or the feisty old gal with the scarlet slash of lippy, high-kicking her way off into the wings from the world's stage?

Usually she can forget all this unless prompted. One of those surveys, perhaps, where she is asked to rank her experience of some hotel or an online purchase, and there are boxes to tick. Gender. Ethnicity. Age. The ages are listed by decade, 20–29, 30–39 and so on. And there she is with her cohort, second from the end, only one to go. She's sliding off the list and her friends are all coming with her, straight over the cliff, *the wheels on the bus* . . .

The tiny trolley with the toothpaste and the chocolates is only a breath away, and she does not want to be reminded of it. She just wants to buy some frigging crackers.

The man mutters irritably at the Tim Tams. He must have noticed her, even allowing for the loss of peripheral vision that comes with advancing years.

'Excuse me,' she says, leaning closer. 'Would you mind if I moved your trolley?' She reaches over and places her hand on the cold metal but the man turns. His eyes are blue and glitter like shattered glass and the whites are mustard yellow. His face is beaded with sweat.

'Why don't you fuck off, you silly bitch?' he says. Politely, as if he were saying no more than 'Good morning'. Spittle foams at the corners of his mouth. 'Cunt,' he adds, for good measure, and puts out his hand to hold his trolley exactly where it is.

Philippa backs off, eyes averted lest he lunge from the leash. This senior is perhaps in the early stages of dementia, the plaques and tangles already curdling the creamy mass of the brain. Social inhibition has been dissolved, memory is shedding like so much dry skin, and all the tiny electrical impulses that are the self are sparking and shorting inside that sticky skull.

She leaves him among the biscuits and walks off down the long aisles, gathering olives and tonic, camembert and baking powder for the cake, although Tom doesn't want one. No birthday cake, no fuss. But she will make a cake. She has invited his oldest friend to eat the cake. Tom can't possibly object to his oldest friend. She will light the candles and they will say — not sing, because singing would definitely be a fuss — Happy Birthday, and she will give him the cunning little multi-tool with fish scaler and pliers and hook remover all wrapped in unfussy brown paper.

She finds her friend Ani by the meat chiller.

The First Day

Ani is small and bright, her hair pure white and curling like a dandelion on the stem of her slender neck. She wears sandals and a shift of brilliant parrot green. Philippa joins her in front of all that dead flesh. The legs of birds and their dimpled featherless breasts, the dainty pointed toes of pigs, the tails of cattle and the livers of sheep. Philippa is planning a leg of lamb, for Tom has conservative tastes. Ani is wondering if she could manage a fillet of beef. She's clipped a recipe from the Sunday magazine for a celebration dinner that featured something called Beef Wellington, which was a whole fillet with mushrooms on top, wrapped up in pastry, which didn't sound too difficult. Ani is normally vegetarian, but her brother is coming down for the long weekend and he is a resolute carnivore. Her little brother, the singer.

'And he's bringing someone!' she says, eyes alight. 'He's being mysterious.'

'Is he indeed?' says Philippa. 'That sounds promising.'

They stand side by side making their selection. Ani, small and bright, Philippa in pale grey and very tall. One point eight metres or, in the pre-decimal measurements she learned in childhood and still privately finds more meaningful, five eleven, thanks to tall Dutch antecedents on her mother's side. Big-boned, hair in the sensible bob she has worn since high school. Her most notable feature are her breasts. They form a mighty shelf, a bust, a bosom, an affliction since they first emerged as two little thimbles on the flat plain of her little girl chest and swelled relentlessly till it was hopeless to try to conceal them by folding her arms. Where once she had run, outdistancing everyone easily on her long striding legs, she became slow, weighted down by jiggle and bounce. Boys noticed. They

The Deck

sniggered as she walked past. 'Boobs', they said, and 'Tits', and she hated them and she hated those stupid words and most of all she hated her own treacherous body.

When she wept, her mother was brisk.

'Don't be silly,' she had said. 'They have a purpose. You will be able to nourish your babies.' As if Philippa were a cow, her sole function to squeeze out her young in its bloody sac and ooze the milk that would feed it.

'But I'm not a cow!' she protested. 'And I don't want babies.'

In time the boys stopped sniggering. They became weirdly entranced instead, wanting to touch and nuzzle. And as she grew older and entered her profession, the breasts took on a kind of independent authority, conferring weight and gravitas beneath her judicial robes as she sailed along the corridors of the district court. This morning they swell beneath a tunic of palest grey and such deliberate anonymity it is as if she is trying to erase herself completely. Leave nothing behind but a faint blur on the retina, a smudge.

She stands with her friend in the cool and they talk about Pete and this 'someone'. There have been many over the years, for Pete is a determined romantic, a serial optimist, but this is the first time he has brought one to meet his sister.

'He says this time it's for real,' says Ani.

'Hasn't he said that before?' says Philippa.

'Yes,' says Ani. 'But this one sounds different. I think he might have found The One.'

'That's wonderful,' says Philippa, because that is what you are supposed to say when people say they have found The One and it's true love and it's for ever. Even though the statistics for divorce and separation cast doubt and the data has been

The First Day

supported by the sorry trail of brutes and victims who have passed through her courtroom, delivering accounts of the utmost intimate savagery.

But still, she stands beside the meat chiller, like some Lilac Fairy wishing the full Disney for her friend's brother, whom she has known since she and Ani first met, sitting on the edge of the playcentre sandpit while their children dug and crashed their little plastic cars. Pete was a singer. He had lived a roaming life working on cruise ships, but now he is back in the country and he is flying down for the long weekend bringing The One, and Ani is going to pull out all the stops. Her trolley is laden with exotic cheeses, fruit and chocolates.

Philippa leaves her friend to her happy selection and heads off for bread and milk before joining the queue at the checkout. The old man is up ahead, carefully lifting one thing, then another onto the scanner. There's a courier between them, Lycra and hi-vis, can of V in one hand, filled roll in the other, leg muscles twitching for the off.

This thing, that thing, this thing to the scanner, slowly, slowly . . .

'Chrissake,' mutters the courier. And then the old man drops a bottle. It smashes on polished concrete, an ooze of glass and mayonnaise, and Philippa can see his face as he turns suddenly towards them, his yellow eyes wide as if he has been taken by surprise. He gurgles, crumples to his knees, slumps sideways. Crimson froth bubbles at his gaping mouth and then there is a gush of blood, so much blood, his dry stick body convulsing and thrashing on the floor.

And Philippa thinks, in the long second as the pool of blood spreads, smooth and glossy as velvet over concrete and the stick

The Deck

legs pedal, frantic for purchase on empty air, 'This must be it. It's here.'

The new variant. Haemorrhagic, lethal, sporting its own genomic barcode, the one she has seen online and in the daily paper she persists in reading from sheer habit among the coffee cups and bagels at the Daily Grind. The variant that has raged out of India and is taking the peopled world, country by country. Borders are falling before the assault, bodies are piling high in the streets, smoke is rising from trenches dug at speed across city parks. And here it is at last, making landfall in the Dunicks Road supermarket.

The courier must have seen the same footage. He recognises the convulsion, the blood. He leaps aside. He races for the door as the queues begin to break and shoppers turn and stare and assistants pause at their tills. He is out the door with his V and bread roll and right behind him is Philippa, the leg of lamb clasped to her chest like a chilly precious child.

Out in the carpark, Ani is stacking love in the boot of a shabby Fiat, her dog barking deliriously in the back seat, paws scraping at the rear window. You're back! You've come back!

'What's going on?' she says as alarms begin to sound.

'We've got to get out of here!' says Philippa, tossing stolen goods into the pale blue getaway car.

'You mean your place?' says Ani. 'Or coffee at mine?'

But Philippa does not mean her place, she does not mean coffee. She means somewhere much further away, far beyond the reach of that red tide which will seep out across the city, touching every corner, every life. Which will inevitably mean cordons and restraint and the deep silence that falls each time the wave sweeps in, altered since its last appearance with some

The First Day

novel tweak which takes time to identify and control.

She means the crib.

Because the alternative is the apartment. Tom's Tower. Long-listed at the time of its construction for the Rosenberg Award, with its ten apartments, theirs the topmost, a masterpiece, the citation said, of sustainable design with its views across the plains to the distant rim of mountains. She really cannot bear the thought of it. Day after day enclosed in that apartment with its perfectly curated view, that interior perfection, that innovative technology that so impressed the judges and reduces all external sound, the sound of life being lived out there in the city, to a buzzing in her ears.

And Tom, sitting in his office, that brown bear of a room, that cliché of a man's lair lined with books he hasn't read in years, listening in his big leather chair to Coltrane on headphones with his eyes shut. Not talking to her.

In company he is animated enough. He becomes Tom, argumentative and adamant, but here in the apartment, just the two of them, he says nothing. They pass each other in silence, sleep either side of an icy white tundra. She cannot bear the prospect of returning alone to that silent place but she says none of that to Ani, whose company she suddenly wants most desperately.

She wants her friend close by, talking or not, however the mood takes them, easy because they have known each other so very long and know when words are useful and when they are too much, and it's just fine to exist alongside each other the way they did when they met, sitting either side of the playcentre sandpit as their children whooped and crashed. They had talked absent-mindedly, dribbling sand through their fingers,

The Deck

intervening when the whooping turned to argument, or wiping a nose, that inconsequential, interrupted maternal talk that had seemed like nothing. They were just chatting. Just passing the time till their children were old enough to go to school when their real lives could recommence. The law degree and the fine arts diploma would be taken up and dusted off and they would become real adults again, with a real job and an IRD number and an income.

And all that time as they were sitting there, they had been doing something. Word by word, they had been building a deep attachment. A forty-year friendship. That was not 'nothing'. It was most definitely 'something'. And now, as that red tide seeps over the concrete, Philippa wants her friend near.

She presents the case quickly, for a siren is already beginning its thin wailing somewhere across the city. She mentions the old man, blood, cordons. The crib.

'Come with us,' she says. 'Before the cordons go up. It's Tom's birthday. The crib's finished and there's heaps of room. Bring Pete. Bring his friend. We'll have a lovely few days. We'll stay there while things get sorted here. We'll forget all about this. We won't even mention it. We'll just relax and have fun. Come with us, till this passes over.'

'I'll pack the hyssop,' says Ani.

'What?' says Philippa, whose parents had been cheerfully indifferent C of E and spared their offspring the wrath and the smiting. Ani, on the other hand, had been steeped in it since birth, raised by devout Baptists on a confusing blend of biblical horrors and the blond American film star Jesus who hung above her bed. He wore a long white nightie and was surrounded by little children, all of whom had suffered and were now

The First Day

presumably dead and with him in heaven, which looked exactly like the Rhododendron Dell in the Botanic Gardens.

If I should die before I wake, Ani and her brother had been taught to pray each night, kneeling on chilly lino, hands pressed palm to palm, *take me to Heaven for Jesus' sake*. Then into bed where she lay in the shadow of all those dead children, staring into the dark and fighting the urge to sleep when death could steal in with its cold fingers and she would stop. It would be the end. She would stop. Stop right there, before she'd even properly begun.

'Hyssop?' Ani says. 'Moses? The Ten Plagues of Egypt?'

Philippa looked blank.

'Never mind,' says Ani. 'Much too complicated.'

She has long ago abandoned the horrors and Gentle Jesus, but the words from long repetition still stick. *And they shall eat the flesh in that night, roast with fire and unleavened bread; and with bitter herbs shall they eat it* . . .

And hyssop. Dipped in the blood of goat or lamb and smeared upon the doorposts so that Yahweh's destroying angel will pass over. He will fly on to smite someone else's first born and leave your child unharmed. You will huddle in your bloodied house, hearing the beating of dark wings pass over.

As she says, it's complicated.

'So?' says Philippa, climbing into her car and slamming the door as the wailing draws closer. She opens her window. 'What do you think? A few days away? A few days at the crib?'

'Okay,' says Ani. Why not? Her brother is already in the air, flying south towards her with his newly beloved and she wants this visit to go well. Not some muddle of cordons and restraint. 'It sounds like an excellent plan.'

THE SECOND DAY

A summer morning. Sun, moon and stars in calm alignment, and on Earth, a car. A black SUV, a rental with shaded windows like the car of a gang boss or the dictator of a small corrupt state. It is travelling through thick bush in alternating light and shade down a narrow gravel road into a bay. Thick white dust rises from its wheels. Ani sits in front, in the passenger seat. Pete had insisted.

'Sit up front, darling,' he'd said. 'Enjoy the view. I'll be fine in the back.'

She accepted, though it meant turning her head to talk to her brother, who sits behind, legs furled awkwardly in the well. As for the view, it has flashed past all the way out from the city at alarming speed. Didi is beautiful, with a halo of curls and the face of an angel. An ambiguous angel, neither male nor female. Not 'he' nor 'she' but 'e'. Not 'her' nor 'him' but 'em'. A Botticelli angel, who drives like the devil, one slender hand on

The Second Day

the wheel, the other arm crooked at the open window, passing everything on the road with a casual unconcern for corners and recommended speed limits. E also has a habit of turning whenever e talks to her or to Pete, maintaining happy eye contact as trucks roar down in the oncoming lane, lights flashing, horns blaring, and motorbikes take swift evasive action. Ani held Raffi close and tried not to notice the view as her brother's newly beloved swept them towards the coast.

Didi is another of those Greek gods to whom her brother has been repeatedly attracted, and the trouble with individuals who look like Greek gods, so far as Ani has been able to tell, is that they often behave like them too, being petulant, faithless and cruel. But Didi seems different.

For a start, e is not Greek but Italian, or, more accurately, Australian.

'Carlton born and raised,' e says. 'Carn the Blues!'

E is a chef who works at one of those lodges Ani has read about in magazines, thousands per night for luxury sheets, luxury spa, luxury dining. But e seems kind, instinctively supporting Ani's elbow as she climbed into the car as if she might collapse with the effort, overcome by senile decay. Ordinarily she would have brushed aside the assistance, but it was meant well, so she forgave em.

Because, best of all, Didi makes her brother laugh. They have an easy familiarity that makes her heart lift.

In Didi's happy company her brother is completely himself. Still the open-faced, guileless boy she remembers from childhood, endlessly trusting, endlessly kicked in the guts by bigger, meaner kids. Her little brother, his hair slicked flat, clad in neat shirt and well-ironed shorts because their mother used to

The Deck

say that they might not be as well off as some, but that was no reason not to make an effort. He was quiet and watchful, and Ani was his staunch defender, the two of them braving the perilous walk to and from school as if crossing a veldt teeming with leopards and lions.

They would see them waiting by the trees on the corner, the mean kids, and as they passed she would hear them mutter. 'Marries,' the biggest and meanest would say. 'Stinking marries.'

She was puzzled.

'Why do they say that?' she asked their mother.

'No idea,' said their mother, who was brisk and Scottish, a McGregor through and through. She had bought Ani a kilt in the clan tartan to wear in the winter and white socks and black patent leather shoes, and she had taught Pete to sing about Loch Lomond and going over the sea to Skye. Ani could see that she and Pete did not resemble their mother, who was pale and ginger-haired, nor their father, who was bald with sharp blue eyes and skin that scorched, but it was years before one of their aunts informed Ani that she and her brother had been adopted.

'Chosen from an ad in the paper,' she said. 'That's how they did things in those days. Your mother saw an ad for a baby. Not from this town. That would have been too public. She went on the train somewhere to pick you up. She was away a few days and when she came back she had you. That was how she found Petey too.'

'So Pete and I are not related?' asked Ani.

Her aunt shrugged.

'Who knows? Maybe. Janet was very discreet about such things. You never got much out of her. She didn't want people

The Second Day

gossiping about her private business.'

Ani remembered it: a Christmas tree with some shiny red balls hanging from branches strung with a few strands of tinsel. It stood in the corner of the lounge and underneath there was a box wrapped in Christmas paper but open-topped, and inside there was a baby. Asleep not on hay, but on a blanket embroidered with rabbits. Was it Baby Jesus? she'd asked, and her mother had laughed and said, no, it wasn't Jesus. It was her new baby brother and his name was Peter.

His little hand curled around Ani's finger. Where did he come from? she asked, and her mother said he was a gift from God.

At the time she had thought it exciting. It was only later that the story became creepy, a denial of origin, a dead end.

Their mother had been careful. She had left no trace behind, no sealed envelope to be opened after her death, not a single document signed with birth names and dates. Even their birthdays might have been invented. Maybe Ani's birthday was just the date when she was picked up from a postal box in the paper. For a while she had tried to find herself, running her finger down the advertisements in Miscellaneous columns from 1947, with their tiny glimpses of a past that made it so very clear that it was indeed another country.

Cow found wandering, Ponsonby Road.

Pianist wishes to meet two musicians with view to forming dance band.

For adoption. Baby girl, half caste. Write P.B. 1442.

Was this her? There were so many babies on offer that year. She gave up.

If asked about her origins, she said with a flippancy that was not quite true, 'Ngāti Miscellany. That's me.'

The Deck

What was true then and is still true now is that she loves her little brother. She loved him walking with his head up past the mean kids, so skinny and so brave. And she most especially loved him on the day of the talent quest.

The school was raising funds for a new hall. It was the usual procession of kids inexpertly strumming guitars and one with a piano accordion and kids tapdancing and doing back flips and a boy who did magic tricks in a black cape. Then her brother stepped up. She had no idea he was planning to do this. He calmly walked on stage, took a deep breath, closed his eyes and sang 'How Great Thou Art', which was their mother's favourite hymn. To begin with, everyone giggled and the big mean kids up the back hooted, but Pete kept right on singing and, strangely, they quietened. His voice soared over them, filling every corner. He sang, and when he finished, people clapped.

He didn't win of course. The book voucher went to the magician. And Pete still got beaten up from time to time, but the mean kids' hearts no longer seemed to be in it. They beat him simply from habit. And when he was fifteen, he became himself. He grew his hair long and luxurious until the principal called him into his office and ordered a haircut. Pete obliged. He had his hair close cut and bleached a startling silvery blond. He looked astonishing. And, with the hair, he took on a defiantly camp persona as if it were a second skin.

'Why are you talking like that?' Ani had asked him.

'Like what?' he asked, irritated.

'All high pitched and flouncy,' she said. 'Like that English guy on TV, that comedian — whatsisname?'

'Oh, piss off,' he'd said and flung a cushion at her.

Their father tried some wrath and smiting, but Pete was taller

The Second Day

and stronger now and not so readily intimidated. Their mother tried tears and reproach and chapter and verse. 'Thou shalt not lie with mankind!' she cried, flourishing the book. 'It says so, right here, Leviticus 18:22. It is an abomination!'

Pete shrugged them off, his whole body a statement, a challenge, an act of defiance.

With Didi, however, there was no need for statement. He draped his arm over his lover's shoulders as he said, 'Hey, Ani, this is Didi. Didi, meet my sis!' She saw his face as Didi bent to kiss her, European-style, on each cheek. Her brother stood smiling, a wide guileless smile of pure happiness. He is loved at last and loving and happy and nothing whatever can go wrong.

Except perhaps a head-on collision with a milk tanker. She sat in the front seat as they hurtled from the city across plains scorched bare and brown, nibbled to the skull by shabby sheep and bony cattle. Hot air shimmered over black ranks of pine. They passed the lake, shrunken within its wide bed to a barren mirror reflecting the sky, patched with crimson algae. They turned towards the hills and began to climb, twisting upwards as Didi took each corner as if this were the Haute Corniche. They raced for the top and the high route that wound along the summit until at last they reached the side road where asphalt gave way to gravel.

Here they are, skidding and bouncing down the road through thick bush where trees have staged a comeback after a century of axe and fire. Branches reach out with speculative fingers, scraping the sides of the car.

'Cazzo . . .' mutters Didi as black lacquer takes a hit, but at least e slows a little.

Ani keeps the window ajar. Raffi is old with uncertain

The Deck

digestion. It's wise to keep some fresh air flowing. He presses his nose to the gap and emits small whimpers of delight at cool air smelling richly of leaf mould, rot and growth. Down they go through green shadow to the valley floor where the trees thin and draw back and they emerge onto a flat. Scrub and flax tangle in broken fences, the remnant of some failed attempt at pasture. The light down here after the bush is sharp and bright.

They lurch across a ford where a creek emerges from scrub and banks of watercress and golden monkey musk. On the other side the road dwindles to a rutted grassy track. The valley widens, bordered on either side by steep cliffs banded with rock and stripes of crimson volcanic ash. The sound of the sea is caught and echoed, and the air through the open window smells of salt and gorse and lupin.

Ani peers ahead through the dazzle.

'Do you think that's it?' she says. The track winds between sandhills and crumpled ridges, and on the highest stands a structure. A rectangular block like a shipping container of rusted Corten steel, tossed up during some fierce winter storm.

'Is that the crib?'

Cribs are supposed to be little makeshift things of weatherboard and dodgy asbestos siding, knocked up by a few blokes in army shorts one long summer holiday after the war. Cribs have a random selection of windows picked up who knew where and a lean-to kitchen and bunkrooms and a water tank on a buckled frame and a dunny set at a discreet distance with a sun-warmed wooden seat, buzzing flies and the best view of the bay.

'Could be,' says Pete.

'Bloody Tom,' says Ani. She should have known better.

The track rises and comes to an end in a parking area beneath

The Second Day

the ridge. A flight of shallow steps leads up between waves of marram grass to a kind of castle wall, not steel, seam and rivet after all but timber siding stained a dark, determined grey-black.

'Oh my,' says Pete. 'This is all a bit dramatic.'

There are no windows to be seen, but midway along the wall a door opens like the gill on some beached sea creature. And here is Philippa — 'Hellllooo!' — in sandy neutrals, shorts and sandals and loose linen shirt. Here is Tom, lean and brown in the male version and 'Hey! You made it!' And it's kiss kiss, handshakes, good to meet you, and here, let me give you a hand with that bag.

They go through the little door. Light slams down upon them. It pours over them as they emerge as if onto a stage. It takes a moment to focus. They are standing on a wide rectangular set of palest plywood. To their left, bare bulbs dangle artlessly from a high ceiling over a kitchen bench, a slab of polished concrete bearing fruit, neon-bright, in big bowls. There's a table, wooden, narrow, with seating for a crowd. To their right a faded green sofa, long and low as a mossy bank, and soft capacious chairs with that open-armed look, all designer scuff and wear and tear, drawn up before a fireplace faced floor to ceiling with smooth sea-burnished stones.

The fourth wall, the one facing the sea, has fallen away. Glass doors have been slid aside and the room opens without a break to a wide wooden deck. More chairs and a barbecue, an ancient ngaio tree lending some dappled shade to one corner. And beyond all this, gleaming, lie sand and sea. The bay stretches before them between twinned headlands till it reaches the chop of whitecaps and the open ocean and the long blue acres that stretch to the horizon where water melts into cloud.

The Deck

Tom stands a little to one side, the conjuror pulling his architectural rabbit from the hat. Ta dah!

'Wow!' says Ani, picking up her cue.

'What a fabulous place!' says Pete, while Didi lifts arms to heaven as if struck speechless.

'Welcome to the crib!' says Tom. 'Your pods are over there, off the deck.'

'Pods?' says Pete. 'So we're in for some interplanetary travel? Deep torpor?'

'People do tell us they sleep incredibly well out here,' says Philippa, who never gets jokes, but Tom is already on the move, trundling Ani's suitcase across the deck towards some black boxes that appear to have been flung by the forces of nature and design across the ridge at calculated angles to the main building. The nearest seems closed and blank but Tom performs some wizardry and there's a click, a whir, and the front wall falls forward in a slow controlled trajectory to form a small deck. Glass doors slide aside onto a pale room, bed plump with soft feather and linen and a pile-up of pillows.

'And en suite,' says Philippa, opening the way to toilet, shower with a head like a drooping sunflower, towels of palest lemon and potions in a variety of wildflower fragrances. 'We're having a bit of a problem with water at the moment, so I'm afraid you'll have to keep the showers short. This is yours, Ani. Pete, Didi, you're over there.' A short distance away another pod, another room of linen and feather. 'Baz has brought his camper. He's parked down by the beach.'

'Baz?' says Ani. 'Tom's friend?'

A third pod remains unopened, like a gift.

'Yes,' says Philippa. 'He's here for Tom's birthday. He's gone

The Second Day

for a surf but he'll be back for dinner.'

'That's nice,' says Ani. 'I haven't seen Baz in years.'

Tom is demonstrating the heating system. Solar, naturally, a 25kW array feeding a 20kW battery bank and the grey-water reticulation and the way in which the shower wall can be opened wide to sunshine and sea . . .

'Fantastic,' says Pete, though not with any real enthusiasm. Technology has always bored him. So Ani adds, 'It's amazing, Tom!'

Tom smiles. He demands such endless quantities of praise. It must be exhausting, Ani has always thought, to be Philippa, having to stoke that faltering ego as if it were some kind of temperamental logburner that requires constant maintenance and regular handfuls of kindling. Ani helps out when she can. It's what you do for your friends.

'You're a genius!' she says.

Tom smiles, and Philippa says, 'Right, we'll leave you all to sort yourselves out. Have a swim, have a walk, come over whenever you feel like a drink. Dinner will be around seven. No rush! We're on Crib Time here.'

And at last they are gone, and Ani can flop on the big soft bed among the pillows and survey her room. Raffi has returned from reconnaissance, sniffing out the land. He stretches out on the carpet in a patch of sunlight. He sighs deeply.

'Isn't this great?' Ani calls to Leo, who has turned up the way he does, a sweet and unexpected shadow in the en suite, peeing into a little circle of germ-defeating aqua blue.

'It is in the fact,' calls Leo, agreeing as he does with that dear echo of his native tongue. *Es ist in der Tat.* 'It is a masterpiece of invention!'

The Deck

She can hear the laughter in his voice, a tap running. He'll be rinsing his hands, his dear big calloused hands. Splashing water on his face. His dear wrinkled face, his grey hair damp.

'I hope Pete enjoys it. And Didi. I like Didi, don't you? E seems really nice.'

But Leo has gone quiet the way he does, turning up without warning, leaving as abruptly. She is used to it now. The glass doors are ajar and a warm breeze noses its way through, catching the white curtain and sending the paper lampshade over her head into a lazy spin, a little way to the left, then back, a little way to the right. She leans back, arms behind her head, the pillowslip smooth against her skin.

Back home the drawing board waits, and the blank white page. Her pencils are in the coffee jar, each sharpened to a workable point, black and coloured. Her brushes, her tubes of paint, the lamp set to shed a diffuse light devoid of shadow. Above the board the orderly shelves are proof that she can do this, in folders of past work and contracts and royalty receipts. She has done it many times, illustrated stories for children about greedy puppies and forgetful taniwha and a little old woman and naughty forest birds — *Out of my way, Kōkako!* — and children who go to the market to buy one big watermelon, two tubby taro, three prickly pineapples . . .

She has drawn the pictures that will prompt the child to find their way through the tangle of line and circle at level one, level two, level three to that moment where the tangle resolves into alphabet and meaning.

She has illustrated the instructions for experiments involving balloons and paperclips and magnets and baking soda and the elements of earth, water, air and fire, and although it was not

The Second Day

exactly the artist's life she had envisaged back when she sat by the kindergarten sandpit, imagining what would come after art school and the diploma, it had been enjoyable.

But not as enjoyable as the drawing she has been doing for months now between commissions. Seated in her studio, the door open to her chaotic garden, she has teased a world from the white page, the story of a little pig. Not a storybook pig, round and pink and pretty, but a tough little kunekune who wears rumpled overalls and a wonky hat and sets out from home across the ocean into a dangerous world.

Great winds puff their cheeks and drive her ship onto rocks surrounding a new island, but she swims ashore among the circling sharks and sets off along a road through steep hills. The road is a bit like the roads near where Ani grew up where white gravel followed a winding course through canyons of limestone pitted with caverns like open mouths and the stone shifted shape as you passed from castle to skull to mythical beast. The little pig's roads are a bit like that and a bit like those roads in the background of Renaissance paintings, where the foreground is occupied by the usual virgin and her plump son but behind them are steep blue hills, walled cities and a glimpse perhaps of the sea. Ani has always preferred the backgrounds.

That's where she takes her little pig as she doodles in her studio, rain falling on the glossy leaves of the kāpuka that self-seeded by the door. The little pig encounters giants and ghosts and demons, she loses things and is sometimes lost herself, and there's no ending to her story. No happy resolution.

Sometimes she has a friend. A goofy donkey or a cunning spider or a dog with one eye. They accompany her on her adventures, crossing deep unbridged rivers, climbing high peaks.

The Deck

And then they disappear. Phhtt! Like that. They are no longer beside her, and the little pig has no option but to straighten her hat and keep right on walking. She's not looking for anything in this landscape. She's not sure where there might be a safe little house made of bricks with its warm fire and comfortable chair. The little pig must simply walk through this enchanting, dangerous, unpredictable world with its dust and explosions and tall trees reaching all the way to clouds thick enough to ride upon.

Ani loves the world she is making. It is not for the children's market. It is hers alone, in black and white, spun from the end of an HB pencil.

When she draws she is surrounded by the beautiful monsters others have imagined. They are pinned to the walls of her studio: a heavy-browed whale with a tiny ship moored upon its back, a marcelled lioness licking her cubs into being from bare clay, a man whose face is on his chest, a man who has one foot lifted above his head as an umbrella. She loves their unlikelihood. There was such scope when they were drawn, such infinite possibility upon Earth.

Now the studio awaits her return, and another commission. It's for a book. There's a decent fee, an American co-publisher, international distribution, but somehow she has been unable to make a start on *One Baby Two*. Those baby animals defeat her.

The two little polar bears playing on the ice.

The two little elephants squirting one another by the river.

The two little calves skipping about in a flowery field.

The two little monkeys hanging by their tails from a jungle tree.

How can she draw them when last time she checked, those

The Second Day

polar bears were at play on a scrap of ice in a warming ocean? Twenty thousand left at last count, and falling. And the elephants are a remnant herd: 28 million in 1800, only 100,000 now, and it is unlikely that either of those elephant babies will live its seventy years but will lie rotting, their tusks sawn off and sold, or surviving in some captive hell, extinct in the wild. And the monkey babies are at play on a brief sunlit morning before the loggers roar in and their tree is cut and chipped or cleared to make way for oil palms.

As for the little calves, they will not live their twenty years chewing their cud in a field among buttercups. If they are males they'll be stunned and killed within a matter of months. If they are female they will be permitted a lifetime of repeated insemination, breeding, lactation, their babies torn from them and the milk intended for their nourishment siphoned off into tankers.

She has researched as carefully as she always does, studying the anatomy of the creatures she draws, their arrangement of bone, their web of muscle and sinew. She needs to know them thoroughly before she picks up her pencils. But knowing their likely fate, how can she do that? How can she make her pencil conjure up little animals at play? How can she keep telling this comforting tale to little human babies, who will point at her drawings with their dimpled fingers and learn the names of the doomed? Who are themselves doomed to life on a planet devoid of elephants and monkeys and polar bears? A planet scraped to the bare bone? It is intolerable to keep telling the lie.

So it all sits and waits, with her editor up there on the North Shore enquiring with increasing concern when she might expect . . . ?

Meanwhile, the lampshade swings lazily in the breeze, the

The Deck

white curtains billow. There's a bumblebee trapped against the window, oblivious to the opening only a few centimetres away. Her furry body bashes at the glass, her buzzing is high pitched, the green world visible but unattainable on the other side. The air is cloying and waxy with the smell of bumblebee panic.

'You could do something about that,' says Leo from somewhere off to the side, but really, what's the point? The bumblebees, the honey bees, the native bees, stingless bees, mason bees, all the tiny buzzing world is dwindling, is dying. Their bodies dry to husks and are vacuumed from the carpet. What's the point?

'Yoo-hoo!' carols Pete in a parody of their mother calling them home when they were children. 'Hey, sis! We're going for a swim. Want to come?' And there they are, standing outside in the sunlight, togs on, towels flung about their shoulders.

Ani gets off the bed, pushes the door wider, waves. 'Yes! Be there in a minute.'

The bumblebee feels the sudden rush of air. Somewhere close by there's the nest where her sisters buzz about their queen who is seated on the little wax throne she has made herself. She is sipping nectar from the wax cup she has placed within reach of her long black tongue. She sits there, fanning the eggs that contain the new generation of her kind, presuming survival. The trapped bee lumbers into flight, lifts away from the mirage on the glass and on her unlikely wings, her thighs weighted down with yellow pollen, she zigzags off into the reality of the bright afternoon.

So Ani opens her suitcase and finds her togs and goes out too, into reality.

THE SECOND NIGHT

That evening they sit out on the deck as the sun sets in a glory of red and gold, great theatrical swags of colour that fade to deep blue as night washes into the valley. The moon hangs overhead, a pale disc, and the stars take up their appointed places as waka and the eyes of gods, or hunter and scorpion, it's all in the eye of the beholder. The white scarf of stars stretches over all their heads, the very image of plenty, the wash of milk spilt from the full udder of the celestial cow as she saunters over the dark fields of the universe. Or the river with its shoals of tuna, their bellies flashing silver and so many in their billions, their trillions and whatever the word is that comes after to signify too many to contemplate.

The sun sets and is, of course, like no other sunset in the history of everything, 'though you can't quite trust a sunset any more, can you?' says Ani. 'You're never quite sure if it's the bushfires.'

Swathes of Australia exploding into columns of flame. All

The Deck

those koalas with their little burned paws in the crooks of burning trees, all those miraculous creatures leaping and creeping and bounding and crawling in flight through smouldering country. And people just like themselves gather on a beach looking out to sea for salvation, because that is where it usually comes from, doesn't it? The rescue craft? The brave little flotilla that will carry them away from smoke and flame to some place that must surely offer greater safety?

'You never know if what you're seeing is smoke and particulates or something beautiful.'

'Opt for beautiful, darling,' says Pete. 'That would usually be my advice.'

The people on the deck regard the beautiful sunset and the wash of blue, and 'Coffee?' says Tom from his station at the bench by a hissing behemoth of a machine, all shiny dials and spouts.

One of them says flat white please, and two say espresso, and one says I can't drink coffee after midday and do you have herbal? And one says gumboot for me, thanks, but don't worry I'll fix it myself, and Philippa says no, no, let us be your wait staff this evening, just relax.

So they relax as the light fades to ash and the birds in the valley go tweet tweet, settling for the night with gnarled claws clamped to the branches of some chosen tree. Tweet tweet they call from the hillside behind the crib, tweet doodly do from the bush-clad hill on the opposite side of the valley.

It is such a tender thing, thinks Philippa as she hands around the coffee. Such a beautiful bubble she has made, light as air. A little group gathered on a deck as darkness falls. Her friend Ani with that awful dog, another of her rescued waifs. And

The Second Night

Tom's old mate Baz, whom she has invited for various reasons, among them that he can be relied upon to lighten her husband's mood. Baz sits on a sofa, picking away at some Blue Mountain inconsequence on his guitar, while Tom, the old animated Tom, hums along as he layers froth on a flat white. And Pete the golden boy who is greying now, but in a distinguished George Clooney kind of way and his friend Didi who, it turns out, is a chef at some luxury lodge up north and said, 'Let me cook this weekend. Please, it would be a pleasure, a thank you for your hospitality.'

E had taken the leg of lamb, deftly cut away the bone, butterflied and basted it with garlic and rosemary and anchovies the way e's nonna taught em, and barbecued it to perfection. E had brought besides some excellent pinot noir, and at this moment e is flourishing a bottle of grappa.

'To correct that coffee!' e says.

'Ooh, a liqueur,' says Ani. 'I haven't had a liqueur in ages. Remember liqueurs? We all drank liqueurs back in the day. Cointreau and crème de menthe that tasted like toothpaste and what was that coffee stuff?'

'Kahlua,' says Pete.

'That's right! Kahlua!' says Ani. 'We drank it with milk. It was a milkshake but god, we felt sophisticated. Until we threw up.'

'Screwdrivers were worse,' says Philippa. 'Orange cordial and rot-gut vodka, ready mixed in a bottle. Ruined my ball dress.' She has a sudden pang of regret for that dress. Blue chiffon with a wreath of silk roses around the neckline. Without a doubt, she thinks, as she delivers the espressos in their acorn cups, the most beautiful dress she has ever owned. There was a photo somewhere. She was wearing that dress with white elbow-length

The Deck

gloves, the way they did then, and her hair is backcombed and flicked up at the ends and she is standing beside a boy who is grinning and has his arm around her waist as if he knows her very well. What was his name again? Richard? Martin? Robert? She thinks she might have been in love with him for a while.

Ani has brought a cake, chocolate and raspberry and incredibly rich. She brings it out to them, shiny ganache and burning candles, and starts the song. Tom usually resists the song, that banal little kindergarten ditty, and all the fuss with candles and the wish. But tonight in front of guests he accepts. He smiles as Ani cries, 'Make a wish, make a wish!'

But what could Tom wish for? Youth and promise, he thinks, looking down at his cake twinkling away in the dark. Youth and promise and a rising star. But what would be the point of that for a man in his waning phase? So he wishes for nothing, smiles at them all, then nips out all his candles one by one between finger and thumb. Tendrils of smoke curl over another year.

They sit on the deck, leaving the lights off as darkness takes the valley and Baz lays aside his guitar and takes out his tin. The red and white Kauri tobacco tin he has had ever since the flat he shared with Tom on Victoria Street back in 1978. It contains some of the best heads he has ever grown on the healthiest plants he has ever cultivated in the patch behind the glasshouse where a jungle of heritage tomatoes has supplied useful camouflage. He licks the paper, rolls and twists and nips the tip, then lights up, draws down deeply, hands it on.

The sky arches overhead, so dense with stars that they leave subtle shadows, not sharp edged like the shadows cast by the sun, but delicate, muted grey-blue. Ani stretches her arm above her head to see her hand reaching for galaxies. So beautiful, so

The Second Night

unimaginably vast, she thinks, and perhaps she says it out loud because beside her Pete says, 'Yes, it is.'

She reaches up her hand, feeling herself shrink the way she does whenever she tries to think about such things. She shrinks to something so tiny, so flyaway, rising up and up and looking back down at herself somehow still there sprawled on the sofa, while her conscious self floats across the universe.

'How big?' she says.

'Ninety-three billion light years,' says Baz. 'Twenty-eight billion gigaparsecs.'

'What's a gigaparsec?' says Ani.

'Big,' says Baz. 'Bloody big.'

Pete says that sometimes when you're out in the middle of the Pacific you can almost forget where you are. You walk about in the body of the cruise ship, along the main concourse among the shops and hairdressers and bars, and you might as well be at Northfield Mall.

'But at night,' he says, 'when I'd finished the gig and was still wired, couldn't sleep, I'd go onto the deck and look out at the sea and the stars, and I don't know . . . I'd think about them, the first ones, setting out . . .'

Ani reaches over, takes his hand. 'Me too,' she says.

She thinks of them. Waiting for nightfall and the star map to appear. Everything stowed on the big seagoing waka, food and fresh water and seedlings and the people the people the people gathered on the shore, excited because people are always excited at the moment of embarkation. Sad to say farewell, of course, but excited too to be setting out somewhere, anywhere. The flex of timber and woven leaf as the ties are unleashed and they emerge into open water where the swell takes them, and they begin to

The Deck

sway the way you used to sway before you were born when you rode along in water in your mother's belly. She thinks about them heading south as the star patterns shift about in their measured, predictable fashion and the air begins to cool. And at last there is that bank of cloud on the horizon and the flights of strange birds.

'I think about them,' says Pete. 'How someone with fingers shaped just like mine, or my eyes, how they got here.'

'Yes,' says Ani, her brother's hand in hers. Her brother who might not technically be her brother but is nevertheless unmistakably her brother. Their feet wading ashore. Their fingers carrying a seedling. Their eyes looking around, seeing this place for the first time. Even when you don't know actual names, or the name of the waka, and you were advertised for adoption, six months old, half-caste, between an ad for a piano player and a lost cat. Even then you think about them. Ngā tūpuna.

'I was on a boat once off the coast,' says Tom. 'This mate of mine asked if I could give him a hand to take a boat up to the Sounds. I'd crewed for him a few times. Sunday afternoons, racing round the buoys in the harbour, that sort of thing. I'd enjoyed that, so I said yes. But as soon as we got out there and started heading north I got seasick. I thought it would go away, I'd get my sea-legs, but I didn't. I just got worse and worse, full-on vertigo. I couldn't stand up, couldn't even lift my head, just fell sideways, and then the weather packed in big time, a huge swell, and my mate had to handle the boat himself and we've never spoken since. That was the end of a beautiful friendship. Not to mention my sailing career . . .'

'But look at them,' says Ani. 'Look at all those stars!'

They look up. And chugging along steadily from right to left

The Second Night

a skytrain passes over. It cuts its banal trajectory across all those complex astral paths. The vision, the dream, the creation of a very rich man. It chugs across their line of sight. And behind it there comes another. And another. Thousands of them, little chunks of machinery going round and round. Down on Earth, the people lean back and watch the traffic.

Philippa inhales. For the first time in years she draws in deep. She is miles away from scrutiny out here, miles away from the life when she spent her days passing judgement on an endless parade of human frailty. Listening to the plea of the thug who raped his wife and left her bleeding on the bedroom floor with a broken spine, the fraudster who stole from the hospital board and fed the proceeds into a casino machine that had been precisely calibrated to relieve her of every cent, the couple cooking meth while a skinny baby mewed for rescue in a filthy cot, the kid who beat a puppy to death with a golf club to impress his mates.

The bruised and broken, the brain damaged and forlorn whose images still haunt her dreams. It is six years since she occupied the high bench, clad in the cloak of sombre gravitas. That cloak demanded that she be restrained in public and unfailingly polite. She must be moderate. She must not drink to excess and she most certainly must not smoke dope, but tonight among friends in this green valley she can kick off her sandals, curl on a deckchair and inhale deeply. And here it comes again: that peaceful indifference she remembers from long ago.

Small clouds of smoke drift, the sea is a gentle pitpat, the colour drains from the hills, and Philippa wonders if she should light some candles, but why bother? She lets the darkness come. It washes over them all where they sprawl on the patio furniture, drinking and smoking and talking of this and that and sometime, late and sleepy, the talk shifts to other nights. Good nights. The best nights. Nights when everything turned out just fine.

It can happen. Ani stretches luxuriously among the cushions, fills her glass and tells a version of this tale.

The wine merchant, the wood cutter and the little silver car
A tale of one who, after divers misadventures, at last attains a goal of unexpected felicity.

Long ago, she was a young woman selling wine.

Her husband's parents in the Wairarapa had decided to get rid of the sheep, stripped out the fences, planted vines and built a big whitewashed winery. Instant Plasterboard Provençal. Wine tastings in the cellar room, lunches on the terrasse, a lot of wisteria, a lot of lavender. The neighbours thought they were mad but busloads turned up at weekends. Wedding parties, corporate functions. It was the decade when wine arrived. It was the decade when corporates arrived. It was the decade of Plasterboard Provençal.

The young woman had been living in the city. Her husband managed waste water for the council. She was training to be a nurse, though she did not like blood, shit or vomit and hypodermic needles made her feel queasy. She had wanted to go to art school but her mother said nursing was a true calling and to serve others was to serve God, and her father said in his opinion modern art was a load of poppycock. So she became a nurse

The Second Night

instead and went home at night to Matt in the flat in Freemans Bay, which was temporary before the inevitable house, mortgage, babies. Until her mother-in-law hinted that they could really do with a hand on the vineyard, so they moved south where Matt got into making wine and she got into selling it.

It wasn't art but she was happy, zipping about in a little silver Mazda. God, she loved that car. She loved wearing cool, sexy clothes, driving her cool, sexy car, rattling off the new language of terroir and herbaceous aromas as if she knew what any of that meant. For seven years she enjoyed herself.

Then one evening she was driving home from a wine and food expo in Palmerston North. It was the decade when expos arrived, and festivals of wine and food. It was the decade when wine awards arrived. She had had a good day. A lot of interest, a lot of orders, all very positive. She should have been feeling great. A summer evening, sunroof down, wind in her hair, the open road. Except at the end of the road was Matt.

Matt and one of the pickers, a French backpacker, such a cliché. Ani and Matt had never been particularly monogamous. Affairs, they had agreed, kept things from becoming boring. They talked about their lovers as they curled around each other in their connubial bed, comparing notes on their sexual habits and preferences and trying out the more interesting ones themselves. They gave each other's lovers silly names.

'What on earth did you see in him?' Matt would say. 'Slow-talkin' Sam? Did he just bore you into bed?'

Or she'd say, 'God, Moronica! Such a ditz! And that laugh! How could you stand it?'

But Melanie was different. Matt had gone very quiet, refused to talk about her, objected when Ani called her Melon Tits.

The Deck

'Don't do that,' he said. 'Melanie's a good person.'

When Melanie was present, it was Ani who was the extra, the outsider. Matt and Melanie's bodies inclined naturally towards each other like two vines intent on intertwining. They spent a lot of time together out in the vineyard and Ani would hear them talking, laughing. When she appeared, they stopped and turned towards her like two naughty children.

She could feel it coming: the slow-motion swerve as she and Matt drove off the road. She knew she should think about what she was going to do when the crash came but she kept putting it off.

So, on this lovely summer evening, she decided to take the long route home, the tourist route that wound through the hills. She had never driven this way before, always gone straight from A to B as fast as she could.

At the top of the tallest hill there was a viewpoint. The sun was setting in the west and there was no question, in that long ago, that it was beautiful with no sinister hint of burning bush. She pulled over into the parking area, got out and climbed a flight of steps to see it properly. There was a trig station up there, and a park bench and a signpost pointing the way to Sydney, New York, Beijing, Antarctica . . .

She had her camera, although there is never any point, is there, in photographing sunsets? Nor is there any point in photographing a wide plain where all the lights are beginning to twinkle. But she took the camera anyway, climbed the steps to the signpost pointing the way to the world and tried to focus.

It was quiet up there. She sat on the bench and listened to the quiet, and after a time she heard a car. It was racing up the road she had just driven, roaring and taking the bends fast, and

The Second Night

suddenly it was there, skidding into the carpark below, the stereo turned way up, the thump of heavy bass and the voices of young men, drunk and very loud, the smash of bottles on stones. She realised suddenly that she was alone up on the knoll. No one knew where she was. It was not the decade of the cellphone. She shrank into the bench and stayed very still, holding her breath. There was the slamming of car doors, the revving of engines, two cars doing wheelies around the carpark, a lot of whoop and roar, and they were gone.

They'd gone and they'd taken her car with them. She could hear it accelerating away around the bends, heading north. She had left the key in the ignition. She had left her handbag on the front seat. She had left several boxes of wine on the back seat. Stupid. Stupid.

And here she was in a thin summer frock and a pair of spindly silver sandals, miles from anywhere. It was getting dark and she had no option but to start walking. She would walk back down the road and hope for a lift.

It was a long way down, in bare feet because that was easier than walking in the stupid sandals. Stones cut her feet. Darkness fell and it was total. No moon and a chilly mist wreathing the hilltop.

She had been stumbling along for a while when she heard the cars again, the doof doof doof as they roared down the hill behind her. She scrambled down the bank and hid among some prickly stuff that scraped her bare skin and tore her dress. She crouched in a ditch, seeing their lights pass by overhead, all that careless male energy, and god, she hated them. Her little silver Mazda roaring along in front, doing a skid at the corner.

They disappeared and she scrambled back to the road, chilled

The Deck

and shivering in her torn dress, her feet bruised and bloody. Below her, she caught glimpses of the plain twinkling with people living their comfortable lives, warm in their living rooms, watching the telly or having a party with drinks and nibbles and music, while she was up here on a hillside, abandoned to a separate reality. She had never felt so desolate, so detached from the rest of the human race.

Then she heard another car. Just one this time, driving steadily down the hill behind her. It could have been anyone, of course. It could have been the guy who picks up the hitchhiker and he has some Ripper fetish and dumps your torn body under a bridge miles away, or he rapes you in the picnic area and leaves you for dead but you manage to survive and struggle to the road where your life heads off in the direction of identification and police inquiry and perhaps, though it's statistically unlikely, a conviction.

Or he's the guy who has prepared a soundproof room in the basement and keeps you there where you are tortured and have babies on your own and none of the neighbours notice anything amiss till you escape ten years later when he leaves the door unlocked by mistake, and you emerge, pallid and unrecognisable, a withered remnant of your former self. Or maybe you don't. You never emerge. You are killed and dismembered and the pieces are kept in a freezer and fed to the pigs.

The stories, the headlines, flickered through her mind as the car approached, but it was that car or freeze up here in the dark, so she put out her thumb and the car stopped. A man wound down the window.

'You all right?' he said.

Of course she was not all right. She was a mess, torn and

The Second Night

scratched and bloody and in tears, which she hated most of all. She never cried in front of people.

Then she was in the passenger seat, the heater on full and a jacket around her shoulders as they drove down towards the twinkling plain. And he said, 'I can run you into town right away, or you could ring the police from my place if you like. It's just at the bottom of the hill. You could stay the night. There's a sleepout, self-contained. You could have a good sleep and first thing tomorrow I could drive you into town to the police. What do you think?'

And maybe it would turn out to be the basement with the chains on the bed, but somehow Ani doubted it. He seemed nice. A square-cut kind of man with big solid hands on the wheel who did not ask a whole lot of questions, but said just enough to reassure. He was a scientist, a zoologist who worked at the agricultural research centre. Had a few acres where he ran some sheep. Pitt Island sheep. He liked old breeds, keeping the genetics going. She told him about the vineyard, which he said sounded interesting, though he preferred beer himself, craft beer. Brewing his own.

The words did not really matter. It was just a soothing babble of this and that, and when they got to his place the sleepout was not some mildewed hovel but a lovely solid little cottage, one of two, each set in its own patch of garden on a terrace above the river. He had built them himself, he said, back when he and his wife first moved out here. She ran them as summer rentals until she became ill, but since she died they were for friends and family. His son was living in one at present but he was out tonight. She would not be disturbed.

Suddenly everything switched to good. A warm bath, a big

The Deck

soft bed. She climbed in and slept like the dead, and sometime just before dawn she woke. There was noise outside. A car door slamming, footsteps stumbling into the other cottage. She looked out the window and there was her car.

The little silver Mazda, parked outside her room as if it had been there all along. She went out to check. Her bag had gone, and all the wine, but the spare key was still in its magnetic lockbox behind the front wheel. So she got dressed in the ripped summer frock and the stupid sandals and drove off into the sunrise to sort out her life.

Turned out it was easily sorted. Melanie had decided to go to Bali, the way young French backpackers do. She'd felt the migratory tug, time to fly. Ani and Matt could have tried to patch things up but they agreed it was over. They had reached the separation point.

So one Saturday a few weeks later she drove back over the hill. She wanted to explain to Leo, to thank him and apologise for running off like that.

He was cutting firewood, chainsaw roaring in a stand of gum trees when she pulled in and the son was with him, stacking logs. They both turned as she drove up, the son looking alarmed. He was pale, pimply, seventeen and stupid. The father was grey-haired but solid, muscled, the sun shining on his bare shoulders, and, well, that was it really. Ani stayed with Leo for the next thirty years. They had Tama. They moved south. They lived in a different city on a different island, they did different things. They painted the kitchen. They donated blood, they bought a dog, they won $800 on Lotto, they helped with the sausage sizzle, they watched Tama play basketball. Then, in an eyeblink, they were waving him off from Departures, an ethnobotanist at

The Second Night

a university in Hawai`i. They installed solar water heating. They had a trip to Tasmania. They learned to salsa. They were happy.

She never said anything about the car, just that the police must have dropped it off. Leo seemed happy with that. The son, Karl, was always a bit wary, but he moved out not long after she moved in, and eventually he grew up and became the manager of an electronics store in Māngere and had two kids who gave him a satisfyingly hard time once they were old enough.

'So that's it,' she says. 'The night everything worked out just fine. My car got nicked and I met Leo.' She leans back and blows a smoke ring. It hovers over her head then drifts away. 'He'd have loved this place. He'd have loved being here.'

And she is struck again by the unfairness of it all. That someone can become so very old. They shuffle ahead of you in the queue and then they turn a corner and disappear and you are left behind with years of living still to do and no option but to straighten your hat and keep right on walking. But every time you smell gum leaves you think of him. And every time someone says something funny, or does something mildly annoying, you wish you could tell him. You wish you could drive home towards him, stopping at the lights on City Road, arranging the story in your head. Making it better so that when you tell him, he will lean back against the bench and laugh. He'll say, 'Ach so!', eyes crinkled with amusement.

That's what she misses, quite apart from bed and sex and all that, though that too: she misses his body, strong and muscled almost till the end, and the clean outdoor smell of his skin and his lovely blocky penis and the way it filled her up and locked them together, his body to hers, for ever.

'Things can work out so much better than you expect,' she says.

'They can,' says Tom, who is suddenly eager to speak. He has a story too. He has told it many times. It pleases him. He wants to hear it again. He fills his glass and begins.

The deer hunters, the sorceress and the muddy boot

A second tale of one who, after divers misadventures, attains unexpected felicity.

They had gone to the island. Him and Gordie. Gordie was his mate from school and a top-class bullshit artist. He fancied himself as the big white hunter, man-alone-in-the-wilderness type and the summer they both turned eighteen he persuaded Tom to come with him to a hunting block on the island, far to the south. He had got a bow for Christmas, one of those lethal-looking crossbows with a scope and all, and he wanted to kill a deer. With a bow and arrow. Twang! Like Robin Hood. Gordie was a bit of a romantic at heart.

'We'll live off the land!' he said. 'We'll have fresh venison! We'll have fish! It'll be great.'

So they packed some gear and a lot of beer and got a boat to drop them off in an inlet. A beautiful place. Dense bush, never been milled, golden sand, little islets everywhere. The hut was a bit rough, but okay. Sacking bunks and a potbelly stove. They got themselves organised and off they went, Gordie stalking the

The Second Night

hills with his bow and arrows, Tom tramping along behind with his dad's old .303.

It had been raining for weeks — the mud was phenomenal and the sandflies were ravenous. And, for some reason, they did not spot a single deer. Not one. Not a sign.

After a few days Gordie was getting grumpy. He had shot nothing with his bow and arrows except feral cats. There were dozens of them, big rangy animals that emerged from the bush onto the beach as soon as he knocked one over, to devour the fresh carcass. He kept on hitting them, and they kept right on coming to eat their mates. Gordie just sat outside the hut in the long southern twilights, beer in hand, killing cats, but it wasn't what he had come all this way to do. He and Tom were not feasting on venison, nor were they eating fish. The bay was stirred up. They were living off dehy chicken curry and packets of biscuits.

Gordie wanted more. He wanted to move. They would head over the hill to the next little bay and see how that went. They packed up and set off. It was hard going, steep country, an overgrown track, rarely used, and a lot of fresh slips and fallen timber. Not a sign of any deer.

But they kept bashing along and, after a few hours, they found a boot. It lay in the middle of the muddy track, a big tramping boot, maybe size thirteen, well worn. Inside it was an old woollen sock, and inside that, a bloody mush. Torn flesh. Snapped white bone.

Tom wanted to wrap it up and take it to the police, but Gordie said, 'Nah, leave it. No point inviting trouble.'

It was not far off dark so Tom chucked it into the bush and they carried on through the mud down into the bay.

The Deck

There was a hut in a clearing, a real dunger of a place. Rusted corro, dark and windowless, sacking bunks, rats everywhere and an open fire.

And this girl. This beautiful girl. Francine, Francesca, something like that, one of those Mediterranean gypsy types with long black curling hair and those smoky eyes. Short shorts, legs that went all the way up and her shirt half unbuttoned. She was a cracker. She was gorgeous. They hadn't expected her. She couldn't speak much English, and they definitely couldn't speak whatever her language was, but there she stood, this bloody goddess in this godawful place, cooking up a stew in a big old black pot over the fire and after several days of dehy and gingernuts, that stew smelled pretty good.

When it was ready, she said in whatever language it was, help yourselves. And from this old metal-frame backpack — it looked far too big for her to carry, she had to be stronger than she looked — she produced a bottle of some kind of spirits. Never had it before, never had it since, tasted a bit like this grappa. And they passed the bottle around and ate that stew and it was spicy and richly flavoured and without a doubt it was the best meal, Tom said, of his entire life. Good food. The fire burning. This beautiful girl. The stuff of dreams.

It was certainly the stuff of Gordie's dreams. He was slugging back the liquor as if it was fruit juice, and it was bloody strong and he was turning on what passed for Gordie as charm. Teaching her to swear in English, asking her what the words were for this or that. My name Gordie. He Tom. You?

She read their palms, told them they would be 'appy, ver' rich'. She did not seem to notice or mind that Gordie was a dickhead so, after a bit, Tom decided to leave them to it. He

The Second Night

took his sleeping bag outside and managed, despite being fairly pissed, to rig up a fly by the beach where he settled into his sleeping bag and tried to sleep. Fed up with fucking Gordie. Fed up with this whole fucking trip.

The sky had cleared, the stars were out, a beautiful night. And suddenly there she was, this girl. She had left Gordie passed out in the hut and there she stood, a silhouette against a billion stars. Naked. She was smiling. Her teeth gleamed in the starlight. And then she . . . well, let's just say it was probably the best night of Tom's life, before or since.

She had gone by morning. Neither of them heard her leave. She had taken that big pack and disappeared into the bush. They took a brief look around, then headed back to catch the boat. Got a deer on the way, a clean shot. Gordie was happy with that. The bow and arrows had proved their worth just in time. The boat turned up as prearranged, and they headed back to civilisation.

And that was that. They never saw the girl again. At the end of the summer Tom left home and went his way, and Gordie left home and went his. They never talked about what had happened on the island. It felt less and less real. A hallucination.

'Though sometimes,' says Tom, pouring another drink, 'I've wondered about that stew. I've wondered about that boot . . .'

'So — what? You think that girl had killed someone? And you might have eaten him?' said Pete.

Tom shrugs. 'Dunno.' He adds a splash of water to the glittering glass. 'Maybe.'

'Gross,' says Pete.

Tom shrugs. 'Best night of my life,' he says.

'Well, for me . . .' says Philippa, who is so very tired of hearing this story, this mystic sex romp under the stars that Tom trots out whenever he is very drunk or very stoned. Because how can she compete with some youthful gypsy goddess with her magical stew, this cracker in the shorts and the unbuttoned shirt — he always mentions the shorts, he always mentions the buttons — who never degenerated into the woman who takes care to separate the glass from the cardboard and remembers to drop off the car for the warrant? How can you compete with the youthful silhouette under the stars when you are big-boned and freckled and have not aged well?

'Well, for me . . .' she says, 'the best night of my life would be the night Rosie was born.'

'Who's Rosie?' says Tom.

But Philippa takes no notice. She adjusts the cushions on the sofa and settles back to tell a version of this story.

The student of laws, the caravan and the marble mountain
A third tale of one who, after divers misadventures, attains unexpected felicity.

She had a summer job. The end of her second year at law school and she was seriously wondering if she wanted to be a lawyer after all. Maybe she should leave it to the private-school boys who had clearly assumed from the start that this was to be their patch. They had been such pricks, ignoring her, talking over

The Second Night

her, knocking her books off her desk, sniggering at their own stupid jokes as she and her breasts passed by.

She had toughened up under fire. There were only three women in her year and they had all toughened up. She worked like hell, got good grades, but after exams she had had enough. She did not want to think for a while. She did not want to have her brain crammed with words. Nothing whatever concerning Ryland v. Fletcher or Read v. J. Lyons and Co Ltd. She did not want to think about her illustrious career. She did not want to think about the future.

She hitched north and got a job in an orchard at the foot of a marble mountain. Ten-hour shifts standing by a conveyor belt watching a million Red Delicious apples rolling by. She had no idea work could be like this. It was a heatwave summer, a relentless sun heating the corrugated iron walls of the packing shed, turning it into an oven. She got vertigo from watching all those apples on the belt, felt as if she were tumbling sideways and she would have fallen except that a woman standing beside her, a nice woman called Polly, big and good humoured, who had worked there for years, showed her how to look up as soon as she began to feel giddy.

'Look at the wall over there,' she said, 'and keep looking till your head settles. Okay?'

She did that, and she was fine.

She had an old caravan to stay in. The owner had promised accommodation, but that turned out to be a shared room in a mildewed cottage with a rotting verandah and a septic tank that had not been emptied in years, or maybe there was a leak, because raw sewage seeped down a ditch outside the front door. The owner had laid down a plank for his workers to cross.

The Deck

Philippa had no idea people could live in places like this. She asked if there was somewhere else?

'Well, yeah,' said the owner. 'There's a caravan up the back of the orchard, but it's a bit rough,' which did not sound promising if the cottage was his standard of habitable.

The caravan sagged and smelled of wet carpet and the windows were covered in cobwebs and at one end there was a bed with a mattress richly stained. But she could spread her sleeping bag over that, and a banana passionfruit vine grew over the roof like a tea cosy with pendulous orange fruit and pink flowers. And, best of all, she had it to herself.

A river ran by, just beyond the fence. At night she could hear it swooshing along over gravel and on her afternoon off she walked along the bank to the place where it surged from under the mountain in an icy translucent flood through marble carved by water and draped in green leaf.

After work she walked back up to the caravan through the orchard. Stripped off her clothes, too tight, she could hardly breathe. Too hot. She sat on the step as the moon rose, eating passionfruit. Then she crashed into bed and slept more deeply, more dreamlessly than she had ever slept in her life. Sleeping on her back, though she normally slept on her side. Sleeping with her feet up on a pillow to rest legs that ached after all those hours standing in the packing shed.

In the morning before the heat of the day she walked back down through the apple trees and everything was cool and damp and spider webs were woven across the rows hung with glistening droplets and the birds sang in the bush up on the marble mountain. At the shed, Polly and the other women would be having a cup of coffee and a ciggie, chatting about

The Second Night

their lives, their families, their kids who were doing all right or hōhā and always in trouble. Chatting in the space before the belts started up and they were off again.

Then, that night . . .

It had been a long day, the hottest so far, over 35 degrees, hotter still in the shed, even though all the doors were open. She had been feeling nauseous. Her legs had become swollen with the standing.

'You need to drink more water,' said Polly, 'even though you'd think water would make the swelling worse. And cut out salt. And when you get home, soak your feet in the river. It's cold, but it's special, that water. It'll make your legs better.'

So that night, Philippa went to the river and soaked her legs in the cold water, sitting on the gravel bank and feeling it surge against her skin, trying to drag her in. Then she climbed into bed, but the pain in her legs was no better. Instead it spread upwards to her back and it hurt more and more, until she began to cry, to howl with the force of it. It was like she was being squeezed, like she was dying up there alone in her caravan and she put a pillow over her face to keep the howling in, and then she became lost in the tears, the pain and the squeezing, and she was a long way off, not here, not on the grubby bed, but in some big wide dark space studded with exploding stars.

And after a bit her body heaved and split apart and there was a baby.

It emerged in a rush between her legs. She put her hand down and felt it there, wet and warm and wriggling, so she gathered it up and it lay between her big breasts.

The moon shone through the window behind her head, a round white eye looking down, and by its soft light Philippa

The Deck

could see the baby's face. Her little crumpled face, her wet hair, her eyes wide open looking back at her. They were dark, those eyes, and slightly crossed and she had these amazing tiny hands with proper little fingernails, in a fist as if she had come out fighting. And she smelled lovely, more delicious than anything Philippa had ever smelled before. Salty and sweet.

The baby lay at her breast and began to nuzzle until she found the nipple and she seemed to know exactly what to do. She opened her mouth wide and began to suck, strongly, deeply, and with each suck Philippa's body clenched, pulsing to the same rhythm, and after a while there was another slither and a big damp meaty thing slid from her that she gathered up awkwardly because it seemed to be attached to the baby. So she wrapped them all together in the sleeping bag and they lay there in the moonlight.

The river rushed past. She lay there not thinking a thing. Her mind for the first time was completely stilled. There was nothing but the sounds of the night, the baby's tiny hands, the smell of skin, her own body as warm and sensate as a dog or a cat. There were no words for things. Just smell and texture. Just her own breath and the baby's tiny snuffling. Just being.

'And that,' says Philippa, 'was the most amazing night of my life.'

She has never said anything of this to anyone. It's a new story. How the baby lay at her breast in the moonlight. There was more, of course. Details she does not want to mention now.

How Polly came in the morning to check why she had not turned up for work. She seemed unsurprised to find Philippa and the baby in their nest. Said after you'd had as many kids as

The Second Night

she had, you recognised the signs, however carefully concealed.

How she called the ambulance and sat quietly admiring the baby till the crew arrived.

How the baby was lifted from her arms by a brisk woman who knew what was best for everyone.

How she was probably right.

How Philippa did her best not to cry or make a fuss because that was clearly irrational and not sensible or helpful to anyone, including the baby.

How she wanted to get a good grade, an A for being rational and sensible.

How she wanted to do her best for the baby.

How she returned to the city at the end of that summer as if nothing had happened.

How she told no one the story of the caravan, not her family, not her friends.

How she took up the law with a passion that surprised everyone. Because all those words, those cases and torts and opinions, were about actual people whose lives she knew now could be much more startling and deep and complicated than she had ever suspected.

How by the time she met Tom the whole story had slid away into a part of her brain reserved for whatever was strange or inexplicable and threatened to tip her sideways into muddle.

But tonight the story has come back. The moon, the warm bundle that was the two of them in the grubby bed, the little snuffling noises at her breast, and that new sensation, glowing and glorious, that she was a mammal in her secret nest, suckling her young. Like the cats on the farm purring in a hollow in long grass, their kittens in a row, kneading at damp fur.

The Deck

'Weren't you worried?' says Ani.

'About what?' says Philippa.

'Well, haemorrhage,' says Ani. 'Or that all the blood could drain out of the baby back into the placenta, something like that?'

'That doesn't happen,' says Philippa. 'Apes walk around for days carrying the baby and the placenta till the cord dries and falls away all by itself. It doesn't have to be cut. Anyway, I didn't know any of that. I knew nothing whatsoever. Hadn't read anything, hadn't talked to anyone. I didn't know enough to be worried.'

'What happened to Rosie?' says Baz. 'Where is she?'

'Singapore,' says Philippa. 'She's not called Rosie. Her adoptive parents renamed her. She's called Felicity now. She lives in Woodlands, works in a bank, she's got three children and her husband is in IT.'

'So you keep in touch?' says Ani.

'Felicity's practical,' Philippa says.

She is. She is brisk. She got in touch with her birth mother when she was pregnant, but only because she wanted to know if there were any congenital conditions that might manifest in her own children. She did not think a meeting would serve any purpose.

'She sends a card every Christmas,' says Philippa. A mother, a father, three children in cute Santa hats and an enclosed letter from The Hu Family reporting the children's progress in music, ballet and soccer. 'That's enough.'

Of course it's not. And Felicity is not 'practical'. She has a bitter core, a hard nub of resentment that leads her to taunt her birth mother once a year with a row of children lined up for the

The Second Night

photographer in Santa's grotto. 'See?' she says, with every banal report. 'This is what you missed out on.'

The woman is such a profound disappointment, and no relation whatever to that beautiful little being at her breast in the moonlight. But Philippa will never admit this to anyone. It would make her seem so needy, so vulnerable, so wrong, and she refuses to let that happen. She sticks to the version of mutually agreed practicality.

Tom gets to his feet.

'Right,' he says. 'Time to call it a day, I think.' And he sets to stacking the dishwasher with more than the usual clatter and bang. The others make some half-hearted attempt at assistance but he shoos them off.

'All under control,' he says, thin lipped and jamming a grubby plate onto the rack. 'See you in the morning.'

'Okay,' they say. 'If you're sure . . .'

'Yes, I'm sure,' he says. 'Sleep well.'

They trail away to their pods under the moonlight.

'So,' he says, when he and Philippa are alone at last on the brightly lit stage that is their kitchen. 'Rosie, huh?'

THE THIRD DAY

A sweet morning, crisp and clear. Sun, moon and stars in calm alignment and on Earth a man in a little boat, cutting a clean furrow across the gleaming of a bay.

Tom holds the tiller, heading for the reef at the foot of the headland on the far side, the shoreline and its complications receding before the simplicity of sunlight and water. He wants simplicity this morning.

How could she? This person he has lain with night after night, that warm familiar presence under their shared cover who all along has held this story within her like a message in a bottle, secret and sealed.

How could she have put him through all those tests and treatments, the see-sawing hope and disappointment, the long trek halfway across the planet to pick up Tashie from that godawful institution?

'So, not infertile after all?' he'd said as they stood, the kitchen bench between them like a barricade.

'I don't know,' she said. 'I don't know why I was able to have one baby and then not conceive another.'

'And not tell me?' he said. 'Did you tell anyone else?' Because that would have been intolerable: that she had told one of those friends he heard laughing sometimes when he opened the door, who paused and rearranged their faces as he entered the room, friendly enough but he had clearly missed the joke. When he asked later what they were laughing about, Philippa was always vague. Nothing. Just something someone said.

'No,' she says. 'I've never told anyone, till tonight.'

'Yeah, great timing with that,' says Tom.

Philippa shrugs.

'Who was the father?' says Tom.

'I don't know,' she says again, she who is always so clear, so certain, who never forgets a single detail. 'Just some boy at uni.'

'Come on!' says Tom. 'You can do better than that!'

He had known she had slept with others before him. Of course she had. There was a pill. It was the decade when the miraculous pill arrived, which had its risks, it had to be admitted — bloating, headaches, blood clots, stroke and in some cases, it had been reported, death — but it stopped the babies in their tracks. It was suddenly possible to have sex with nonchalant disregard for consequence. People did. Tom did. Philippa did. They exchanged their tallies one night, sitting naked on Tom's bed, dealing previous lovers turn and turn about like kids playing Snap!

Holly Tredgold. After the school formal.

My friend Hanna's Uncle Ted, a young uncle with an MG in British Racing Green, married of course, total bastard.

The Deck

Girl on Stewart Island.

Boy in her torts class, good looking and good sex, but when they were out with his mates he totally ignored her, turning to look at her when she spoke with a kind of cool disregard as if the back of the chair had suddenly decided to venture an opinion.

Girl he'd met at Kaiteriteri, New Year's Eve.

Et cetera.

Et cetera.

But this boy? The father of her baby? She has never mentioned him, not once.

'Just some boy at a party. I really don't remember.'

He's a blur, a heavy insistent blur after some sweet pineapple-flavoured punch specially concocted 'for the girls'. A student flat. A crush of people. Music, noise, hilarity. She remembers dizziness, and weight and the feeling of being pinned down, though she didn't want to be pinned down, and fumbling and juddering and sweaty gasping, sharp pain between her legs, a heave and some sticky residue. But his face? His name?

'Sorry to be so vague,' she says.

And was she sorry also for the hours of discussion when, after years of trying, it became clear that they were unlikely to conceive a child without assistance? It was the decade assistance became available. The decade of clever reproductive technologies, the eggs removed by specialists from splay-legged women, the sperm jittery in the Petrie dish. Should they try that experiment? But would a child born of such technology be truly human? Would it be thin and alien? Would it have been distorted by its gestation under laboratory lighting? There was that girl, though, the one born in the UK, she seemed normal enough. Or what about hormone injections and sperm recovery and surrogacy and, if so, who? And, if so, how?

Was his wife sorry for all that debate, and the cost of all that doubt? For it did cost, not only in dollars but in their confidence in themselves. Their viability as a breeding pair. It cost in energy, too. The effort of it all as they maintained busy professional lives, his architecture, her law. And it cost in grief — the tears every month at the menstrual blood. He simply could not bear her grief.

Then the talk shifted to adoption. He was not keen but Philippa became fixed and focused, the way she could, and he went along with it. It was some deep female thing, he decided, this desperate urge for maternity. He would not thwart that. He loved her.

Adoption was complicated but possible. It was the decade when the world became a global marketplace of babies. The offspring of the poor and disadvantaged of a dozen negligent states were advertised for adoption. Would they choose a baby from Romania? Ecuador? China? Russia? It would not be selfish to do so. There were too many babies. The world was groaning under the weight of babies. The great mass of humanity was destroying the planet and quarrelling over dwindling resources. Tom and Philippa would not add to the pressure by having more babies of their own. Instead, they would act responsibly. They would reach down from their lives of immense privilege and lift one of those neglected babies from the inevitability of destitution and despair.

Was she sorry now for the endless paperwork that entailed, the interviews and telephone conversations and at last the long journey flicking through day and night to a brown-eyed baby in that terrible room, those rows of small children caged in their

The Deck

cots, weirdly silent because who would come to comfort them?

But one looked up. She was beautiful, with big brown eyes and a pink rosebud mouth. She raised her arms to them. Help me! Help me! And he watched as his wife fell in love. He watched her enraptured face as she cradled this baby amid the stink of stale milk and dirty nappies and boiled cabbage.

They rescued her, this one little child from that clanging indifferent place, and they crashed into parenthood. He remembers how it was, standing in a featureless hotel room, the alien city below punctured by streetlights. He remembers holding his daughter, doing that thing that always seems to work in movies. Rocking back and forth till the baby quietens, snuggles and sleeps peacefully till dawn.

But this baby did not snuggle. She arched away from him, she beat at his chest with tiny fists and she opened her sweet mouth and howled. All the way home, across all those lines of longitude and latitude, Natasha howled.

Once home, she rocked in her cot and banged her head and devised means of escape, tumbling up and over any barrier with the agility of a gymnast, a circus acrobat. She learned to crawl through any gap in the defences Tom built to keep her safe. She went to school and swung by one hand from the highest bars in the playground. She jumped from bridges into untested water, rode her bike out into the traffic, indifferent to risk or consequence.

Other children stood by fascinated as she lit match after match and set the classroom rubbish bin on fire or climbed to the ground from a third-floor window. And later, when she took to stumbling home dishevelled in her big black boots and tiny skirts, mascara streaking her beautiful face, indifferent to anger,

The Third Day

tears, threat, restraint, curfew, she remained an object of their amazement.

'Tash is a fucking legend!' said one little vampire, pierced and tattooed with ripped lace leggings and nails like bloodied claws. Then came the nights when she did not come home at all. Tom caught glimpses of her as he scoured the city streets at 2am, the loudest, the most extreme in the mob of kids milling about outside Burger King. He watched her bend down as a car pulled up to the kerb. He watched his daughter climb in, as if she had done this many times before. He watched her leave. And then came the misdemeanours, the police, the juvenile court, until suddenly one day she was gone.

She stole Philippa's credit card and bought a ticket to a concert in Brisbane and they never saw her again. She flew away to that big red continent and disappeared.

You would think it was impossible in an era of data collection and digital record, but if someone really doesn't want to be found, said the police officer when they lodged the missing person report, it can be surprisingly difficult to track them down. And there was always, of course, the possibility of the shallow grave in mulga scrub, the cloud of flies, the beautiful skin withered to dry leather containing a pocketful of bones.

They had handled it all, thinks Tom as he heads towards the reef. They had handled it together, as a couple. It had been exhausting, a source of professional embarrassment to Philippa: she who passed judgement on other people's wayward children was not even capable of controlling her own!

They had handled it with dignity. It was a private grief, shared only with their closest friends. In an odd way it had even lent them status. They were the couple who, unable to have a child

The Deck

of their own, nobly adopted a child who proved to have been profoundly damaged. But they had behaved throughout with decency. He had done his best to be a patient father. Philippa had been a loving mother. They had turned their infertility into an attempt to do good in the world and they had suffered a tragic outcome.

And all of it had been based upon a lie. All along, Philippa had had her baby. She had a daughter to whom she had actually spoken. And every year she brought this daughter's children, her grandchildren, into their home, among the line-up of Christmas cards on the mantelpiece, leaving Tom to assume they were the offspring of some grateful client.

She had never said a thing.

He squeezes down on the throttle, feeling the boat slap down hard. How could she have chosen that moment to tell him, in front of witnesses? How could she have calmly readied herself for bed, moisturising her face and neck with that expensive goop she favours, as if nothing had happened?

He had slept on the mossy-green sofa and got up at daybreak, walked down to the rocks where mussels formed orderly ranks like the tiles on a roof, from the tiniest, no bigger than a fingernail, to the big buggers that clung to the most inaccessible crannies where the surf surged, their shells gnarly with barnacles and their feathery old beards protruding, and who knew how old they were? Sixty? Seventy? His exact contemporaries.

He had knocked a few loose with a sharp blow and forced their shells apart, scooped out the flesh, white for males, palest pink for females. He had baited the rod that now lies beside him in the boat as the cliff looms ahead, lacy with white bird shit. He takes the boat in close, near enough to find the moki at their grazing, not so close that the line could tangle in the dense forest of kelp that waves its long brown branches just beneath the surface.

He finds his hunting ground, lining up with the headland, the cave mouth and the dead tree that hangs over the lip of the cliff, and drops anchor. When he switches off the outboard, the silence falls around him like silk. The lap of water at the hull, the soft breath of the wind on his bare neck, the calm purpose that always accompanies the moment when he deals out the line and feels the sinker drag it down. He waits, hand on the reel, jigging.

He waits.

And then the tug.

Not the nuisance nibbling of herring making off with his bait but a strong, decisive gulp. His fish is down there unseen, a big one with a bit of weight, its every move transmitted through the fine filament that connects them, his hand to its snagged mouth. He feels it tug, struggle, make small darting runs away from him as he lifts it up. He is the hunter, calm and implacable. He draws his quarry forth into the harsh light of day. It breaks the surface into the breathless realm, a grey-blue iridescence, flapping wildly from the hook that is firmly embedded in its puffy lip. He draws it close and there is that tender moment of regard, eye to eye, as he removes the hook, twists and tugs. Its round unblinking eye regards him without expression, but surely with some flicker of hope. Right to the final second hoping for release.

He takes a firm grip.

'Sorry, mate,' he says, because a part of him always does feel sorry. He has watched such fish for years, witnessed their beauty

The Deck

and assurance when he has dived down into their domain. Now the fish's gills flap as it chokes on alien air. It writhes and threatens to slip from his hand, and there is nothing for it but to be quick, grab the iki, an old screwdriver he has ground down to a sharp point for just this purpose. He strikes down onto the skull. Just above that round unfathomable eye, a single decisive blow that smashes through bone to the creamy mass of the brain where he whips the blade about, reducing reflex and whatever passes for thought in this creature to a mush. It jerks and lies still in his hand.

He guts it then, quickly, drags out intestine and kidneys and heart, tosses the scraps into the ocean, where gulls swarm and squabble over the choicest bits. He lays the emptied body in the chilly bin, baits the line and starts over.

The fish have never been so willing. The fishing has dwindled along this coast. Often he has returned empty handed, but on this clear morning he has chanced upon a school busily popping shellfish from the rocks below and careless of risky temptation. He lifts them up, one after another, and he knows he should stop. He has more than enough for tonight's dinner. But it's just too easy. The moki are lining up for their own demise. They are practically asking for it.

So fucking stupid. No wonder they're dying out. He fixes the bait and drops the line over and over, and only when the bin is full can he stop. His skin is scorched, arms and legs and face a scarlet flush that will be painful later. He has been unaware while his attention was so narrowly focused on line and bait and tug, but the sun is hammering down and the glare on the water is making his head ache. He needs to go back in to shore. He wants to bear his miraculous catch up to the house.

The Third Day

But when he makes his entrance, no one is there.

He had been anticipating Wow! Amazing! A triumph! Applause. A chorus of ululating women, but instead he arrives to silence. The beautiful room he has made feels desolate for all its perfect proportions. Without the chorus it is an empty stage.

Instead, he must carry his fish down to the bench he designed for just this purpose, at a sufficient distance from the house to deter flies. A stainless steel bench angled to drain into the sink. Magnetic rack with knives ready to hand, a whetstone, a smoker, everything ready to go.

He chooses his favourite knife and sets to work, and the scales fall away in sticky sequinned threads. Some fish he leaves whole and places on platters in the fridge for the evening meal, but the rest he has to fillet and wrap for the freezer and the magnitude of his achievement becomes less visible, bit by bit. He scales and fillets with the gathering certainty that, by the time he has finished, the morning and his catch will be just another fishing yarn. Exaggerated. Faintly absurd. An old man's empty boast.

And now that matters. When he was young he was unaware of this need for praise. He accepted it as his due. He was the scholarship winner, the first-class graduate, the new recruit to the firm whom the senior partner, an avuncular booming man, introduced to clients and colleagues at gatherings of the Institute of Architects as 'our rising star'. In meetings, members of the firm turned towards him and paid attention, rather than turning shoulder on and interrupting as they did to others less gifted or less agreeable.

When he left to join another couple of rising stars striking out on their own in an independent practice, the senior partner wished him well.

The Deck

'Good show,' he'd said, slapping his protégé on the shoulder as he ushered him towards a glowing future. 'Now, let's see what you can do when left to your own devices!'

What the trio managed was a practice with a local reputation for quiet, meticulous competence. Not, after all that initial promise, one of the illustrious firms in the city with international reach and major civic contracts, but a middle-of-the-road kind of company designing unadventurous practical suburban shopping centres, offices, houses, renovations, apartment complexes.

When Tom retired, there were speeches and thanks from the rising stars he had recruited, the young graduates of architectural schools and some years of experience in practices in London, LA or Singapore, with all their style and confident ambition. Tom was stepping aside into a life he planned to fill with fishing and golf and travel to see what other architects had done when left to their own devices. The tickets were a retirement gift, an opportunity to stand before the high arch of La Défense, the nun's wimple of Notre-Dame du Haut, the Sagrada Familia, the Aliyev Centre in Baku . . .

Their chief impact had been to make him feel rage. Building by building, masterpiece by masterpiece, Tom became more and more appalled at his own profound insignificance. What a con-trick life was! The way it persuaded you of possibility, dangled it just out of reach before finally defeating you.

'Come on,' he had said to Philippa who was reading the guidebook, eager to get to Gehry's Guggenheim early before the crowds. Sunlight ricocheted from the complex of gleaming shell. It gave him a headache.

'I need a drink,' he'd said, walking away. He was frantic. It

The Third Day

was all he could do not to run, howling at the sky like those crazy old stinkards who swore and raged at lampposts and trees along the boulevards.

'What? Now?' she'd said, bustling to keep up. 'It's not even nine o'clock.'

'Yes, now,' he'd said.

A dark bar. Something very plain and very ugly whose only purpose was to serve shots of some very powerful liquor.

At recent meetings of the institute he had found himself standing next to young men and young women who looked blank when he introduced himself. They abandoned him mid-sentence when the senior partner, now ancient, honoured and revered, was wheeled into the room.

The sun beats down as he drops the freezer lid at last on his unacknowledged triumph. He pours himself a drink, even though it's not yet whatever-the-hell. A strong drink. A tumblerful of indifference. Then he sits in a patch of shade on the deck with his burning skin, and the warm air settles like suffocation over his aching, irrelevant head.

At the far end of the beach by the creek, Baz kneels by the van, scraping wax from his surfboard. The bay was dead flat when he first woke, a wide glassy expanse viewed through the open door of the van from the doggy warmth of his bed. But the wind would shift eventually and the waves would build because that's what they always do.

Yesterday when the van heaved itself, heavily laden, over the crest of the hill, he had seen it for the first time. He had surfed other places along this coast but never here. A narrow inlet of blue lay between twinned headlands and a perfect left-hand

The Deck

break peeled from the southernmost point, the waves driven by an offshore wind into the beautiful mathematics of orderly progression.

> *Let the wave move at the constant speed **V**, let the surfer sliding across its surface be the particle with the mass **M**, let the essential forces acting upon the surfer be gravity **G**, buoyancy **B**, and drag **D** . . .*

The seductive tension between order and chaos.

He had driven down as quickly as the van would allow, crashed over the ford — some damage there, but it could wait — and parked up by some raggy macrocarpas at the far end of the beach. Then he had dragged on his old wetsuit and run, big bare feet padding through marram grass, over sand and broken shell before water and wind could change their minds. He'd paddled out, the particle subject to the functions of form and energy, and his board had bucked beneath him like a live thing. His body lay prone, his arms reached out, pulled back, as head down, he punched through successive walls of water, sunlight snagged in his eyelashes.

He paddled hard, feeling the grating of bone at hip socket and in the shallow cup of each shoulder joint that was part of it all now. Whenever he knelt, his right knee clicked in protest. Whenever he stood, twisted, switched weight from foot to foot, it was to an internal chorus of clicking and grinding he could hear with complete clarity, though the sounds of the outer world were becoming muffled. Other bones, tiny pink stalactites, were growing in the caverns of his ears, closing the canal against these icy southern waters.

The Third Day

He knew he should make an appointment to deal with the grinding and the clicking and the stalactites. He should sign up for examinations, X-rays and medical procedures involving drills and chisels and incisions behind the ear, or across the buttock, or at knee joint and shoulder. He had glanced online at accounts of corrective surgery intended to reassure with their casual mention of plastic or ceramic replacement parts and steel rods, and it all seemed very straightforward. Really quite routine.

But it was a matter of time, wasn't it? On that wave of time the particle also slides, subject to inexorable forces.

> *Let time move at a constant speed V, let the human borne upon its surface be the particle with the mass M, let the essential forces acting upon the human be survival S, hope H, and the drag of knowledge K . . .*

He knew there were only so many clear days like this day, the waves lining up row on row, the sound of water rushing in his surf-damaged ears, the basalt cliffs high on either side, a shag poised on the branches of a dead tree overhanging the water, its wings spread wide like Jesus on his crucifix. Except this little bird-god lifted off its perch and rose up, up. It dropped like an arrow headfirst to the water then bobbed back after an interval, something fresh and wriggling in its beak.

On that first day Baz had paddled out to meet the bay. Every beach, every break, every wave had its own distinctive rhythm. He had sat out the back beyond the breakline feeling the sea breathe beneath him. The shoreline was far away, his friends'

The Deck

crib a collection of small black boxes on a terrace above the sandhills. There was some clamour off to his left, close to the cliffs, a squabbling cloud of gulls, the water broken by slap and fuss, a shoal of herring perhaps.

And then the shadow. Not a shoal. That would glitter and twinkle, all the tiny fish driven as if by a single mind. This was something bigger and more purposeful. Something grey and sleek. Maybe it was benign. One of the dolphins that were endemic to this stretch of coast though in rapid decline, down to double figures. He had seen them often enough over the years, sweet-faced little creatures at play like himself with those essential forces. *G, B, D . . .*

The shadow passed beneath his board, too big to be a dolphin. A seal perhaps? Some still dozed on the rocks at the foot of headlands, their big soft slug bodies accommodating every jagged ridge. A sealion? Or a leopard seal with its wide deceptive smile and savage teeth?

Or a shark?

There were more of those these days. Dogfish and blue sharks mostly, some rigs, a few hammerheads, and in season the big sevengills making their way south to the island inlets and rivers where the little jelly pups would stream from those grey torpedo bodies. And great whites. More of them each year as the waters warmed and fish stocks out at sea dwindled, hoovered up by trawlers flying a rabble of flags, national and international, all taking advantage of chaos and distraction to ignore laws and quotas and conventions. The crumbling of order. The destruction of social contracts.

Baz preferred not to think about sharks. Long ago he had bobbed about on a long board trying out this new thing. It was

The Third Day

the decade when California arrived with surfboards and woody wagons and girls in bikinis and the Beach Boys in close harmony on the soundtrack. It was the decade of the loose-limbed, sun-warmed endless summer. He and his mates were trying it in a cooler climate, a hundred metres out from an unforgiving southern coast.

There was a sound. A cry, high pitched, that cut right across the day, and somewhere off to his right there was a commotion, everyone paddling fast for shore.

Except one. There was one who did not head straight for shore. He turned instead towards the one who was screaming out there in the water, his leg torn to the bone, his board damaged, the shadow circling.

It was not Baz who made the decisive move. He was the one who sat frozen out the back, his legs drawn up out of the water onto a board that seemed suddenly very frail. He was the one who at the moment of terror proved incapable of action. He could only watch while someone else did the thing he had learned about since childhood, the heroic, noble thing, obeying an impulse that overrode the natural instinct towards self-preservation.

The hero did not scramble for his own safety but instead paddled towards his wounded comrade. He loaded him somehow onto his own board and then, amazingly, heroically, set off kicking strongly for shore, pushing the board and a mate whose blood was coursing freely. While an animal circled whose every instinct was to tear and kill and devour. An animal that could detect a single drop of blood in seawater from five kilometres away.

While Baz sat and watched.

The Deck

It is curious to witness your own failing, your total absence of nerve. 'Nerve' had been much valued when he was a child. His father had been a soldier. He had fought in the desert, and it went without saying that he had displayed nerve. He had tossed a grenade into a slit trench occupied by German soldiers when the Kiwis were making a run for it, bayonets fixed, straight through the enemy lines, and Gerry thought they had us boxed in, the bastards, thought we were done for. The Brits had given up on us too, typical bloody Poms, just like they did on Gallipoli, back when his old dad, their grandfather, was a soldier. He too had fixed his bayonet and he had charged up a cliff face, straight at Johnny Turk.

Their grandfather had had nerve.

He had been commended for it in a special certificate in which the King 'wished to record his high appreciation of services rendered'. He had signed the letter with the royal signature, 'George', which sounded almost casual, as if the King were an affectionate uncle. The King's letter was framed and hung alongside the photo of the Pope above the dining table.

Their grandfather had survived the charge up the cliff face but he was not so lucky some months later in France, despite all his nerve. He copped it, hit by a sniper only weeks from the end of the war, and all their gran got was a few bob and that letter from the King. But when the time came, their father had not been deterred. He had stepped up because someone had to put a stop to bloody Hitler. He had gone off to fight in the desert in those baggy shorts he still wore in the summer, his legs bowed and knotted with blue vascular threads, his chest bare, a hanky knotted on his head and a cigarette, a doofer, half smoked, tucked behind one ear for later.

The Third Day

He had nerve. Nerve was what was needed in war, and in peacetime it was needed on the rugby field. Baz's older brother had nerve. He rushed in to tackle kids twice his height and weight. He lost two front teeth but he had what it took. Baz did not have what it took. He was a nancy-boy who needed to toughen up, which was why their father tied him to the verandah post and bowled at him, hard and fast, over and over all one summer till he learned to stand steady at the crease. Baz learned to bat, and to loathe both cricket and rugby and as soon as he could choose for himself, he chose this.

The solitary engagement with the wave rising in its unique formation at his back, its white crest rearing over the smooth blue trochoidal curve in a ratio determined by water depth and gravity. And him paddling, the particle, pushing hard to catch it on its run in to the shore. He chose to be gathered up by the forces of gravity, buoyancy and drag, the beautiful mathematics of natural forces, and to find his point of balance upon them.

That was yesterday. Today it's flat. The waves have shrunk overnight and the wind is soft. He kneels on warm sand waxing his board, waiting for things to change as they always do. The grey shadows are out there, all manner of shadows, some benign, some threatening, but that is how it is.

If he were to be torn to pieces by some sea creature, at least it would be savage and quick. An ocean death on a sunlit morning, consumed by a creature simply following its instinct for survival, would undoubtedly be painful and terrifying — he has never forgotten that scream — but better that by far than other deaths he has witnessed. The damp-rot creep of cancer and the protracted and ultimately futile chemical resistance. Or the choking death as the lungs fill with fluid, and the trundle

The Deck

of the oxygen tank. Or the decline into senility and the La-Z-Boy recliner and the listless screen with some baking competition on endless repeat, or worse, a wildlife documentary from which all the wildness, all the life, has been deleted. Nothing but the imagery of waves breaking with the sound muted and no hint of the beauty of the sting of sea spray on bare skin and the fishy reek of seals and the keening of seabirds and the cloud a high arch overhead. The whole great breathing world of sea and sky.

Better a shark than a death devoid of that breathing world.

Baz kneels in the sunlight. He has scraped the board clean. He flicks the old wax into the marram grass and turns to applying a fresh coat, tracing a lattice of firm diagonal lines across the surface that will hold him steady when wind and water agree. When he can pad again on his big bare feet across the sand to the sea. He will run and plunge headfirst. He will ignore click and grind. He will give himself, body and soul, to the ocean. And he will pay no heed to shadows.

You could, if you wanted, call it nerve.

From up on the hillside Philippa watches him moving about contentedly by that awful van of his, when he could have stayed in one of the pods with a comfortable bed and a shower. Baz has always had a van. A series of them, each an identical kennel on wheels where he has kept all his stuff. Wetsuits, boards, tools, gardening gear, guitar, disgusting mattress and cooker.

'I prefer the van,' he said when she suggested the pod. 'Thanks, but I like my own space. I like knowing where everything is.'

When she first met him years ago, Tom's flatmate, she wondered what anyone saw in Baz. Tall and quiet, a science

The Third Day

student, pre-med, who didn't seem to have any opinions about anything at a time when everyone had opinions about everything and the arguments were long and loud and segued into marches and sit-ins and protests. Baz just sat, cradling a beer, listening.

'He's just so *annoying*,' she said to Tom as they lay close-cupped in his bed, the lamp casting a crimson glow through the muslin scarf she had draped over the shade. It was her first contribution to the décor. 'I mean, that strong, silent man act. Does he really not have any ideas at all? Or does he think he's superior to everyone, the smug guru sitting there passing judgement on us all?'

'He's not so bad,' said Tom. 'He won't be passing judgement. He's not like that. He's just quiet, that's all.'

'Well, I think he's boring,' said Philippa. In his presence, before that silence, she felt herself to be too voluble, too loud. She had been reading stuff. It was the decade when women began reading stuff. Books about women and how they had been controlled, ignored, persecuted, deleted from the historical record. It was a revelation. Her life, her mother's life, her grandmother's life and the lives of all the women who had been her antecedents, all the way back, were lived within a system, invisible but vice-like in its grip.

It was as intangible as the air they breathed, but its effects could be measured, studied and recorded. Studies showed, for example, that if a woman spoke more than one third of the time in a mixed group, she was perceived as having talked too much. The figures were backed up with pictures of ducking stools and nags' bridles with that cruel tongue plate and vicious metal spike.

So when the male students with their supreme assurance

The Deck

interrupted her or the other two women in her year, when the lecturers ignored her or addressed the class as 'gentlemen', this was no accident. Such things were the superficial evidence of a massive underlying system.

Philippa began to keep count. It was the decade when women began to keep count. She wrote nothing down but she began to notice and remember slights and insults, personal and historical, everything from witch burning to the way she had to present Tom to the doctor at Student Health when she wanted a prescription for the pill, with a guarantee that they planned on marriage. She noticed and she counted how the doctor talked only to Tom, kept eye contact only with Tom, even though it was her body that was being discussed here, her ovaries that were about to be chemically manipulated, her hormones, her womb. From such data she assembled a case. A case for the indictment, for the prosecution. Though when exactly she would present this case, or to whom, or for what purpose, was not exactly clear.

Baz's silence was more difficult to categorise but she noticed and counted it. It was a highly effective silencing strategy. It was as effective in silencing her as an interruption, though it was a bit more subtle than a spike through the tongue, and she hated him for it.

Other girls were not deterred. Baz's room was next to Tom's. At night they heard the headboard of his bed hammering on the partition that divided a grand Edwardian dining room in two.

'Ooh,' moaned that night's girl as the headboard accelerated till she cried 'Yes yes yes!' and Baz emitted a grunt and it was over. And Tom reached for Philippa, his hands grabbing her big breasts, his erection hard and urgent, and she'd turn towards

The Third Day

him, her mouth, her tongue soft and wet and probing, and their bed squeaked and rattled in its turn.

And all the time a part of her was distracted, thinking of Baz and the girl a few inches away through the wall, and it was as if they were engaged in a kind of competition: Baz and the girl versus her and Tom. She let herself moan more loudly than she had before, and Tom reared up in response and his cock was punching harder, faster and she was coming, she was coming, oh yes yes yes! And it was weird, but if there was a competition going on, then Philippa most definitely wanted to win.

Out of bed, however, Baz was a bore. She did not see the point of someone who had no opinion whatever about American imperialism or the validity of anarchism or the future of religion. Until the afternoon at the beach.

She cannot recall which beach or who was there, just a tangle of arms and legs in Baz's ancient Kombi van among boards and wetsuits and a mattress stinking of unidentifiable but definitely unsavoury residues. They lurched down a road of bumps and potholes, taken by surprise each time for there were no windows in the back and they tumbled about yelling, 'Ahhh!' or 'Fuuuucckkk!' or 'Slow down!' until the van lurched to a halt and they all scrambled out into the chill wind of a dazzling autumn day. Baz and a couple of others were suddenly full of purpose, dragging on wetsuits, lifting boards from the van, running towards the ocean. The waves were huge that day, a southerly swell running.

The rest fooled about, considered a swim but the water was *sooo* cold, it was *freezing*, their feet went numb on contact. They pushed one another, made half-hearted forays up a rocky outcrop, gathered driftwood, made a little camp in a cave. The

The Deck

back of the cave was damp and dark and smelled of seaweed. It was somebody's birthday and someone had brought a carrot cake, which was a new kind of cake, healthier than the marble cakes of childhood. This cake was made of grated carrot and had cream-cheese icing, so it was packed with protein and vitamins and therefore good for you. It was the decade when carrot cake arrived. It was the decade when food was divided into categories, healthy or unhealthy. In Philippa's childhood you ate what was on your plate — usually mutton, roast, stewed or fried — with potatoes and boiled carrots. On birthdays you ate marble cake.

Philippa sat with the others around their fire, eating her healthy cake and drinking Cold Duck, while out among the huge waves Baz and his mates swooped and flew. After a time he came in. He walked up the beach towards them in his tight black skin, the sun catching in the wild tangle of his hair, and Philippa looked up and maybe it was the Cold Duck, which had left her light and fizzing, but suddenly she saw what all those girls moaning in the room next door must have seen. Baz was beautiful and who cared if he had no opinion concerning the Domino Theory?

And here he is again, older, heavier, the hair thinned to a fuzzy grey tonsure, and yesterday she had watched him swoop the length of the bay before stepping down into the smash of white foam, then turning, paddling back out, over and over. Still, to her eye, beautiful.

Baz, whom she has invited because it's time Ani stopped pining for Leo, who was a nice bloke, admittedly, but he has been dead for eight years now and that is long enough to mourn. Philippa believes in process. Everything can be broken

The Third Day

down into manageable stages, including grief. She has read a book by a woman with a reassuringly authoritative European name, double barrelled, with an umlaut: the five stages of grief from Denial (Stage One), to Anger (Stage Two), to Bargaining when the bereaved attempts to alter reality by making a deal with God, to Depression and ultimately to the desired state of Acceptance, when a new plan is in place and the bereaved can move on.

Ani, she thinks, should be approaching Acceptance by now. Maybe it was significant that last night she chose to tell that story about meeting Leo? Philippa had heard it before, several times, but then it was told as a duet for two voices, Ani and Leo taking turns to supply the detail over some chaotic meal at their place, with the latest dog begging for scraps of lasagne because they never trained their dogs properly. Philippa has never approved of dogs inside. They belong in a kennel down behind the macrocarpas, the way they were housed on the farm. But she had sat with the latest dog pressing its damp nose into her crotch under the table and listened to the story of the stolen car, the dark hillside . . .

'. . . and then this woman I see at the side of the road with her thumb out, all messy —'

'I looked an absolute wreck —'

'— and I think, Leo, I hope this woman is not, you know, crazy, or drunk. I hope she doesn't throw up all over my —'

'I was just so relieved when he pulled over.'

'I say, "You okay?"'

'And obviously I wasn't okay, but —'

'It's freezing up there so I say, "Hop in" —'

'And I thought, he looks nice, but you can't really tell, can you? I mean, I've seen photos of the Yorkshire Ripper and he looked nice enough . . .'

They told such stories, taking turns to add this or that, but in a kindly fashion. Not as Tom does when she is telling a story, interrupting to correct the timing of some event, or the exact mileage between places or the names of people who are barely relevant, so that before she knows it her story has degenerated into a confusion of argument over detail and contradiction and the whole point is lost.

Ani and Leo told the stories of their shared lives in a happy counterpoint that ended only when Leo began to miss his cues.

When Ani said, 'And then I heard this car coming down the road behind me,' Leo's eyes remained vague and glassy. He had no memory of the hillside, the woman on the road. Who was she? And who were these people seated around the table, these friends who had become total strangers, menacing, unrecognisable?

Ani was watchful, supplying names, identification, helping him locate knife and fork, leaning over to wipe his mouth free of tomato sauce, as steadily, inexorably, Leo disappeared. He became small and frightened and unpredictably angry, wandering from the house without his trousers, or clad in random garments, his and hers.

And the friends stood by watching, like a chorus, like the extras in a movie who are the background crowd in the bar or at the traffic lights, the frame to the leads who are caught up in a drama of dangerous emotion and human frailty and the will of whimsical gods. These extras, this chorus, interrupted from time to time, popping around with a casserole or apple cake. They talked among themselves about the protagonists in the

The Third Day

drama in their midst with a mixture of awe and pity. And when the drama reached its climax they put on the black suit, the black dress and attended the funeral.

They sat in a chilly suburban Catholic church because Leo, after a lifetime of atheism, had put it in his will years ago that he should be buried in the church he had last willingly attended when he was twelve. They had sat listening as a dry little priest rattled through the service, referring always to their friend as 'Leopold'. 'Our dear brother Leopold' who became, with that change of name, a stranger to them all. The priest spoke rapidly in a flat Irish accent, clearly irritated at having to deliver the ministrations of the church to someone who had never, to his certain knowledge, turned up once for Mass. And afterwards the friends said, 'I'm so sorry for your loss,' and made donations to the memory care unit.

But all that was years ago, and Ani still has Leo's voice on the answerphone. She still actually has an answerphone. She still has his outdoor boots on the rack by the back door. His bowls trophies still occupy the shelf in the living room. It was as though Leo had merely stepped out for a moment, leaving Ani stuck in Stage One, Denial.

'It's not healthy,' Philippa had said to Tom. 'Do you think we should introduce her to someone?'

Tom said nothing, his eyes on the screen.

It was not easy to find a suitable man. The flurry of midlife separations had long passed, and everyone they knew was settled into coupledom. Even the couples who had squabbled endlessly in public for years seemed resigned to sitting it out for the duration.

'Don't you think you've had enough?' says the husband to

the wife who has just accepted another pinot and is already slurring, sloppy and sentimental.

'Piss off,' she says, but without rancour. She can't be bothered to defend herself, and he can't be bothered any longer to care.

The long-term philanderers seemed to have settled down, hormones calming after a lifetime of not-so-secret liaisons. The men who placed a speculative hand on the bum of the wife's best friend, just testing. Was that a flicker? Was that a hint of 'All right then!'? Would a phone call be a good idea, opening the way to another series of delightful afternoons in motels at a safe distance from the city? A surreptitious weekend away that was supposedly being spent at a conference in Rotorua? Even those old roués had slumped back into coupledom and spent their afternoons at golf or pruning the hedge.

As for the widowers, they remained single for no more than a nanosecond, swiftly reclaimed for coupledom, or sinking into a contented bachelorhood that permitted restoring an Indian motorcycle in the hallway and bugger the carpet, or nights spent with one eye glued to the telescope mounted on the garage roof for the observation of celestial spheres.

And then there were those, very few, who had remained single all their lives with no apparent attachment to another, male or female.

Baz, for instance.

Philippa has invited them both, Ani and Baz, and this morning she suggested they might like to take out the kayaks.

'It's so calm and there's a huge cavern midway down the bay,' she said. 'You should see it. It's amazing. You can't always get into it, but it would be easy now, at such low tide.'

But Baz said kayaking had never really been his thing,

The Third Day

specially now his shoulders were packing up, and Ani said she'd rather come with Philippa to pick raspberries. Pete and Didi said they'd come too.

From where she stands by the walnut tree Philippa can see them, just their heads visible among the overgrown canes in what remains of Bimmi's garden. She can hear the murmur of their voices. The walnut tree at her back is old and ample, with leaves like wide-open hands, and every branch is studded with the green knobs of unripe nuts.

When she was a child out here visiting her great-aunt, this was her tree. It had broad branches set at even intervals and was easy to climb, and once up there, high above the ground, your back firm against the trunk, you became invisible. You could look down on the world and see everything, the whole length of the bay, but no one could see you.

Your sister, your brother trailed about calling, 'Hey Plip! Plip Plop! Where are you?' They could stand right underneath at the foot of the tree and still not find her. She could look down as they gave in and she'd won, but she could not be bothered to come down and claim the victory. It was nice up there in the tree. She'd stay right where she was till Bimmi rang the gong and they all trooped down to the house, the old house going to rack and ruin, her parents used to say, such a shame, but what could you do? Bimmi was so stubborn.

Bimmi had been a city-bred girl who arrived in the bay as a young bride soon after the First World War with her piano loaded onto a dray. Not from the district — no one knew where she'd come from, no one knew her people. And definitely not cut out, the neighbours opined, for mud and sheep and cattle.

But Bimmi had proved to be made of sterner stuff than first

The Deck

appeared, living into her nineties, long after her husband had his heart attack at the height of the shearing. She stayed on in the bay alone, in gumboots and saggy vest and old trousers held up by knotted string, sole inheritor of paddocks hacked from bush a hundred years earlier by her husband's ancestor, a rough little brute from Exeter. He had clear-felled the hills of their trees and the bay of its whare, its people and its long centuries of children waking to birdsong, centuries of the voices of women weaving kete in the sunshine, men drawing in a net, the flicker of fish on silvery sand.

The brute in his bun hat, equipped with guns and dogs and the full force of new laws, saw them all off. He burned their whare, set fire to their hills and strung fences of barbed wire over the smouldering earth. He planted hedges of gorse, watering the seedlings with tender care. He knocked together a house on the hillside where he fathered a brood on a solid little woman with heavy haunches and a glare no one would broach.

Bimmi stayed on in the bay, and under her guardianship, to the grave misgivings of family members and neighbours, the fences disappeared under a golden cloak as the gorse exulted, scenting the air with toasted coconut. Through its spiny tangle prodded kānuka and puahou, kawakawa and kōtukutuku, spears of green taking back the hillsides. Bimmi sat on her ramshackle verandah cracking walnuts and watching it happen, all this quiet determined regrowth. Birds flocked. Kererū in their white vests sat on the branches of the plum trees emitting their small contented ooh ooh. Chaffinches flew about inside the house, picking crumbs from the rotting carpet, while pīwakawaka took care of the flies who had become trapped in the cobwebs that draped in luxuriant swathes over the windows.

The Third Day

So beautiful, so astonishing that something so tiny could spin so much from its body, don't you see, Pippi? And Philippa had been entranced. She lay soaking in the bath, which was filled with water that was not like ordinary water back home but ran a rich dark brown, the exact colour of Bimmi's tea, which she never drank with milk, just a slice of lemon in a tin mug.

Her sister and her brother were doubtful about the bath and the brown water, just as they mistrusted the stinking dunny behind the house and Bimmi's meals, which were odd and appeared at random intervals, sometimes very late at night. Potatoes cooked in the ashes of the open fire, black as coal. They left smudges on your fingers and face and made your teeth squeak. They were to be eaten cut in half, with an egg spoon, sprinkled with salt. Philippa thought the potatoes were delicious, and on bath night she lay happily in the tub with the eagles' feet, tea-brown water up to her chin, watching the daddy long-legs that lived in the corner of the ceiling walking about upside down, and was enchanted.

She even liked the bad bits. The wild cat that emerged from the bush with matted coat and eyes glued shut with pus, dragging its hind legs painfully, appallingly, across the yard. The children stood on the verandah, watching. 'Ugghhh,' they said. 'Yuk.'

Bimmi appeared with the gun, an ancient .22 kept among the cobwebs in a cupboard in the barn. It looked long and mean and heavy with its polished wooden stock, its grey metal snout.

'You two stay inside,' she said to the younger ones. 'But you,' she said to Philippa, 'are old enough for this.'

'If an animal is suffering,' she said, fitting a bullet snugly into its little metal nest and snapping the gun straight, 'it's your duty, if you can, to put it out of its misery. Do you understand? The

The Deck

power over life and death lies in your hands.' She held Philippa close as she raised the gun.

'Keep breathing,' she said as she placed the gun against Philippa's shoulder. 'Nice and steady.' The cat sensed the closeness of the muzzle and raised its ravaged head, making a final effort at a snarl, its gummy eyes weeping. Bimmi's old hand closed over Philippa's and placed her finger on the trigger. A soft, gentle squeeze. The sound was shocking, and the gun bounced against her shoulder, but Bimmi held her still. The cat jumped and fell sideways, twitching, its feet running fast on empty air then becoming still. The little kids' faces were a pale blur at the sitting-room window.

They buried it with some ceremony, flowers, a cardboard cross, under the broad beans because Bimmi said you must never let good fertiliser go to waste and a dead animal was about as good as it got. It's all a cycle, you see. Death and growth, and when she died she wanted to be put in a hole in the ground up there by the barn and an apple tree planted on top. All right? Will you remember that?

Yes, Philippa said. She'd remember.

Then Bimmi died, and it was discovered that she had ignored all custom and precedent and willed the house with its chaos of books and papers, its dubious outdoor dunny, its floors so rotten they had to be crossed on planks laid down over the holes, not to the oldest available male but to her great-niece. The one she loved best. She bequeathed house and spiders, walnut tree and kererū, the overgrown remnants of the brute's farm, to Philippa.

And when the dodgy wiring shorted and the house burned to the ground one winter day, Philippa wept. The ramshackle barn was untouched but the house had gone. Only a square of black ash and charred timber remained, and a single chimney like a skinny admonitory finger. Tom kicked about in the ashes, scenting potential.

The chimney still stands up here on the hillside among poroporo and the overgrown remnants of Bimmi's garden: plum trees and lichened apples, feijoas and lemon trees laden with yellow fruit, thickets of raspberry and blackberry, and the walnut tree where Philippa stands now looking down at the bay. She's in no hurry to return to the house. Tom will be in a mood.

Part of her is regretful. She should probably not have told him about Rosie in front of others. But a greater part of her feels not regret but relief. The day feels somehow brighter; she feels giddy and light as a bubble. It's as if she has emptied a cupboard, cleared some shelves, got rid of stuff. It's something she finds herself doing a lot these days.

Her mother did the same at this age. She remembers visiting and finding her seated on the carpet in front of the china cabinet carefully printing the initials of her children — P for Philippa, M for Maria, J for John — in indelible felt tip next to the hallmarks on the base of the Royal Albert teacups and saucers, the Dresden shepherdess, the pair of Delft candlesticks inherited from her great-grandmother.

'I don't want any squabbling after I'm gone,' she said, picking up a hideous Staffordshire parrot and printing 'P' on the bottom. 'I don't want any nonsense.'

As if the lawyer, the filmmaker and the chartered accountant would find themselves tussling on the rug over a teacup. Everything in their mother's little unit became labelled. A folder in the dresser drawer contained bank records, a highly detailed will and a funeral invitation list with names, addresses

The Deck

and phone numbers, most of them irrelevant by the time she did eventually die. She outlived the list, descendant of good breeding stock.

Recently Philippa tossed out the Staffordshire parrot. Gone too is the painting by the famous artist, which she had never really liked and is now certain is both oppressive and pretentious. She has cleared the shelves in the apartment of books she will never reread and things she has kept simply from habit or because they were a gift. She has tossed out clothes she will never wear again — too tight, too short, the wrong colour.

She has also made a start on clearing out stuff that is intangible but nonetheless real: friendships with people who irritate or depress her. Rules and rituals maintained purely out of habit: the getting-up-before-7am-or-you-miss-the-best-of-the-morning rule. The rule of reciprocal invitation — you-must-have-them-to-dinner-because-they-asked-you, even though they bore you to tears with the doings of their children and adorable grandchildren.

Gone are the people who bore her with disgustingly graphic recitations of intimate medical disorders. Or tedious rants about the failings of central government, or the city council, or the regional authorities. Or amusing anecdotes from the courtroom that everyone has heard a hundred times before.

Gone are the insistent monologues that must not be interrupted on the shortcomings of current immigration policy, the best moorings along the eastern coast, the case against minimum pay agreements. For years she has sat, being polite, because that was another rule: the don't-be-disagreeable, don't-say-what-you-really-think rule. Instead you must sit, longing for the moment when the guests will look at their watches and

The Third Day

say, 'My goodness, is that the time?' when at last you can leap to your feet, find their coats, chivvy them out the door and retreat to bed, lamp on, a good puzzling murder mystery to finish the day, the dishes left any old how on the bench.

She has tossed out all that. She has tossed out Christmas and New Year's Eve and her Pilates class and her Tai Chi sessions and any compulsion to reply to emails within the hour or, in many instances, ever. And she has retrieved other things in the process.

Last night was the moment when she took down from the high shelf where she had stored it all these years, the caravan at the end of the apple orchard. She lifted out the little dark-eyed baby, the moon, the icy gush of the river, dusted them off for the first time and held them up for others to see. And ever since, she has felt light and giddy and girlish. As light as a bubble.

She is in love with this bright day. She is in love with the crimson raspberries in the white bowl, in love with the leaves she has picked from the tangle of Bimmi's garden, sorrel and sage and feathery fennel. In love with the murmur of the voices of her oldest and dearest friend and her friend's brother and his beautiful companion among the arching canes below. In love with the lick of damp grass at her bare legs. In love with Baz moving about down there by the macrocarpas at the far end of the beach. In love with the sunlight and how it falls over her, filtered through the green leaf canopy of the walnut tree.

She is leaning against the branch that had always been the first step up. The smaller branch that was the handhold is still there. She sets down her bowl and reaches out for it. It feels firm so she pulls herself up, her old body that today feels just fine, because she herself is so empty, so light.

The Deck

She lifts her lovely bubble self up among the leaves until she finds the sitting place. It's there too, broad and smooth, the place where she can sit with her back secure against the big trunk. Safe, invisible, looking down and seeing everything and everyone, the whole length of the bay, from the perfect hiding place.

THE THIRD NIGHT

That night, sunset fading, they eat fish. Didi barbecued the moki whole, stuffed with wild fennel and sliced lemons, flipping them at just the right moment to ensure the skin was crisp, the flesh sweet and juicy.

'Pesce alla griglia,' e said. 'Another recipe of my nonna's.' But e knew to hand the platter to Tom for delivery to the table. E has had years of training in the detection of mood, sensitive as a quivery greyhound to nuances of feeling: the barely concealed revulsion, the glance that hints at the prurient curiosity lurking just beneath the business suit, the significant detail, the slight groove in the flesh of a finger that means a wedding ring, the barely audible comment where the good-humoured banter and hilarity is about to segue into something vicious, when it would be unwise to leave the safety of the bar.

Unless, of course, e was in a mood for self-destruction, wanting the intricate satisfactions of pain and contempt and disfigurement. The tremulous excitement that compelled em to step out, over and over, onto the fine wire strung over the abyss of e's own annihilation. Sometimes e has wanted that. E wanted it very much.

So e has read this room as e has read many others. E has seen Tom's wounded pride as he surrendered these five fish, fresh and silvery, still with the bloom of living disfigured by the bloodied mark of the hook.

'Beautiful fish, mate,' e says as e hands the platter to Tom to hand around, standing aside wiping down the grill as Tom receives the chorus of ooh and ahh and, for a moment, blooms.

So the planet rolls over and the purple shadows wash into the valley and the stars circle overhead as on Earth they mop their plates and talk. They eat raspberries dusted with icing sugar, then Didi brings the grappa to correct the coffee, and Tom produces the Glenfiddich, and Baz brings out the guitar. He picks his way through the soundtrack of their lives while they talk. Talk the way they used to talk a long time ago when the world was very wide.

What did they talk about back then?

Other people mostly, because that is what everyone talks about mostly. Friends and people who were no longer friends. People they had met at work or in class or playing for the same team or in the same band. People who were total strangers but encountered in weird situations. Famous people — actors, musicians, politicians, activists — whom they didn't know and would never meet but whose faces and voices and mannerisms had become globally recognisable among the 3.682 billion clambering about the planet at that time.

They talked and they laughed the way you never laugh again

The Third Night

in your entire life, that helpless hilarity as they tumbled about on the carpet in some grubby flat, at some crazy stuff they'd done or the crazy stuff other people had done.

They talked about places they wanted to go and places other people had been. They talked about music, about Dylan, and what was that about the herd of moose he gave his girl and how did they manage to fly? Or Lennon, and what the hell was Yoko Ono all about? And then there was that cake left out in the rain. What? Why? It was the decade of inscrutable lyrics.

They talked about stuff they'd seen on TV and stuff they'd seen at the movies. New movies, brightly coloured. Two men stripped and wrestling naked in the crimson firelight, or the long, dark opening shot that zeros in on a pinprick of light that is the Siberian prison camp, or the wide blue sky and the big bikes riding that endless highway to cross the bridge coming into Nazareth. And old movies too. Truffaut and De Sica and *Jules and Jim* and *Bicycle Thieves*, which was just the most powerful movie ever, and, nah, that's just because it's in black and white and why does black and white always make things look more important than colour? Why does colour make things look at the same time more real but less serious? And how come they could make movies like *Bicycle Thieves* when Rome lay in ruins, while the best this country seems able to manage is Film Unit crap about hot pools and mountains and farming on the Desert Plateau?

They talked about stuff they'd read. Some of them talked about Borges and Gabriel Garcia Márquez and Pirsig and Chomsky and some of them talked about Betty Friedan and Germaine Greer, and was what she said true? That women who played at being meek and guileful, and repressed their actual

The Deck

power, were fools? They talked about nuclear testing and the frigging French and ohu and back to the land and Laing and Skinner and the brain and its amazing potential.

And sometimes, because some things are eternal, some of them talked about the line-up for Saturday's test.

Some of them talked about *Finnegans Wake* versus *Under the Volcano* and why can't we write like that and yeah yeah, there's Frame there's Mansfield, but she doesn't really count does she, she wrote in France, and of course she counts, say some others, she wrote her best stuff about here, and who can compare with her, who will be like her, still read in fifty years' time? A hundred years' time?

Because a hundred years viewed from that carpet was an immense amount of time. Why, it was 52 million, 560 thousand minutes! And all those little minutes stretched ahead like tiny leaves of grass on a vast plain.

They tried marijuana as soon as the dental student next door started offering some for sale, and little blocks of sticky hash a mate of his brought back from Kabul, and sometimes those tiny paper dots that made the wallpaper in the flat dissolve and the lampshade explode like a supernova and their hands became huge, they were elephantine, they would never be able to move again, they became slug-like, inert, trapped in their slug skins on the grimy carpet.

They talked until birdsong.

And alive and breathing underneath all the talk was the unspoken question. The only question that matters.

Do you like me?

Will you be my friend? Will you talk to me? Will you hear me? Can I say whatever I want to you? Can I be who I am with you?

The Third Night

And tonight, here on the deck in the moonlight, they ask it again. The only question. Do you like me? And they wait for the answer.

Yes. Probably. Why not?

They sit and talk. About other people mostly, because that is what everyone talks about, mostly.

They talk about people they used to know, people with whom they worked for forty years but never really got to know. They talk about people they know now, with whom they play golf or bridge. They talk about total strangers encountered in odd situations and about people they don't know personally but it feels as if they do because their faces are everywhere. In magazines and on screens large and small, their names and mannerisms instantly recognisable among all the 8-point-whatever-billion individuals who currently cling to the skin of the planet as it rolls through the firmament.

They could talk about friends who have undergone disaster, the failure of body parts, joints crumbling or calcified or cracking like the dry timbers in an ancient house. Brain cells melting to mush. They could talk about people they know who have endured the worst thing: the deaths of children, who should remain behind in the queue, waiting their proper turn for the edge.

But not tonight because such things are far too sad for the warm air and the moonlight and the soft breathing of the sea. They talk instead about friends who are enjoying unexpected felicity. The friend who lost her licence but is now having an affair with the taxi driver who has been picking her up from the supermarket since the cataracts. He's Iraqi, younger than her by at least a decade. Faris. Incredibly handsome. And she's so happy but her children are furious because they fear, probably quite rightly, that she'll leave the taxi driver the house.

They talk about places where they have been happy, places they have visited and how lovely they were that first time, thirty years ago. The Greek island. The Indonesian beach, palm fringed. The canals, the gondolas. The glacier, the mountain top, the hill village. Before the crowds, the Hidden Gem rating on Lonely Planet, the cruise ships, the tour groups.

They talk about places discovered by accident at the end of frustrating days or when lost in confusing country, wonderful, curious places. And other things that turned out better than expected: parties they hadn't wanted to attend, or journeys they hadn't wanted to make where they met this amazing person, or movies that didn't look at all promising but were fantastic after all. They talk about brilliant books picked up at random from bargain bins. All the delights of accident and chance, and how dreadful it is that chance is being taken out of the equation. It's all targeted marketing now and how irritating it is to become a target to whom movies are delivered that have been selected by a clever machine and complex algorithm and analysis to meet precisely determined individual taste.

They could talk, of course, about the line-up for the test on Saturday.

They could talk about politics, trading one received comment for another to build their arguments. They could talk about politics, international, national and local, expressing allegiances formed fifty years earlier, their opinions still tinted red, blue or green depending on that choice. They could talk the politics of a small country compelled for ever to make a choice between the juggernauts: whether to side with America or China, which

The Third Night

wasn't any kind of choice at all, was it, like having to choose whether to be flattened by one great fat hippopotamus rump or another.

Well, if we have to choose a rump, says one, I'd go with America. At least they pay lip service to democratic principles, freedom of speech, freedom of the press. They've got that tradition of the wilderness, *Walden* and all that.

But none of that's true, says another. It's an oligarchy. The press uses its freedom to publish outrageous propaganda and *Walden* was a lie! Thoreau was sitting up there in his glorious solitude having his dinner brought in every day by his mum, while all around him nature was falling back before invasion and land grab and genocide.

But at least there's a nod in all that, says one, in the direction of Rousseau and those eighteenth-century philosophers admiring untrammelled nature. At least you can see where that part of America comes from, the idealised, best part of it, unlike a culture that seems to have no philosophical basis whatever, just getting rich and powerful by any means, fair or foul, and scraping the planet raw in the process.

That's just cultural ignorance, says another. Have you never read Lao Tsu? The *Tao Te Ching*? 'Heaven and Earth and I share the same root. Heaven and humanity will act in harmony and transform themselves in the same way.'

Jeeze, you're not still quoting that hippie shit . . .

They could talk the way they talked until very recently when seated around tables like this one: about war and famine and economic collapse and fire and storm and tornado and how they used to swim in the rivers when they were kids, just hop out of the car on trips into the mountains and swim wherever they liked, and now the rivers have been drained and there are only dustbowls, tyre tracks, plumes of dust rising.

But that kind of talk belonged to a time when they had seemed like concepts, topics for discussion rather than urgent reality. That talk belonged on the other side of the hilltop, where they have argued, quoted, debated for years. It doesn't belong here, not now, not tonight in this miraculously green valley where the moon lays down a smooth white path across the southern ocean as if it were offering a way out.

'April sun,' sings Baz, riff to familiar riff, '. . . in Cuba, *nah nah nah* . . .'

'This is so nice,' says Ani, stretching luxuriously, her old dog asleep with his head on her lap, her brother beside her, his friend curled up close as Baz picks his way through the soundtrack. 'Maybe everything will turn out all right after all.'

'. . . ever' little thing,' sings Baz, '. . . gonna turn out righ' . . .'

And, for proof, he stops singing, sets aside his guitar and tells a version of this story.

The three brothers, the wave and the soldier from the war returned
A fourth tale of one who after divers misadventures at last attains a goal of unexpected felicity.

There were three brothers. The oldest was tall and tough and was their father's favourite. The youngest was a curly-haired clown and beloved by his mother. And the one in the middle was smart and skinny and tried to keep his head down.

The Third Night

Their father was a heavy-set miserable bastard whom everyone excused on account of the war. He was a great one for the war. He marched to the memorial on Anzac Day, a row of medals pinned to his best jacket and his hair Brylcreemed flat, then off to remember them at the going down of the sun in the bar at the RSA. He was a regular there and at the Brian Boru on Palmerston Street, life of the party, before he staggered home to knock around the wife and any child unwise enough to get in his path.

The three brothers built huts of old boxes and scraps of corrugated iron in the scrub behind the house, and there they lay, curled up on coal sacks, listening to thud and smash down in the house and the voice of their mother, high pitched, trying to talk him down and muffling her cries lest the neighbours hear because, as she said repeatedly to the three brothers, this was nobody's business but their own. They were not to breathe a word, not to the neighbours, not to their friends, not to the priest or the nuns at school, and specially not to Dr Morgan, who paused as he wound a strip of white bandage around the middle brother's broken wrist. 'Now, laddie,' he said, 'tell me the truth. Was it really the bike this time?'

His glasses had slipped down his nose and his eyes were mild and kind. His big blunt hands were deft and the bandage was firm. But their mother's injunction held. They all stuck to the story. Their father was not well, on account of the war. He had been through a lot. No one had any idea.

And in the morning, early, the sun rising through mist and dew beading the grass, the brothers would emerge from their rough shelter, shivery and stiff, and go back to the house, where their father would be passed out on the sofa, snorting like a pig,

The Deck

while in the kitchen their mother moved about, wincing quietly, a black eye, a bloody nose, a smashed wrist roughly bound in rags torn from an old sheet. She would be standing at the stove stirring their porridge and their grey school shirts would be hanging from the clothes rack, all nicely ironed. She would pour golden syrup and top of the milk onto their porridge and cut cold meat for their sandwiches, wrapping them awkwardly, one-handed, in lumpy parcels of greaseproof paper.

And she would offer it all up to Jesus. Her little cross to bear. The flower of Catholic womanhood.

The three brothers tried to keep out of his way, but it was not always possible to escape to the hut. Their father's wrath simmered and exploded at unpredictable intervals. His huge hands lifted them up and swung them from their feet. The brothers were notably accident prone. They turned up at school with stitches and bruises and limbs in plaster. The oldest had snapped a rib jumping from the coalshed roof, the youngest had broken his leg on a swing, and the middle one had got concussion not just once but three times, by falling off his bike.

The oldest learned from the master, and dealt his own kinds of cruelty, pinching and punching and bending the fingers of his younger brothers till they cracked. The youngest ran to their mother, who held him in her arms and gave him a teaspoon so he could eat condensed milk straight from the tin. And the middle one kept his head down.

One night, the house in an uproar, the middle one slid headfirst out the bedroom window and rode away. The street stretched ahead lined by lampposts with puddles of light at their feet. The houses on either side stood back a little behind hydrangeas, their eyes closed tight against the dark. His bike was old, an

The Third Night

ancient Raleigh with rusted mudguards and a creaky chain that went *cawww caww* as he pedalled into the deep dark silence.

The road ran down to the place where the lights stopped and scrub and sand and gravel began. Out there was the sea. He could hear it waiting, the in and out of its breathing. He dropped his bike among the African thorn and slid down the bank, walked barefoot over broken shell towards the dark water, breathing, waiting.

But then, a flame leaping. The sound of talk and laughter, driftwood spitting sparks into the air, and a voice calling, 'Hey, kid! Hey! You! What are you doing? Get over here!'

So he turned that way instead. Not to the darkness but towards the warmth of the fire and the surfboards stacked against a low-slung Holden and the waves rolling in, each one new and never to be repeated, not once in the whole history of the world.

There was an alternative, he discovered that summer and in the summers that followed. He discovered it on days of sunlight and seagulls, and days too of frozen fingers and chattery teeth, on days of early-morning mist and evenings when he could turn to find the moon rising over the mountains, and he was out there, gloriously alone, flying in on the curve, towards the shore where there was an alternative to the roaring house, in the warmth of the group around the fire, the easy talk of friends.

The three brothers grew and set out to make their way in the world. Their mother had hoped for a priest in the family but they had other plans. The oldest brother became a soldier, marching off to the north to fight the commies. Not a reluctant conscript but an eager V Force volunteer. The youngest brother moved south, worked for a bank and married a nice young woman from loans. And the middle one raised his head and

The Deck

bought a van and headed east over the mountains.

His hair grew long, down to his waist, and when he came home just that once for his younger brother's wedding, his father met him at the gate and said, 'What the hell do you think you're doing here? Go on: get out, you long-haired lout. You're not welcome here,' and turned his back and slammed the door. He had given the oldest brother the rosary when he embarked for Vietnam, the one he had picked up somewhere in Italy. It had kept him safe, he used to tell them with tears in his eyes at the maudlin point before the roar, when Gerry was knocking them about at Monte Cassino. It was his greatest treasure.

It did not prove efficacious. The oldest brother returned from war damaged and raging. He lived sometimes in a boarding house in Newtown, but more often it was the sheet of cardboard on a city street, the urine-soaked sleeping bag, the impotent tirade at the lunchtime crowd.

The youngest brother said, 'Leave him there. He can rot, as far as I'm concerned. He's a prick.' He had not forgotten the broken finger, nor the pillow over his face as he had lain too frightened to sleep under his Superman duvet in the lower bunk. But when their father died, their mother said, 'Bring your brother to the funeral. I know he's not well, but he's been through a lot and he should be here. He's family.'

So the middle brother picked him up, and he was on his meds so he sat calmly on the ferry as they crossed the water and drove back over the mountains to the mean little cottage on the long straight road. The church was crowded for our dear brother Joseph, rest eternal was requested, and their little mother, bent double with arthritis and a rough life, sat with her three sons, sniffing into a hanky scented with lavender.

The Third Night

The oldest brother sat beside her, wearing his beret and a black artillery cravat with an embroidered silver fern and his medals pinned to a clean shirt. The youngest brother sat on the other side with his nice wife and three children and held his mother's hand.

And then the three brothers and three of his mates from the Brian Boru carried their father from the church and lowered him in his box into heavy clay in a plot off Utopia Road. The Last Post wavered over the marble rows of regret, and the old soldiers filed past, dropping poppies into the gaping hole. And all the middle brother could think was, 'Make it fast, get it over, shovel on the dirt and get him buried good and deep.'

Afterwards there was tea and sausage rolls in the little cottage, and whisky for the men, and Sorry for your loss on all sides, exactly as if something or someone had actually been lost. And after an hour or two of that, the middle brother could not bear a moment more.

He sidled off, drove down the long road to the beach where the surf was up, one of those mighty Tasman swells that come out of nowhere from a still, evening sky. It surged and broke, the kind of surf that can make or break, but the middle brother did not much care which. He never had. That was the key. He took his board and his wetsuit from the back of the van and made his way over the black sand, thinking as always that he would let the waves decide.

The sea was big. The rip took hold of him before he had gone a few yards and swept him out the back, then curved off to the south and left him there. He turned, as he always used to, and looked back at where he had come from.

The town was a row of lights on the flat by the river, all

The Deck

switched on and far away in tiny houses, where people lived their tiny lives and none of it mattered. Particles in an immense universe. And then he felt his board lift and there was a roar, a thrumming in the air behind him, and this wave came up on him from the twilight, a massive curving left-hander, without a doubt the largest he had ever encountered. It came in, its white crest way above, and took him in its mighty grip. He was riding this mountain of a wave yet poised perfectly within the tube, finding that sweet balance between control and chaos. He was flying, carried towards the shore, where the wave broke like thunder and his board smashed in two, and it was a miracle he too was not broken, his neck or his back. The wave flung him up onto the beach, then drew back and left him lying there, his skin grazed and his wetsuit shredded. He lay there, winded, gasping for each lungful of air. Then he picked up what remained of his board and drove back to the house.

The mourners had gone. The lights were on. His mother was in the kitchen with the oldest brother, who sat at the table drinking a cup of tea as if he had never left and would never leave again. Across the hall in the sitting room the youngest brother and his nice wife were sitting with their three children on the sofa eating pizza and watching a video. One child was sprawled on his knee, another was curled up between them, and the third was playing with the nice wife's hair, tying it up with a ribbon that looked as if it might have fallen from one of the funeral wreaths. And as he watched, they laughed, all at once and all together.

The middle brother knows the theory. He's read Einstein, knows that 'the distinction between past, present and future is only a stubbornly persistent illusion'. But standing there with

The Third Night

his grazed legs and wet hair, looking in at the little cottage, he knows that that is not how it feels to be alive.

The past is buried in a box.

The present is no illusion.

And the future can take any shape you choose.

'And that,' says Baz, strumming that easy familiar loping A D A, 'was a good night, because for a while there I thought that every little thing, you know, is gonna turn out just fine.'

'Yep,' says Pete, because tonight he feels it might be true.

And for further proof, he tells a version of this story.

The singer, two ships and the angel at the bar

A fifth tale of one who, after divers misadventures, at last attains a goal of unexpected felicity.

There were two ships and they sailed the sea, one at the beginning of the story and one at the end. The *Principessa* was first, a former transatlantic ferry designed for the efficient relocation of huddled masses from postwar Europe to the land of the free, but in 1980, newly renovated, she was redesigned to cater for 670 tourists cruising the Mediterranean.

It was the decade when cruising began. The decade of *The Love Boat* and Captain Stubing in the white shorts and knee socks. Every week on TV he greeted a new consignment desperate for romance, because romance lay out there, pink

The Deck

and frilly and resolutely heterosexual, just over the twelve-mile limit. Remember Loretta Swit? Loretta as the Russian Commissar? Transformed under the influence of a tropic moon and a taste of American values — not to mention Doc Bricker in the regulation tight white shorts — into a vision of capitalist loveliness? Long blonde hair and a strapless white gown. That was Loretta. That was cruising.

There was a singer. Pete. It was his friend Sarah who suggested the cruise ship. She had come to London planning to become the next southern songbird, storming the opera houses of Europe, while Pete would be another Inia Te Wiata, only in a higher register. They would become famous and fêted. Instead they found themselves sharing a grimy flat in Victoria along with an assortment of other New Zealanders. He paid the rent by pulling pints in a pub. Her career highlight was singing Cinderella in a panto in Chelmsford wearing a costume worn by several previous Cinderellas with an awkward crinoline and a decade or more of staining under the silken armpits.

She found the gig as an entertainer on the *Principessa*, and when the tenor left abruptly, nose smashed to a bloody pulp in a punch-up in a nightclub in Marseille, she called her friend.

'Come on down,' she said. 'You've got the repertoire, and it's seventeen degrees here and sunny.' So the singer hauled out the tux and flew down, and together he and Sarah sang the 'Some Enchanted Evening' programme, a bit of Rodgers and Hammerstein, a bit of Bernstein, a bit of Bing and Grace Kelly warbling 'True Love' as they sailed away to connubial bliss. Plus 'O soave fanciulla' for the opera fans and because, well, it was Italy right there, wasn't it? The home of romantic opera? That port-side sparkle of coastal lights. Later in the evening,

The Third Night

the singer slicked on the hair gel and, glass in hand, channelled Frankie and Dean, the early Dean in his Rat Pack prime before brain fade and kidney failure.

The *Principessa* was packed to the gunnels with romance. Candlelit dinners for two in the atrium, red roses on every table, heart-shaped pillows on every bed, and the singers supplied the soundtrack. *Oh, my love, I tremble, I can't help falling, I will always, for ever and ever* . . . When the reality was that one in three, or maybe more, romances would implode, mostly within the first eight years.

But he dragged on the tux, delivered the love songs, the Sinatra and Martin retro set, and one night an old lady came up to him while he was having a quiet drink in the bar after the show.

It was late, the party over except for a few sad stayers like himself, alone in the bar while the loved-up were off having ecstatic hetero sex in their cabins. He had a table tucked away in a corner where he could see the barman who was new and might have possibilities, but the old lady found him and pressed a note into his hand. People did that quite often. Approached him for some special song, a dedication. The entertainment director kept a close eye out for such transactions and took his cut, but Mrs Bloom — Claudia, the accent North American, maybe Canadian — was discreet.

The envelope was fat with $50 bills, and there would be more, she said, if he would come to their cabin and sing for her and her husband.

She was a very ordinary little woman. The *Principessa* was small, not like the cruise ships that came later with their passenger lists of 4000-plus. It was possible to notice people,

The Deck

even people as determinedly ordinary as Mr and Mrs Bloom, two dumpy little grey-haired people, neatly dressed, she in a plain cotton shift, he in chinos and a short-sleeved shirt tucked in at the waist. The singer had seen them at their table for two and walking around the deck hand in hand and dancing cheek to cheek to the showband. She seemed to do all the talking, while her husband nodded, smiled, said nothing.

And now she was handing over an envelope and asking him to come to their cabin and sing. There was a piano in their suite. He could play the piano? Yes, he said. He could play the piano. He could sing.

The entertainers were not quite crew, but they were not quite passengers either. Private performances, fraternisation with the guests was strictly off limits, but it was late, no one was around and the envelope was plump. The barman did not look up as he followed Mrs Bloom — it did not seem right to call her Claudia — to their cabin.

It was a part of the ship he had never visited before. A hush fell as they neared the Trevi Suite. The carpet was thicker underfoot. The suite was vast, with big leather sofas and crystal chandeliers and a baby Steinway grand. Glass doors opened onto a private balcony with a view of the sparkling coast.

'Nightcap?' said Mrs Bloom as Mr Bloom poured hefty shots of Balvenie, still without a word. Then they settled themselves down with their drinks on one of the big sofas, she curled up like a kitten, her hand in his, while the singer took his place at the piano.

'Right,' he said. 'What would you like to hear?' And Mrs Bloom said, '"Night and Day". Very slow. Sing it real slow. That's the way Jack played it in the band.'

The Third Night

Jack had played sax in a band the singer had never heard of, in some midwestern town the singer had never heard of.

'Do you still play?' he asked Mr Bloom but his wife was brisk. 'Cancer of the tongue,' she said. 'Just sing.'

So the singer sang. 'Night and Day' and 'Strangers in the Night' and 'Everybody Loves Somebody', singing them more slowly than he had ever sung them before, but giving them his best shot because she looked so tiny sitting on that overstuffed sofa, snuggled up beside Jack who had his arm around her shoulders.

They looked so happy, the pair of them, their bodies folded into each other, like a single entity. He wondered how that happened and how they had come to be here, in this plush suite. Despite appearances, they must have made a lot of money. Had they sold the house? Sold the hardware store on Main Street and blown the lot on this trip of a lifetime? Who knew? But they were prepared to pay him well to sing, so the singer sang. Half a dozen love songs at the grand piano.

Mrs Bloom had kicked off her shoes. She was not wearing stockings and her legs were skinny and blotched with brown skin and a web of blue veins. From all those hours standing at the counter, the singer thought in a momentary vision: Claudia at the till, Jack out the back putting in an order for lightbulbs or U-bolts. Or, maybe if there was a lull, practising a tricky phrase on his saxophone.

He reached the end of 'Love Me Tender' and Mrs Bloom set aside her glass and got to her feet.

'Now,' she said, 'let's try something a little different.' And the singer thought, oh no, here we go, the real reason he'd been summoned to the Trevi Suite at 2am. Was it to be geriatric sex

The Deck

on the plush pile, a threesome with old Jack?

But no. Mrs Bloom walked a little unsteadily to an ormolu side table and took something from the drawer.

'Just you singing,' she said. 'No piano. Just stand there and sing.'

It was the way his gran used to ask him to sing when they visited on Sunday afternoons. 'Give us a song, boy,' she'd say as soon as they arrived for tea and cake, and she'd stand him by the fireplace and he would sing 'The Holy City' and she would join in the chorus in a wavery soprano and cut him an extra-large slice of cake afterwards.

Mrs Bloom asked for 'True Love', Bing and Grace on the yacht, suntanned, windblown and at last alone . . .

'And this,' she said, handing him a mask. 'Wear this.' It was one of those black eye masks they hand out on long flights.

'Slowly, remember! And no peeking!' She giggled, and he could see her suddenly emerge from behind her old crepey skin: the younger woman, not beautiful but with a nice smile, standing at the counter, the kind of girl an ordinary boy might fall in love with and live with for the rest of their lives.

So he put on the mask and stood there in the middle of the room and began to sing. As he sang he could hear some whispering, some footsteps, a click, a little rush of air and then . . . nothing. He waited. Should he sing something else? Should he remove the mask? Not a word. He could hear only the background throbbing of the ship's engine and the rush of water against the hull far below.

He began to feel awkward, embarrassed, irritated, and finally he dragged off the mask. There was no one there. Just another envelope on the ormolu table addressed to 'The Singer' in

The Third Night

blue ink and, inside, a sheaf of American $100 bills and a note written in the same neat hand on the cruise liner's heavy linen notepaper. For services rendered, $5000. Dated. With thanks, Jack and Claudia Bloom.

The singer took his pay. No one had seen him enter the Trevi Suite and no one saw him leave. He washed his glass and returned it to the mirrored drinks cabinet, he wiped the piano keyboard clear of any traces of his visit. When there was an inquiry, and there was an inquiry, he was not called in for questioning. Mr and Mrs Bloom had chosen well. The currents in the strait were strong. Their bodies were never recovered.

That morning they docked in Naples. Sarah was keen to see Pompeii but it didn't sound promising: a dead city, buried in volcanic ash, dead people face down, cast in plaster and a little dog twisting on its leash.

'Not really my thing,' he said. 'You go. I'll look around Naples.'

He wanted a live city. A cacophonous, grubby, peeling place where he could walk among people who were very much alive. People who shouted to one another across narrow winding streets strung with washing from the balconies. People talking and laughing, busy little shops and hole-in-the-wall pizza places. Alleyways that opened suddenly into open spaces with churches and grand façades.

The kind of space where a composer in his frockcoat stands slouched against a marble plinth clutching the manuscript of his most famous opera amid car horns and the whine of Vespas.

A coffee at a sidewalk café.

A young man like himself seated alone at a neighbouring table, who asks in a strong Australian accent for a light.

Danny DeCicco, over here for a family wedding, louche and

The Deck

handsome, George Chakiris, *West Side Story*, dancing, click click finger click.

A strange ecstatic afternoon behind drawn curtains in a cheap hotel.

That evening, the singer returned to the ship, dragged on the tux and sang some more romance and all of it — Mr and Mrs Bloom hand in hand on the sofa, the Australian, the beauty of a body in filtered summer light, the stone composer on his plinth clutching more romance, another aria, 'Meco all'altar di Venere' — it all seemed unreal. It lodged in the singer's memory as a kind of fever dream, a hallucination . . .

Many years later there was another ship, the *Hibiscus Queen*. The Valentine's Day cruise via Bali, Komodo, Nouméa, Lautoka, Apia to Tahiti. The romance of the South Seas, wreaths of frangipani and garlands of silver cupids strung over tables set for dinner à deux. And best of all, the opportunity to renew your vows on board with the captain officiating in white tropical kit as the sun went down over the Pacific. Or, for a considerable premium, making those vows for the very first time on a beach on a tropical island, barefoot in white sand, and one of the singers from the nightly cabaret knocking out a soulful, slow slow tempo 'Unchained Melody'.

The singer was no longer officially a singer. He had graduated to administration, organising the acts, though he still sometimes obliged. Some couples liked his retro 1960s Dean Martin at the Sands lush-in-a-tux crooner cool. He had perfected the routine over many years, and romance was his stock in trade.

He had sung a thousand versions of it, right through the time when plague raged through his world and love and sex became a terrifying proposition, full of risk. The antiretrovirals

The Third Night

took time to develop and, in the meantime, the young men, his friends, died. But through it all, this time of plague, he dragged on the tux and sang. He sang through that and he sang through a life punctuated by a succession of failed affairs, disastrous attachments, unreciprocated infatuations, embarrassments, humiliations, ecstasy and ensuing disillusion, bubbling hope followed by bleak despair, until finally he had had enough.

The singer had reached the conclusion that there really was no point to any of it. This sensation celebrated as love was no more than an itch. Ecstasy, orgasm — they were no different to a sneeze, a clearing of the passageways. Love and romance were simply fancy packaging for the heave and grunt and goop of brief congress. He could live without love. He could observe his body's twitching instinctive responses without being enslaved by them. He had reached the state of calm detachment recommended by the Zen masters he read about in self-help books, paperback titles repackaging age-old philosophies for a modern market. It was the decade of the paperback bestseller recommending techniques to allay sadness, fear, anxiety, loneliness, financial impoverishment.

He would retire. He would return to shore, decorate his apartment, cycle out to the Waitākeres at the weekends, invite a few chosen friends over for dinner from time to time, live a quiet, retired, gentlemanly kind of life. The *Hibiscus Queen*, the Valentine's Day cruise would be his last.

Some 3500 passengers signed on for romance, seventy per cent of them over fifty-five, plus the full complement of hospitality staff and crew. All of them stacked like so much merchandise in cabins that increased in size above deck and decreased in size and comfort below deck, before dwindling into the warren of cramped quarters that accommodated the unfortunate citizens of the world who kept the whole business afloat. The anonymous mass of international labour whom the decade had determined should perform humanity's least desirable tasks.

The singer was relatively comfortable. He had a cabin to himself and an office from which he fielded complaints, contracted performers, handled difficulties, technical and personal, soothed and deflected and kept everyone smiling. The company's policy was to deliver freedom from care. Their customers had signed on for romance and, by god, romance they would have.

But on the third day, far from land but still on course for Nouméa, Lautoka, Apia and Tahiti, one of the passengers turned up at the dispensary with a headache. A blinding headache. Light was intolerable. A rapidly accelerating heartbeat, high temperature. He was followed by another, and then another. They developed seizures, began to bleed from the nose, ears, mouth, anus. More and more of them until, one of the waiters told the singer, whispering lest he be overheard, they had had to clear a couple of freezers to hold the overflow from the morgue.

The *Hibiscus Queen* became a place of quiet withdrawal. Silent corridors, trays stacked outside doors kept firmly locked. The frangipani faded and fell. The restaurants with their festoons of silver cupids were empty. The casino twinkled but no one was playing. The blue waters of the pools slopped a little way this, a little way that, undisturbed by swimmers.

The theatres with their programmes of romantic favourites became dark caverns, and the entertainers, dancers and musicians, being crew, donned disease-resistant gear and were set to

The Third Night

distributing 3500 breakfasts, lunches, dinners and quantities of booze to the guests who, confined to their cabins, watched endlessly repeated footage of the islands they should be visiting. The imagery flickered on big screens, a virtual balcony showing white-sand beaches, swaying palm trees, smiling locals and shoals of brilliantly coloured fish darting about in lagoons of impossible blue.

In the open ocean out of sight of land, the news feeds were blocked. The passengers knew nothing of the blockades at port after port as officials denied the *Hibiscus Queen* entry. They did not see the media headlines reporting their cruise as The Plague Ship! The Ship of Horrors! They did not hear the comments of islanders who were no longer smiling but remembering with great clarity old tales of introduced contagion, abandoned villages, overgrown gardens, the skeletal figures of the dying, the grief of the handful of survivors.

Day after day, the silent ship drifted. The singer and the waiter pushed the food trolleys along the silent corridors. Ernesto was young with a lively, smiling disposition. He cheerfully ignored the official prohibition on gossip. The freezers had become so full, he muttered as they stacked the empty plates, that they had to carry their contents after dark to the deck behind the casino, a brief word from the captain before the swift drop into a commotion of fins and thrashing tails in the water below.

Confined to their rooms, passengers died swiftly, silently and without medical attention. The crew in their cramped quarters sickened and sweated, delirious in fever. The second officer died, and the quartermaster, a dozen deckhands and galley hands, ordinary seamen, several cabin stewards, the photographer and casino manager, entertainers, dancers, one of the drummers . . .

The Deck

Ernesto kept the singer informed as they gathered up the trays from the empty corridors. The virus floated in the stale air about their faces, seeking a way in, an orifice where it might lodge, latch on, multiply, set to its genetically ordained task. The singer, sweating with fear within his inadequate protection, longed for release.

And then, miraculously, it was granted. On dwindling supplies of fuel, the *Hibiscus Queen* limped home to port, where the remaining passengers and crew were able at last to disembark. The singer walked down the gangway into a couple of weeks of further restraint in the muted neutrals of a former hotel room repurposed for quarantine before at last he was free.

He emerged into the bright light of a warm spring afternoon in an Australian city. The new variant of the virus had yet to make its mark but the streets were already quiet, anticipating its arrival. He walked away from the port and dived into the dark burrow of the first bar that was open.

And there, frowning at his cellphone, a lager to hand, taking a break before his shift at the restaurant across the road, was the beautiful boy, click click finger click. Danny DeCicco. Older now, with tinted hair and wearing glasses, but still recognisably the boy with the George Chakiris smoulder, louche and loose and leader of the Sharks, click click finger click. He looked up.

'Pete!' e said. E had cast off the chrysalis in which e had been cocooned for so long. That dull confinement that was not e's authentic self. No longer Danny DeCicco, but Didi. Beautiful, unrestricted Didi.

'Jesus! *Caspita!* What took you so long?'

The Third Night

'And that,' says Pete, 'as Dino used to say, was amore.'

The others on the deck, hearing this story, sigh because love has found a way across a great span of time and many lines of longitude and latitude. It is proof that all will be well.

'Sing something, Pete,' says Ani, because she has always loved to hear him sing. 'Sing us something beautiful.'

So the singer gets to his feet, stands on the deck as if it were his stage, and sings the aria, the one everyone recognises, about the night when people could not sleep, wishing for a good outcome despite all that history has taught them, despite the odds.

He sings Puccini, though it's not a given he can make that final high B any more. It's a while since he has done this, but he stands up on the deck the way he used to stand when his gran asked him to sing in front of the mantelpiece.

He sings it for the beautiful creature in the piazza, in the faded hotel, glittering in the dark inner-city bar and now miraculously here. He sings it for his sister and her stinky old dog and these friends of hers here on the deck, and the moon path leading out over the ocean.

'*Nessun dorma,*' he sings. '*Nessun dorma.*

Tu pure, o Principessa,

Nella tua fredda stanza . . .'

He sings of the stars that tremble with love and hope and he sings, heading for that high B, of defeating the curse, avoiding death, winning the hand of the terrifying princess.

'*Morir, morir,*' he sings. '*Dilegua, o notte.*

Tramontate, stelle.

Tramontate, stelle.

All'alba vincerò.

Vincerò . . .

The Deck

Vincerò!'

He's getting old, his voice past its best, but somehow he finds that high B. It floats on his breath out over the bay. I will win! And the note is echoed from the rocky cliffs behind the house.

Vincerò . . . Vincerò!

Oh, they sigh, the people on the deck. How beautiful. Pete mock-bows and Ani reaches over and takes his hand as he collapses onto the sofa beside Didi.

'Oh, Petey,' she says. 'Oh, darling Pete.'

'. . . and ever' little thing,' hums Baz, 'gonna be all righ' . . .'

'What's that sound?' says someone.

'Hey now,' strums Baz, starting the song about something going down . . .

'No, listen! Really — what's that sound?'

Raffi has lumbered to his feet and taken up his post, barking.

'Shut up, Raffi.'

Pause.

There is a sound. A car. They turn and look up the valley into the darkness. Car lights zigzag down the road through the bush, flickering in and out of view.

'Are you expecting anyone else?' Ani says.

'No,' says Philippa.

They are quiet, listening as the car crosses the valley floor. They can hear it slowing for the ford, then following the track over the flat towards the parking space below the house.

The engine cuts out and there is the sound of car doors slamming, and voices. Two voices, two people climbing the steps. Tom switches on the lights and in the sudden blinding glare everything looks unreal, as if cut from plastic. The plastic

The Third Night

people on the deck blink as two people open the door and enter the light. A woman. A girl.

A pause.

'Maria?' says Philippa.

Her sister, with long curling grey hair, trundles a suitcase on wheels out onto the deck.

'Hey,' says Maria in that lazy affected drawl of hers. 'Thought you might be out here.'

Behind her, with another suitcase, a skinny girl, dark hair trailing over one eye so she seems like some wild bird nervously surveying predators through dense foliage.

'This is Zoe,' says Maria.

Zoe lifts one hand in a languid wave but keeps her eyes down.

'Zoe?' says Philippa.

Last time she had seen Zoe was at the funeral, years ago. The old man was lying in his box, not so very old when considered from the perspective of her own advancing years. A heart attack at the eighth tee. She had sat in the front row at St Martin's while Zoe in a blue fairy frock ran up and down the aisles with her brother, with no evidence whatsoever of parental control.

The children's squeals rang from the rafters throughout the service and Philippa had found herself willing the old man up there to emerge from his mahogany box and roar, 'Cut it *out*, you kids, or you'll both get a clip around the ear!'

She had sat in her neat black suit, knowing that such threats were not ideal. There had been far too much of that sort of thing in her day. The razor strop hanging in readiness in the bathroom, the heavy leather strap in the teacher's desk drawer for the girls, the whippy length of cane for the boys. She remembered the sting on the palm of the hand, the tears, the choking sense of injustice. In her professional life she had witnessed, over and over, the aftermath of that old regime. She has listened to tales of the most appalling cruelty vented on little children and been filled, over and over, with amazement at the human capacity to survive brutality and even to rise to forgiveness. She had approved of every law designed to protect the vulnerable from attack. She is a liberal, for god's sake. She aspired to be good and kind.

But as Zoe and her brother squealed and ran she had wondered if she should perhaps have a word with her niece after the service. Sophie looked lumpen and bad tempered, but perhaps a little hint would not go amiss, a gentle suggestion that children really did need to be instructed in appropriate behaviour and consideration for others? She had sat planning how she might do that without causing offence, knowing full well that she was always on doubtful ground, having failed so spectacularly in her own attempt at parenting.

The fairy frock is long gone, replaced by a black puffa jacket, trainers and skinny jeans so ripped and torn it looks as if the wearer has been attacked by a knife-wielding assailant.

'Nice to see you, Zoe,' says Philippa, as if her arrival were expected, a pleasant surprise, along with that of a sister she has not seen in forty years. Who had not even bothered to attend Poppa's funeral, nor their mother's. She had stayed right where she was in LA or Sri Lanka or wherever the hell, citing a heavy workload, a shoot in Guangdong, a festival appearance in Toronto or some other unavoidable engagement.

'Even for your mother's funeral?' Philippa had said, talking down the line to this voice which had taken on a weird North American cadence so that it felt like talking to one of those

The Third Night

faces on a big silver screen. 'Surely, even big-shot Hollywood types can get leave for that?'

But now here she is, her hair long and grey, and it could look bag-lady, she could look street-drunk hauling her worldly goods about in a tattered plastic shopping trolley but she doesn't. She looks arty, like Jane Campion, or that photographer who bracketed Lennon and Yoko Ono together like twin foetuses in a tight womb. She's wearing black of course. Black jeans, loose black shirt, clunky black boots despite the summer heat, but she looks cool and right and her legs are long and slender and her skin is clear and unwrinkled and she's wearing tinted shades, for god's sake, even though it's after midnight.

She stands coolly surveying them as they blink back into the sudden blast of light.

'Your neighbour said you'd probably gone to the beach so I thought maybe she meant out here, to Bimmi's. I'm glad I guessed right. It's one hell of a drive. I'd forgotten.'

'It is,' says Philippa. 'It is a hell of a drive, but you're here now, so come in, come in. You'll recognise some faces.'

It takes time. Faces swim into focus. Grey hair where once it had been long and lustrous. Tom balding now with a beard, though it's pointed and grey and French intellectual where once he'd favoured Old Testament mad prophet. And Pete. Is that Pete? With his arm around the shoulders of some angelic creature? And this woman in a brilliantly coloured dress who seems intent on hugging her, although she doubts they have ever met. And off to one side, lanky and a bit knocked about since she last saw him . . .

'Hey, Maria,' says Baz, laying aside his guitar. 'So, where's my bloody camera?'

The Deck

But that moment fades rapidly into the next, which is all fuss and bustle. A drink? Coffee? Juice for Zoe? A sandwich? Because they have driven for ages across the island, managed to bypass the cordons in the city, taken the back roads, but now they're here and there are beds to make up in the last remaining pod, which is set up with single beds and smells a bit dusty, unaired.

Zoe drops her bag by the door and takes out her phone.

'Sorry,' says Philippa, stuffing a pillow into its case. 'There's no reception here.'

'Real?' says Zoe, looking alarmed. How can life be conducted without reception? Without messages ping ping pinging into view?

'If you go further up the hill you can get coverage,' Philippa says. 'It's a bit random but there are places. We'll show you tomorrow.'

'Though it's probably not a good idea,' Maria says to Zoe after her sister has left the room and is safely out of earshot. 'You wouldn't want to reveal our location.'

'I know!' says Zoe. 'I know all that!'

'You won't be able to go online, but it's just for a few days,' says Maria. 'Till everything settles down.'

'I know!' says Zoe. 'I know that! I've got heaps of stuff downloaded. I'm fine!'

And she does seem fine. When Maria leaves her to go back to the house she is sitting up in bed in panda print pjs, earbuds in, swiping happily at the screen.

The others have dawdled off to their pods. There is just Philippa wiping down a bench and Maria who stands by the open door of the fridge picking delicacies from the interior — a slice of

The Third Night

cold lamb, a tomato, the remains of some potato salad — with her bare fingers. A habit Philippa remembers only too well from childhood. Maria picking with her fingers at the Sunday joint and their father yelling and the way she persisted, seeming to enjoy the upheaval.

'So,' says Philippa, 'what's all this about? What's going on?'

Maria shrugs. 'Nothing,' she says. 'Thought I'd come and see you, that's all.'

'I don't hear from you in decades and you turn up here, no warning. Why?'

'Can't this wait till morning?' says Maria through a mouthful of potato and mayonnaise. 'The cross-examination?'

'No,' says Philippa. 'It can't wait. And Zoe? What's she doing here?'

'Look, I've been driving for hours,' says Maria, 'including that damn goat track up there, in the dark. You've obviously spent a fortune on this place. Why didn't you upgrade the access? It's a nightmare.'

'Yeah, yeah,' says Philippa, feeling herself revert in a split-second to thirteen with a kid sister who drives her insane.

'We'll get on to the case for the prosecution tomorrow,' says Maria, filling a glass with water. 'The summing up of all my shortcomings and the bloody sentencing. But right now, I'm going to bed. I need to sleep. Okay?'

She sets off across the deck, pauses midway and turns.

'This place,' she says, 'by the way, is hideous. This whole fake scruffy kiwiana simple-crib-at-the-beach schtick. I mean, are you kidding me? I preferred the real thing, Bimmi's place. It was old and dirty and it stank, but at least it was real.'

'What do you mean?' says Philippa. 'This *is* real!'

The Deck

But she's gone. A shadow crossing the deck to the third pod. The glass door slides open, a rectangle of light, then shuts with a click.

THE FOURTH DAY

Early morning, just before dawn. Moon and stars in their customary alignment and the night air still and warm. Maria lies on pastel linen sheeting twisting a strand of hair into a tight dreadlock, the way she does when she's thinking. She's kicked aside the duvet and slid open the doors to sounds she recalls from years and years ago: the regular breathing of the sea, those strange sad cries she used to wonder might be people trapped in the cave under the cliff, maybe the people Bimmi had told them about who got shipwrecked on this stretch of coast and washed into the cave and couldn't be reached, no matter how hard the rescuers tried.

Bimmi told you things like that as if they didn't matter, as if they were merely interesting facts, but for Maria they were only too vivid. Their skin became her skin, shivering in wet clothes. Huddled on a ledge, trying to keep warm, calling and calling and hoping someone would hear. Maria knows now that the

The Deck

sounds are the calls of seabirds or seals barking, but still some echo remains of those voices crying Help! Help!

Across the room her granddaughter sleeps quietly, emitting tiny whiffling sounds as she breathes out, her phone on charge on the bedside table.

Maria lies on the neighbouring bed, feeling the warm air wash around her bare legs, and she thinks, What the hell have I done?

It's all because of Sophie.

Plain, mulish Sophie. Maria has always been a little frightened of her daughter. There had been an initial period of passionate attachment. Sophie had clung to her whenever Maria attempted to leave, late for a meeting, late for the airport, late for a date, the taxi idling at the kerb. Off for only a few hours, a day, a two-day shoot, a week tops, but she'd be back, she'd bring a present and, look, Valeria is here, she's going to read you a story, she's going to make you chocolate milk, she's going to take you to the zoo to see the spider monkeys. Sophie had wrapped her arms around her mother and had to be peeled away, howling as if her skin were being ripped, as if she were an extra limb.

And then, abruptly, when she turned five, she changed. Maria had taken a morning off especially to escort her to her first day at school, holding her hand, anticipating tears. But Sophie had surveyed the kindergarten class at Pauling Elementary, their faces turned like flowers towards the open door. She had dropped her mother's hand.

'Go away now,' she said, and she shut the classroom door firmly between them. Maria could see her through the glass panel, taking her place as if she knew exactly where she belonged.

The attachment had gone. As Sophie grew, it seemed more and more obvious that she did not like her mother very much.

The Fourth Day

She regarded her with cool distaste, said little unless it was to criticise.

That haircut's awful.

Why don't you wear makeup?

Why are you dating that creep?

She retreated to her room, told her mother nothing of her life.

When Maria moved with her back to New Zealand, the gap widened into a chasm. Sophie missed friends she had known, like, for ever, with their Madonna hair and crop-tops and Levi 501s. She missed hanging out at the mall, daring one another to steal eyeliner or scrunchies. She missed the way everyone talked at once, and everyone was ON all the time: Lights Camera ACTION! She missed her cat and the California sun and the big old house in the canyon they shared with all these cool people who did cool stuff and she was never ever lonely.

It rained a lot that first winter and the flat on Dominion Road, just her and her mom, was cold and damp. Sophie tramped off to her new school in her ugly tartan skirt and a hideous blue shirt, her feet shod in lumpy regulation black school shoes. Her shoulders were hunched and the kilt bulged awkwardly at the waist around her plump hips. In the afternoons she came home alone and when Maria returned, usually late, usually in a rush, Sophie would be sprawled on the sofa, curtains pulled, watching *The Bold and the Beautiful* or *Beverly Hills, 90210*, watching them intently for the drama of their lives and the boys and love, but also because this was as close as she could get to America. Her lost paradise where a girl could turn up in a new school and she might not be all that pretty but she met all these new friends who were funny and talented and good looking and everything turned out fine.

The Deck

On the worn blue carpet beside the sofa the takeaway containers piled up: chicken nuggets, pizza (always Hawaiian, with pineapple), sweet and sour pork in sticky red sauce from the Hot Wok on the corner. Maria had to put in long hours. It had not been easy breaking into local filmmaking. It was a small world where everyone knew one another. Jobs were tightly defended. She had to work at it, devise a strategy, be available whenever, wherever. Sophie ate a lot of chicken nuggets and sweet and sour that first year.

Eventually she found some friends. Religious friends who swayed on Sundays babbling in tongues of fire, but at least she seemed happy in their company. She settled in at school, began wearing the regulation jacket and marched about clanking with medals like some five-star general. She passed exams and enrolled in business studies at university. She married Jason under an arch of white roses, reading vows to each other that they had written themselves.

'I promise to love you for ever. Together we will be a team. We will follow our dreams and achieve our life goals.'

Yeah, yeah, thought Maria, seated on a spindly white chair with a ridiculous confection of netting and feathers perched on top of her head like a roosting fowl. Sophie had gone out and bought it herself when Maria refused to wear a hat as Jason's mother planned to do. She had pinned it to Maria's head irritably so that the pin scratched.

'Owww!' Maria had cried, squirming away as their roles did a complete flip on all those years when she had stood behind her daughter plaiting her hair and pinning the thick curls absolutely flat as requested. Sophie hated untidy ends.

The fascinator perched up there, trembling in the breeze

The Fourth Day

blowing in from the Pacific. Jason's mother had gone for the full royal cartwheel in palest primrose, which threatened to levitate entirely, but Maria knew that in her borrowed plumage she looked far more ridiculous.

Sophie and Jason embarked upon adult life as Team Brown. She casually tossed aside her surname, the one she had inherited from her father in faraway America. Ostrowsky.

'It's simpler,' she said. 'No one ever asks me how to spell Brown.'

Team Brown moved south. They set up a business escorting wealthy tourists to view the wonders of the country. They supplied guides and luxury vehicles, and Jason flew them in a helicopter to mountain tops where they picnicked on pavlova and champagne, and then he flew them down again. Sophie kept track of the finances. They had five children because God willed it. They had a house with a view of the lake. They prospered because God meant them to prosper.

They expanded, employed more staff, opened an office on Frankton Road, received industry accolades. And then the tourists stopped. The cordons came down across the world and the airports went silent. The business faltered. Team Brown stopped spinning through the clouds to the mountain tops. They laid off staff and sold off the Range Rovers and the helicopters. They collapsed into disappointment, anger and despair.

Sophie's body puffed and bloated.

Until Ezra touched her. He was a youth leader at their church, cleancut and handsome. He saw her with her family at Sunday's Joyful Noise, her face grey with anxiety, consumed with worry about money and economic collapse and their failed business, fearful for their children's future and terrified by this disease that could kill them all. He came to her home, sat at her kitchen table and placed his hand, smooth and cool, over her plump fingers and said, 'Sophie, you don't have to be afraid. None of it is true.'

Ezra had been doing some research of his own, and he had discovered amazing things, facts that completely contradicted what everyone was being told on the news. Truths that were being deliberately suppressed by powerful interests, this megawealthy cabal who were really in control of the world. He invited Sophie to join a study group of investigators like himself, independent thinkers who questioned what they were being told and met each week to share their discoveries.

Sophie felt his hand close over hers. She looked up into his kind and reassuring eyes and a great flood of something that felt like hope flowed over her. He laid his hand upon her sad flabby flesh and made her whole. Jason, too, joined the study group. Team Brown began to jog together, to eat raw unprocessed foods. They became lean and glowed with good health. They researched and discovered the truth.

It was Ezra who told them about the coming of the new era. The Transformation. The dawning of Year Zero of the Metanoia. It will begin on an island 700 kilometres off the coast of Chile. Más a Tierra is the tip of a massive volcano, dormant for many centuries, but all that is about to change. It has been predicted in Chinese oracle bones, on the walls of Egyptian tombs, in Sanskrit writings dating back 1500 years. And in the Mayan Calendar where the island appears as Q'aq'awitz, the fiery source of life. From its fires will emerge a global awareness of the commencement of a new cycle.

The scoria-covered slopes of Más a Tierra will swell, and

The Fourth Day

when all the planets and stars are in conjunction, great eggs will crack within its mighty walls, eggs that were seeded long ago when a meteor entered our solar system and disintegrated into billions of particles. Seeds rained down upon the earth. They nested in the caldera where they have been growing ever since, but now the time is ripe. A swelling has become evident on one side of the mountain, the eastern side facing the sun, and the time of birth is upon us.

All these new beings will emerge. Beautiful creatures, iridescent, immensely strong, with the resilience of the dinosaurs who preceded us on Earth. They will appear before the people gathered to witness their emergence while overhead a huge cloud will rise from the volcano to spread across the planet. In an eyeblink, the cabal and all the presidents and prime ministers and the corrupt institutions of world government will be struck dumb and shrivel away to little mounds of dust.

The new era will begin and all the things we've got so wrong will be set right, Sophie said, her eyes brilliant with anticipation. All that filth and overcrowding and global warming and sea-level rise and the way we've weakened ourselves as a species through unhealthy living. The way we've permitted hordes of people who should never have been allowed to breed to produce babies. All that will stop. And she and Jason will be there to witness the beginning. They will follow Ezra to the mountain.

'But is it safe to travel right now?' Maria said. 'Isn't Chile in chaos, with revolution and famine and rampant infection everywhere, hundreds of thousands dying every day?'

'You shouldn't believe everything you see on the news,' said Sophie, calmly folding a T-shirt into a suitcase. 'They're paid to exaggerate.'

The Deck

'Really?' said Maria. 'Who pays them?'

The shadowy overlords, that's who, who control the media, the United Nations, the World Health Organization, the World Bank, who want everyone to be fearful, because when you make people frightened they're easy to control. You can make them do anything.

'I thought you'd be on to it, Mum,' said Sophie. 'You were the one who taught me to mistrust big business. You were the one who made the movie about birth defects from Nausagon and the coverup, those pharmaceutical companies lying so they could make massive profits. And, yes, people are dying, but that really doesn't matter. In fact it's a bonus, because it will leave room for a new, superior hybrid species to flourish.'

'So these volcano egg people are here on Earth to interbreed?' said Maria. 'Who with? With you?'

'Not with us, *obviously*,' said Sophie as if her mother were particularly dense. 'We're too old. Forty-plus is way too old for safe breeding. It's the younger ones who will benefit.'

'So you mean Zoe? You mean Josh and Evie and the twins?'

Sophie shrugged. 'Well, not right away, but in time, when they're ready, yes, of course. If they're lucky enough to be selected.'

They are leaving in a few days for Valparaíso where a boat has been chartered to carry the faithful who are gathering from around the world to witness the end of history and the dawn of the new era. They have sold up here and bought a place in the settlement that is being built on the slopes of Más a Tierra.

They have photographs. See? Doesn't that look absolutely beautiful?

Sophie was giddy with excitement. She had country music on

The Fourth Day

rotate, she hummed along, she twirled about the room, packing socks and shorts.

'When will you be back?' said Maria.

'Never,' said her daughter. 'Why would we come back here?'

They have their passports, though such formalities will be irrelevant come the Metanoia. Once the new world order is established, old boundaries will be swept away. They will live high on the slopes of the volcano among the egg creatures.

Team Brown is ready for departure, and Maria had been invited down for the weekend, not to celebrate her daughter's forty-fifth birthday as she had assumed, but to say goodbye.

'Why didn't you tell me?' Maria asked, hearing herself sound pathetic, needy and weak.

'Because you would probably have tried to talk us out of it,' said Sophie. 'That's what people do. They just quote all that media crap about riots and plague, even smart people. This whole country is consumed by fear. Once the dogs start barking, the people run, and if you try to offer them some alternative reality, some facts they haven't encountered before, they shut off or tell us we're crazy, that we're putting our kids at risk.'

Maria had to tread this minefield carefully.

'Do you think they might have a point?' she said. 'This new variant seems virulent, there's millions dying . . .'

'And how many of those people,' said Jason, leaning in for emphasis, jabbing the air with his finger, 'were old and would have died anyway from the common cold? How many had diabetes because they've abused their bodies for years? Did the newsreaders mention that? Break down the figures?'

'No,' said Maria, 'but . . .'

'Why not?' said Jason. 'Why not? Because it's not politically

The Deck

acceptable to say that the world is overpopulated. Billions of us fighting for space, scrapping over resources and yet we persist in trying to keep all these people alive who are weak or old, long past their useful term. It's crazy! And then there's this bug — whether naturally evolved or deliberately designed, who cares? — that comes along and does us all a great big favour. It culls the herd of the weak and old so the herd can move on. We'll be stronger, healthier. And I know that makes me sound like a Nazi, but, to be honest, they had a point.'

'Really?' said Maria, who had never liked Jason from the moment he first turned up with her daughter. Sophie alight with adoration, he too handsome by half in a smooth blond, brushed-back, boy-band, Nick Carter kind of way. Too stupid. Whenever the conversation touched on politics, he professed to be an anarchist.

What the fuck? Maria had thought, though she didn't say it out loud. Not while Sophie smiled and nodded as her new boyfriend leaned back on his chair, laying it down as if he were delivering some profound and original insight that all political parties were crap and indistinguishable as agents of repression and all politicians were useless and corrupt.

And now he's saying the Nazis might have had a point.

'Not about the Jews of course,' he added.

'Oh, that's a relief,' said Maria. 'Given that Sophie is part Jewish on her father's side and your kids would likely have been loaded onto Hitler's trains.'

Jason waved aside that tiny detail. 'Not the Jews, but the rest — the subnormal, the ones infected with incurable diseases. I mean, it was tough, but humanity is going to have to deal with all that sooner or later, and that moment is now. It's been taken

The Fourth Day

out of our hands. A virus is cleansing the planet and it's lucky for us really. But if you say that, you just bring down a hail of abuse.'

'Even friends,' said Sophie. 'People we thought we could trust. They wade in. When we tell them about Q'aq'awitz and the Metanoia, and that we're going there, they tell us we're terrible parents when we're not! We're giving our kids this incredible opportunity!'

'Whoop de do,' said Zoe, who had been sitting quietly through all this, breaking her slice of cake into chocolate crumbs, not eating a morsel.

'See?' said Jason. 'Even our kids have been filled with fear, turned into sheep.'

'I am not a sheep!' said Zoe, knocking her plate away. Chocolate crumbs rained down on the table. 'I just don't want to go to this stupid island. And the only thing I'm frightened of right now is you!'

She crashed from the room, slamming the door so hard the walls shuddered. Another slam from upstairs as she stamped into her bedroom.

Later, Maria knocked tentatively at her door. Her granddaughter was seated on her bed, tapping at her phone. The room had been stripped bare of its posters and photos. A suitcase stood packed in the middle of the floor.

'Everything okay?' said Maria.

''Course not,' said Zoe. 'I mean they're mad, aren't they? My friend Rakaia says they've gone mad.'

'Convinced, I suppose,' said Maria, seating herself on the edge of the bed. Still the gingham duvet cover with the horses. Still the glow-in-the-dark stars stuck to the bedhead.

The Deck

'No,' said Zoe. 'Quite definitely mad. Certifiable. You don't believe all that stuff about the volcano, do you? The dinosaur people?'

'It does sound a bit unlikely,' said Maria.

'And you haven't met Ezra,' said Zoe. 'He's the creepiest dude in the world.'

Suddenly she flung her arms around Maria, clinging.

'Please don't let them take me,' she whispered into her grandmother's neck. 'I want to stay here. Please don't make me go.' She trembled, her whole body one frantic vibration.

So now they are here in the bay, as dawn breaks and the birds cry Help! Help!

Yesterday was the hasty escape, the note scribbled and left on the pillow, Zoe's suitcase loaded stealthily into the boot of her car, the two of them driving away down long empty roads past the shining acres of moonlit lakes, the lurking fear of detection, sirens and police lights in the rear-view mirror. They never materialised. Maria had tossed her phone into some roadside scrub, while Zoe's phone had been safeguarded for weeks, location disabled, private network installed. The entire family had been safely concealed behind a thorny thicket of encryption. Her parents were taking no chances.

They swooped unimpeded from the high country down through the pass onto the plain, following a winding road that evolved gradually into arrival in this place, the most remote place Maria could think of where they could hide out until her daughter and her husband and the creepiest man in the world had gone off to meet the future.

There had been a moment, an hour or so into the drive, when she glanced across at Zoe, curled up on the passenger seat, phone in hand, flicking through songs by bands Maria has never heard of, but they were good songs with great instrumentals and interesting lyrics. Zoe had downloaded heaps in readiness for the long journey to the source of the new era. Music filled the car. Her granddaughter had great taste. She played drums, she said, in a band with Rakaia and some other dudes. They've been writing their own stuff, people seemed to like it, there was a competition coming up. They'd been practising. Her face, reflected in the glow of the screen, was serene.

Maria drove through the dark knowing that Sophie would leave exactly as planned, regardless of Zoe's absence, regardless of the criticism of friends, regardless of reason and argument. She and Jason would be on that plane. Her daughter had had that look that Maria learned long ago meant there would be no compromise and no retreat. She would leave as planned, and she will never ever speak to her mother again.

Fair enough, thinks Maria now as the dawn breaks over the bay and the birds waken. She lies on her tangled bed, twisting her hair. I've never been the perfect mother. Too caught up in my work, not to mention a lifetime of ridiculous relationships.

But as she had driven with Zoe through the dark land, she had felt herself filled with a novel sense of purpose. She could make up for previous failings. She could do something good and self-sacrificing. She could save her granddaughter from a dubious fate. She could sell up her place in the city. She could move south and care for her until her parents recovered their senses. Sweeping around a curve in the road she had felt heroic. She was like the sort of older woman who would once have been played by Frances McDormand. Someone the promos called 'feisty'.

The Deck

But now, lying in the pre-dawn, she is not so sure.

What the hell, she thinks, twisting her hair in a knot, have I done?

Her sister does nothing later that day to reinforce her confidence.

'You realise you've kidnapped a minor?' she says when Maria finally confesses to the escape.

They are walking to the waterfall. The sun had beaten down all morning from a flawless sky. Too hot for the deck, too hot for the beach where the sand burned bare feet. The waterfall, Philippa said. It would be cool in the bush. They could swim.

Three women, a girl and a dog set off up the valley. Zoe and Ani walked ahead, Raffi waddling beside them making pleased little detours into the undergrowth.

Maria and Philippa dawdled behind as Maria made a swift impromptu edit on the storyline. She cut swathes of dialogue and distracting backstory and tightened the narrative arc to just a story of a very necessary rescue, featuring her daughter and son-in-law as deluded individuals in thrall to a madman, and herself as a reluctant but determined heroine.

Her sister is not convinced.

'Kidnapping's a really serious crime,' she says. 'Fourteen years maximum.'

'Yeah, yeah,' says Maria. As if that fact were irrelevant.

'And what's worse, you've made me an accessory!' says Philippa. 'You've made all of us accessories to a serious crime. You've always been so bloody inconsiderate.'

'It's just for a few days,' says Maria. 'I think your reputation will be fairly safe. All right?'

Philippa sighs. 'I suppose . . .' she says.

The Fourth Day

It really is too hot for argument.

The track veers off into the bush and green leaf arches overhead. The creek runs alongside, lower than it used to be at this time of year but still sufficient to cool the air. They can breathe more easily here. They follow one another along a narrow track, talking of this and that.

'That white flower. What's it called? I can never remember the names of plants, can you? They just don't . . .'

'My sandal's falling to bits . . .'

'Nice to see Baz again. He's looking . . .'

'Hey, Raffi! Get out of that . . .'

Raffi has been renewed by the cool and the shade and a new path. He rolls in the stinking ecstasy of a dead possum.

'Raffi, that's disgusting . . .'

The waggy optimism of a walk with a dog.

The track winds at a gentle incline uphill over tree roots and stones. Spiders have spun their webs across its width, long sticky threads that catch on their faces and snap one by one, so it's as if they ascend by breaking one barrier, then another.

The creek tumbles downhill beside them around boulders worn smooth since they emerged as molten bubbles from the vent. There's birdsong and all those trees in all their variations of green and kōtukutuku dangling long strips of red-gold bark like streamers and houhere raining down upon them, covering their path in white lace. And then the track flattens and emerges into a clearing.

Knee-high grass and bracken and ahead a wall of basalt over which the creek tumbles in a narrow plume of white, down through rock and fern to a pool deep enough for swimming. Around its edge lie flat-topped rocks, water smoothed, where

The Deck

they might sit or stretch full length in the sun or in the dappled shade of a single ancient tree that reaches over the water, bent and bowed. In spring it would be golden, brash and bright. Birds would flock and feast. But now, in late summer, its flowers have fallen and what the tree offers is a tracery of grey-green leaf, the subtlety of light and shadow.

They take off their sandals, dangle their feet in the cool water. Dragonflies of brilliant emerald hover, hunting the meniscus and the air is alive with the buzz of other species in the tall grass and the rush of water over stone.

Maria stands and drags off her shirt. A black bikini on a body that is lean and tanned, the skin still smooth and puckered only at the belly where a ragged line marks the place where she was cut open to reveal a baby, tucked like a little bean in the bloody pod. She lifts her arms and, without checking, though she really should, executes a neat duck dive, then rises, flicking her long grey mane into a flurry of icy droplets and yelling, 'Ooh ooh, mercy me that's cold. I'd forgotten how it's always bloody freezing here!' Then she's under again and striking out for the far bank in a rapid crawl, kicking furiously.

Ani follows, and her body too bears its marks. The white-line curves from armpit to breastbone where she has been stitched and mended. She clasps her arms over an empty pocket and goes in bit by bit, to the ankles, to the knees, to the groin, before surrendering with a happy sigh, falling backwards and spreading her arms. A perfect starfish, looking up at the azure blue of the sky.

When Philippa first suggested a walk, Ani had been reluctant. She had been caught before by one of Philippa's little walks, slogging up some hill to look at a view they could have seen just as well from the comfort of a car on a road. It was all a bit earnest, she thought privately, this enthusiasm for sweat and effort, healthy mind in healthy body.

But this wash of cold water, this breathing air . . .

She can feel the scar tighten across her chest where the soft mound of her breast had once been. She had been offered reconstruction of course, but she had declined. Partly it was because she could not bear the thought of staying a single day longer than necessary within the confines of a hospital. Not after all those days sitting in a La-Z-Boy chair with a needle in her arm delivering reprieve and a nurse enquiring from time to time if she's okay and she says, 'Yes thank you' because she must be polite, even as the cocktail floods her body.

But the other reason she declined was because she did not see the point. Her breast was gone. Her breast with all its ducts and lobes and ligaments, all its history and purpose. It seemed important to see that each morning in the bathroom mirror and acknowledge its absence.

The long scar meant something, just as the little scar under her chin meant something. The little scar where a swing at the park had hit her when she was four. It knocked her over and she needed two stitches. She remembers her dad gathering her up and carrying her, bleeding copiously, to the car. Except he wasn't her dad and her mum wasn't her mum. They had picked her from a newspaper, choosing not the baby of good parentage who will become available in July, nor the fair-skinned baby, but her.

When she sees the scar she remembers that complicated fact, and her blood sticking to the green and brown pattern on a man's jersey.

The Deck

She floats on her back on the water's surface, arms spread. It is without doubt a Perfect Moment. She collects them: moments that are not remarkable for any reason — not some moment of intense emotional connection, meeting a long-lost friend, achieving a long-held goal, surviving some great horror — but perfect just the same. A moment where everything seems to stop for a second and there is nothing but beauty and stillness and she'll remember it for ever. She drifts in the stillness and from somewhere behind her up on the bank she hears him laugh, a kind, gentle amusement. 'Yes! It is in the fact a Perfect Moment! It is a cracker!'

Philippa goes in last, cautious over the stones, the pale skin of her freckled gingery inheritance puckered where the sun has nipped too close, and beneath the navel the four horizontal marks where the scalpel so delicately, so precisely, entered and pruned away the empty sac of her defective womb. The tufts of hair at her crevices look sun-worn too, faded from red to white. She dithers on the bank, arms clasped over her breasts, saying, 'I wish I could swim! I wish I could swim properly! It's because of that time I nearly drowned in the school baths and I've never learned.'

Maria lies on her back paddling lazily. 'No, it's not,' she says. 'It's because you wouldn't try. You were always such a wuss. You never learned to swim, like you never rode your bike with no hands.'

It's too soon yet to engage. Philippa ignores her and concentrates on feeling her way into deeper water. The bottom of the pool is covered in a smooth layer of tiny stones that glint in the sunlight. The others swim from side to side, splashing extravagantly on passing and laughing, while she looks down

The Fourth Day

into the depths and suppresses the knowledge of the eel. They caught one here, she and her brother and sister. They threaded a dead hedgehog onto some binder twine and dangled it in the water and a huge eel emerged from the shadows under the bank. Bigger by far than any eels they'd ever seen before. Its huge head rose up and then it undulated towards their bait, opened its jaws wide exposing rows of needle teeth, and dragged the lot, hedgehog and twine, from their hands.

Maria tried to hang on but Philippa cried 'Let go, let go!' For the eel could have taken her little sister. It could have dragged her under like the princess who was seized by a dragon and taken down to a castle beneath a lake from which she could never return.

She remembers that blunt grey head, the strength of that slimy muscled thing on the other end of their flimsy lure, and despite years of listening to accounts of the most appalling injuries human beings can inflict upon one another, it retains its special horror.

That eel will have gone by now. She was huge, a big old female, full grown, maybe seventy or eighty years old when they tried to drag her out onto the bank with their cruel bait. She will have made her way long since back down the creek she had first entered as a tiny silvery thread. She will have headed downstream, drawn by some mysterious alignment of moon and stars and the scent of the sea to cross the beach and enter the open ocean.

She will have headed out into dark waters, swimming thousands of kilometres north to the tropical sea where she had first burst into this thing called life. She will have risen to the surface when she reached that place, and all those eggs will

The Deck

have streamed from her dying body, as it begins again. That silvery thread, the sweep south to this creek, the long life by the waterfall. How could they have planned to beat her to death on the bank with their silly sticks and stones?

Philippa inches into the pool, not mentioning the eel, not wanting to supply further proof that she is a wuss. The chilly waters lap at her shoulders. When she looks down, her legs have become shortened and bent by refraction and her hands look like little white fish. But finally she's under and executing a clumsy dogpaddle across the pond to the place where they can clamber out, pass through the curtain onto the narrow ledge at the foot of the waterfall, where it is possible to turn and see the world blurred and flicking rainbows.

They dive and splash and swim back and forth and say this is gorgeous and Maria says, 'Bimmi used to bring us here, remember, Plip? She was a great believer in the virtues of cold water, that it was good for our constitutions, better than any bath. Silly old bat, such a puritan.'

'But it is, isn't it?' says Philippa. 'Better than any bath.'

Zoe had sat for a few moments on the bank with Raffi, watching the old ladies splash and squeal. It was all a bit embarrassing really.

'Come in!' they called. 'It's lovely! It's refreshing.'

'I'm okay,' she said, getting up. 'I might walk a bit further up the track.'

'But aren't you hot?' they said, their hair slicked down on their old heads like so many seals looking up.

'No, I'm fine,' she said. 'I don't feel like a swim.'

'Well, don't go too far,' they said. 'Stay within earshot. We'll call when we're ready to head back. Okay?'

The Fourth Day

'Okay,' she said, setting off across the clearing and into the trees. Her phone was in her pocket.

In the clearing, the old ladies stretch on the rocks to dry, then they swim again, they drink the clear water falling from above, they lie on the rocks, and after a while Zoe returns without having to be called (there was no signal whatever and the track had become steep and blocked by storm-damaged trees). The old ladies have looked up and seen a little cloud the shape of a rabbit sailing in over the lip of the waterfall. The air has become noticeably cooler. It is time to head back.

No one knows what time it is exactly, the hour, minute, second. Time is just one thing happening after another, the speeding arrow that flies from past to present to future. It is just one sensation then another. Hot. Cold. Wet. Dry. It's just a track through trees, downhill alongside a creek. It is the air cooling as the bank of fog that has hovered on the horizon for days begins to roll towards the land.

They cross the ford on the road where they stop and pick watercress and fennel and monkey musk because it is beautiful, and they return with leaves in their arms and tangled hair, and as they enter the house it is to find the others gathered.

Tom looks up and says, 'Good, you're back. Sun's over the yardarm. How about a drink?' And time comes bustling back, tick tock, neatly carved into base twelve. Twenty-four hours, sixty minutes, sixty seconds. Or determined by the sun, by that yardarm.

Tom is happy. He has been solving a problem. He has spent the day with Baz, making something work properly again and the thought of that gives him immense satisfaction.

The Deck

On the first day before everyone arrived, he had walked up the hill to check on the water tank. It was part of the routine. An inspection of facilities to guarantee that they could supply the needs of the little group of humans about to gather in his house. There must be water for the kitchen sink and bathroom showers and lavatories. Sufficient to flush away their waste, their flaking skin, their shit and piss. Down it will go on the cascade, around U-bends and pipes to the septic tank in the scrub below the house. And there it will plop and bubble as the seething multitudes get to work, the billions of bacteria of several species, the microscopic worms and tiny creatures no more than a single cell who have always had the planet under their complete control.

When Tom came up the hill that first day following the old farm track, it was to find the tank half empty, the feeder pipe from the spring kicked aside and the ooze emptying into a muddy wallow. The air smelled rancid, sweaty like old socks, like the most pungent of cheeses, a dense cloying stink.

Deer tracks were everywhere, and pig root, the work of the feral descendants of that old bat Bimmi's stock. When she felt herself approaching death she had opened all the gates on what was left of her farm, releasing her chickens and a deer, a hind she had kept as a pet and its fawn, and her little kunekune Enid, together with her latest litter of plump spotted piglets. They had wandered off into the bush-clad valley where they set to breeding exuberantly, incestuously or with the renegades who arrived, drawn by an instinct for survival in a parched land. They produced a mighty progeny, feral and intractable. And in this hot season they ventured down to former pastures in their search for water. They wallowed. They left their heady stink.

The Fourth Day

Tom knelt in mud, one arm shoved into the mouth of the spring, dragging away the mass of root and weed that always formed when the boulders he piled to protect the pipe were knocked aside and light got in. It came away in a tangled hank. The spring dribbled onto his bare skin, a steady flow, though a mere trickle compared with earlier years. Springs everywhere, even in this valley, had dried completely. Beyond the hilltop, riverbeds snaked over the plains as dirt tracks, where dust rose in plumes at every puff of the dry winds blowing from the mountains. But this spring still ran, and the creek too, though the levels were dwindling.

They'd have to watch every drop if they were not to run out of water entirely. He would have to build stronger protection around it, and he would have to cull the marauders. Hunt the deer and pigs till their numbers were more manageable. He'd have to get out the gun.

He'd reconnected the pipe, and today he made a start on a post-and-rail enclosure, strong enough to resist the most determined intruder. He and Baz had dug postholes in the heavy ground around the spring, sweating mightily in the heat. Baz was good to work with. He never objected or made useless suggestions for alternative schemes of his own devising, as others did. He was always content to let Tom take the lead, he was quick and accurate and strong, and he didn't waste time on idle talk. He was quiet and got on with the job.

Baz had been thinking. He was adjusting to the person who turned up last night, who, beneath the mane of grey hair, was Maria. Tom's girlfriend's kid sister whom he had first seen several lifetimes ago in a line-up of girls in identical pink dresses

The Deck

with posies in their hands and their hair puffed up.

Baz had been seated out in the body of the church among Tom's mates, all of them a bit the worse for wear after the stag night. Not that there had been a lot of scope for debauch in Dunshea, but they had hit the pub and done their best and it was all a bit of a blur, including the obligatory fight in the pub carpark.

It was puddled and dark and one of Philippa's cousins had had his knee pressed painfully on Baz's spine, still raging about the Tour, though it was months past. Still furious at the cancellation of the game in Timaru and those fuckheads in Hamilton and Eden Park. That particular war was not yet over, not here in Dunshea. It would never be over. He had Baz in a savage headlock, face down on the tarmac, but he had mistaken his mark. Baz may have looked vulnerable with the long girly hair but he had learned at the foot of the master, his older brother, how to break a hold, go for the balls or the nose, squirm and kick and jab. In a fight he was like an eel on a riverbank, slippery and impossible to hold.

Now the cousin sat two rows over with a black eye, giving him the evils through his Ray-Bans. Baz would keep his distance in case he decided to bring in reinforcements for another round. Up the front of the church Tom stood waiting, fenced in by flowers, with a couple of other survivors of the Dunshea pub, all of them in suits. Tom was even wearing a waistcoat, for fuck's sake, and a tie, and a pink rose pinned to the lapel. He looked docile, slicked down like a dog that's been brought to heel. A dog wearing a champion's rosette. Best in Show. Watching him standing there, Baz made a solemn vow.

Never.

The Fourth Day

Never would he wear a suit and a tie that clamped the neck like a leash. Never would he stand in a cold grey church stinking of lilies, that sweet reek that was so close to the offal pit.

Baz's leg jiggled uncontrollably. He was desperate to move, to get out of there into the open air. He was wearing his flares, passably clean, and the old leather jacket he had nicked when his brother marched off with V Force to deal to the commies, and a pair of cowboy boots from a second-hand shop in Lyttelton, elaborately tooled and heeled.

Up front, the organ squawked and gasped, pedalled frantically into life by one of Philippa's aunts. Red-faced with the effort, she fumbled into the wedding march and everyone turned to watch as Philippa, fully rigged in white, advanced. Arm in arm with the lump of fat and gristle, the former loose-head prop and provincial rep, current president of the local branch of Federated Farmers, the Nat, the fascist whose sperm had somehow managed to infiltrate the formidable fortress that was Philippa's mother and engender Philippa.

They bore down on the altar, Philippa and the lump, to where Tom stood waiting, apparently unaware of how fucking ridiculous he looked. He stood grinning like an idiot as the girl, the future, the whole disaster closed in on him.

After it was done, signed up and no going back, everyone filed out into the sunshine, where a photographer from town recorded the wreck on the church steps and in front of the roses by the war memorial. *Now, everybody, SMILE! It's not a funeral. Not yet anyway. Now — say SEX!* Philippa's mother did not approve of that. No. Not at all. Totally uncalled for.

Baz also had a camera, a little Kodak Super 8 movie camera with which to record the momentous occasion. He used it to film his mates surfing or performing in various permutations of the same band in pubs and dingy basement clubs around the city where the floor heaved under the mob. Weddings were not really his thing, but Tom had asked. Philippa wanted a record of the day, and Baz worked in television.

'Working in television.' It sounded cutting edge. As if he had morphed from boring physics student to glamorous creative type, when the reality was that he had a menial job sweeping the floors and moving sets and lights around an old downtown mercantile building roughly converted to deliver the new technology in black and white to the living rooms of the city. It was the decade of the new technology. Of the gardening show with pruning tips, the show for the kids with puppets, the quiz where you might win a car or a trip for two. And Baz was there, at the cutting edge, in his white techie coat with his broom.

So he roamed about with his little Kodak, trying to keep out of the photographer's way, snatching film of the bride, the groom, the guests, the maids in a row by the memorial that listed the names of all those dead boys.

She stood at one end of the row in her pink frock, holding her posy as if it were a grenade. She glowered.

'Maria!' Baz heard Philippa's mother hiss from the sideline. 'Stop slouching and smile!'

Maria engineered a brief grimace. She was tall and awkward, her hair short and choppy, not puffed up like the hair of the other girls. Her brows were dark and drawn in a frown and her lips pouted. She was not beautiful, but Baz's camera came to a stop when it reached her. And later it searched her out, seated at the top table in the hall where toetoe and ferns wreathed the honour boards and there was a choice of roast lamb or chicken.

The Fourth Day

She glowered, fiddling with her glass as the speeches droned on until at last the Delta Tones, out from town, set up in a racket of reverb and the dancing could begin.

At last Baz was free to sidle off across the cricket ground over the road and down to the river for a smoke. He slid down a bank tangled with willow and white silt and found a convenient log. He took out the tin and the Rizlas and lay back, out of sight. The Delta Tones were a distant echo. His camera lay on his knee. He drew in deeply.

There was a scrabbling overhead and a hail of clay and small stones, and suddenly she was there too, in her pink dress, sliding down the bank. Twigs and dirt clung to her hair.

'I thought I saw you sneaking off,' she said. 'Ooh, is that that stuff? Marijuana?' (She pronounced it with a hard 'j'.) 'It smells funny. Can I try some?'

'No,' said Baz.

'Why not?' she said. 'I'm over sixteen. Age of consent. I can do what I like.'

'No,' said Baz. 'Your dad would kill me, or one of those cousins of yours.'

'So can I try your camera?' she said. 'That's actually what I came for.'

'Umm,' said Baz, relieved that she had given up so readily on the dope but reluctant to hand over something that had cost him several hours of sweeping floors and dragging around the set for *Garden Time*. But she reached down, took it from his hand and carefully pivoted to pan across the scene. The river, the willows, and then she turned the lens towards him.

He raised a hand to block the shot. 'No!' he said.

But she said, with surprising authority, 'Stay still,' and kept

The Deck

right on filming. His feet. He had kicked off his boots. His legs. Slowly tracking the length of his body. His hand rising to his mouth, the puff of smoke between his lips, closing in on his face, acne scarred, the wind catching a lock of his hair and blowing it over his eyes, his eyes looking back at her through the camera, alert, amused.

He saw himself later, tacked onto the record of a wedding that could have been any wedding anywhere. Unremarkable footage that pleased Philippa, though 'Why did you have to include her? Being bad tempered and upsetting everyone as usual?'

He had not shown her the ending. He cut the long slow footage of a man smoking by a river, a beautiful sequence that had used up all his film and left none for the dancing and the going-away car with the shoe tied to the fender and JUST MARRIED daubed in white paint over the rear window. He had missed the bit where Tom and Philippa headed down the road towards their happy ending.

And later, after Maria had turned up at his door, after she had moved into his flat, into his bed, after that last night and the old man riding down on them through the winter dark, after all that, when she had packed and gone, he had also missed his camera.

And then, many lifetimes later, here she was again. Older, greying, but unmistakably herself and she was saying, 'Baz? Is that you?' And it had all come flooding back.

All that long, hot day he lifted the mattock, over and over, bringing it down hard onto resistant earth. He tore away grass and root. He got on with digging a hole and tried not to think of her.

The Fourth Day

And Pete and Didi? What did they do on this long, hot afternoon, the others safely distant, the place to themselves? Philippa had suggested kayaking. Some cavern out there in the bay.

'It's so beautiful,' she said. 'It's amazing, a marvel. You can hardly ever get inside, but today would be perfect. So calm. You could take the kayaks.'

Didi shook e's head. 'It sounds lovely,' e said, letting her down gently. She was always so enthusiastic, like some overbearing Akela driving her little cubs into outdoor activity. Thank god they were leaving in a day or so. 'But it's too hot. We'll just potter about here.'

Pete nodded in agreement, relieved. Kayaks? Really? He never intended to get on a craft of any kind bobbing about on any stretch of water again for as long as he lived.

'You go and enjoy yourselves,' said Didi, 'while we stay here, nice and cool. And we'll make some delicious drinks for you all when you get back.'

E could feel Pete beside em, his beautiful body. E had stood shaving in the en suite this morning, for though the follicles had become softer and more delicate under prolonged treatment, chin and neck persisted in producing a black shadow. That thick Italian beard refused to lie down and disappear without daily rituals of removal, facial scrub and moisturiser. The windows behind e's head stood wide open and in the mirror e could see Pete out on the deck saluting the sun, the bay, the gleaming expanse of sand.

Pete's body, bare to the waist, bent and stretched. He breathed and his lungs, twin sacs, inflated, deflated, inflated, while his heart beat a steady tattoo and glands made their minutely calibrated adjustments, adding a dab of this, a soupçon of that to

The Deck

the efficient working of the whole system, and the furled gut forced from mouth to anus the sludge of his consumption.

He stretched and twisted in the sunshine, believing that by doing so he could wring himself clear, return his body to some primal state of perfect purity. He reached up, believing that by doing so the prana would enter through his stretching fingers and through the soles of his bare feet. He breathed slow and steady with the sea, with a bird trilling up and down its scale, as his body flowed from silhouette to silhouette, urdhva mukha svanasana, adho mukha svanasana, virabhadrasana, upward-facing dog, downward-facing dog, warrior . . .

He's kept himself in shape, thought Didi, as e watched Pete's reflection while conducting the routines e hoped would confer perfection on e's own body. E has always loved the glimpses, those moments when Pete was unaware of being watched, from the very first moment when he wandered across the piazza, took his place at a table, ordered a caffè and sat, looking somehow sad and alone behind those dark glasses.

Didi had watched him covertly from the bar, where it was dark even at noon. Danny DeCicco was making an escape from family. From the overwhelming mass of cousins, aunts, uncles, all animated, all exclaiming over him, how handsome he was, like someone long dead, like Zio Renzo, like Fortunato! As for the girls, *le ragazze*! How they must all be in pursuit! It went on and on until he simply needed to get away for a little while and be just himself, Danny DeCicco, leading his own private, secret life.

So no, they did not kayak to any cavern in the hours when they were alone, all the others safely distant attending to the water supply, or viewing a waterfall. The body that was Didi seized the body that was Pete in close embrace. These two sleeves of skin with their remnants of primate hair. These faces the remnants of the gills of ancient fish. These bones that took formation half a billion years ago when, in some warm primeval ocean, a worm turned. It began swimming upside down and slowly, over aeons, its spine rearranged itself from front to back, and here it is, a spine within a sleeve of human skin, bending towards another sleeve of skin. And the rope of nerve within the spine and all the many nerves that radiate about the body, those fine wires, those neurons, that surge of sodium within the cell, that electricity of positive and negative, that switch of ions, the complexity of receptor and synaptic gap, that whole miraculous chemistry fired within the sleeve.

Blood flooded the corpus cavernosa, the caverns within the penis. The glands exuded their sweat of salt and fat and water. The orifices of the body opened to receive. The eyes within the sockets in the skull were wide. The twin tunnels into the skull that were the nostrils flared and caught the scent. The four muscles that open the jaw flexed, and the mouth opened pink within its vermilion border, its delicate mucosa the same at either end of the furl of gut, at the mouth and at the anus, puckered like pleated silk.

Skin touches skin, sensation sparking along clustered nerve to the deepest crevices of the brain, with their names that are like the names of the craters on some new planet: to thalamus and amygdala, the little almond, to hippocampus, the little seahorse, and the zona incerta, that 'region of which nothing certain can be said'. The deep inner mystery of the self.

On the bed that long, hot afternoon all is sweat and urgency and grunt and thrust and release and caress and sleeve against sleeve, body wrapped around body, till they lie side by side and the day flows in again, the sound of the sea, a breeze billowing white curtains. They are back upon Earth.

And when the afternoon cools and the others return, they are showered and dressed already, and Didi is making everyone margaritas.

THE FOURTH NIGHT

Fog has rolled in and blanketed the bay. Ever since they arrived, the fog had been a grey wall at the horizon, but over the afternoon it had advanced, blanking out the sea before it reached the headland where it rose up like a wave and poured down over cliff face and hillside until the whole world was milky. The temperature dropped abruptly and sound became muted. The birds were silenced. The people too became quiet. When they ventured outside, things loomed up: a tree, a flight of steps, the corner of a building floating free of context. They encountered one another as strange elongated creatures who emerged from the fog like babies bursting through the caul. It was unnerving.

That evening they closed the doors on the fog. They preferred a lighted room to the deck where the fog laid its damp fingers upon them. They sat in their wooden box, looking out at the swirl of nothing.

The Deck

'I think we need a fire,' says Philippa, and Baz says, 'Good idea.'

He likes fires. Ever since the flame on the beach that was his salvation he has liked fires. There was never any shortage of driftwood on that wild coast. Whole trees beached and bleached to white bone. Twigs and branches tangled with hanks of dry kelp that spat green and blue at the touch of a flame as the salts exploded. Baz and his mates made fires up and down that beach, and once, more spectacularly, among some pines planted in the dunes, where, at first lick, the flame raced in multiple directions through dry needles and began climbing trees until the whole plantation was a roaring inferno from which they ran like hell.

They were just kicking about by the dairy as the fire engine heehawed through the intersection, all the volunteers in their fireman's hats looking strong and purposeful and Mervyn Davies looking down at them as the truck roared past. His eyes were cool. He knew it was them. No one was ever positively identified as the culprit but one night Mervyn grabbed Baz as he was sorting papers for his delivery round. He seized him by the neck of his jumper in one mighty paw, lifted him clean off his feet and leaned in close. His breath smelled of fried onions. 'You watch it, sonny,' he said. 'I've got my eye on you.'

Many fires. That moment when they came in at the end of a good day, feet and hands numb, head aching from the icy water, and set to crisscrossing twigs to form a teepee in shingle or sand over crumpled paper, centring the pile so that the draught even on a windless night would gulp the flame from a single match. Always just a single match. That was the challenge. And then feeding it slowly with bigger pieces of driftwood, bit by bit as if it were a baby, coaxing it into life. And finally the circle

The Fourth Night

of warmth and light on a stretch of dark coast as the mates gathered around.

'Ooh yes!' says Ani. 'I love a fire. We always had an open fire and a woodburning stove. Leo spent hours cutting and stacking. You should have seen his wood piles. He made these round structures, wood houses he called them, with all the logs cut to even lengths and stacked in a ring with a kind of pointy roof on top. He said the wood dried best that way, but I think he just loved the look of them. They were hard to get right. They were a work of art. People stopped on the road and took photos.'

But now she lives in the city and the council does not approve of fires. They release particulate matter. The particles rise into the atmosphere and contribute to the diminution of the ozone layer, and who wants to do that? Cause drought and famine, the collapse of the ice shelf, the extinction of species, the deaths of children under a burning sun? She has a heatpump now on the wall next to the abandoned hearth. It whirrs into life at the flick of a switch and releases eddies of warm air like a nor'wester howling through the living room, setting everything to agitation. Her house is warm. Her house is dry. But no one would ever pull up a chair by the heatpump. No one would sit late at night in its calm reflective glow, staring into gleaming caverns that flare and fall.

'Heatpumps are efficient,' she says, 'but I miss the fire.' She hopes Leo will hear.

Out here, however, so far from the city, they can have a fire. There's a basket by the fireplace filled with logs, though there is nothing small enough to use as kindling so Baz takes log and hatchet out onto the deck and begins to chop. Neat fingerlings of macrocarpa peel away.

The Deck

Tom appears at his shoulder.

'We don't usually do that out here, mate,' he says. His task, cutting kindling. His hatchet. His deck. 'There's a chopping block at the foot of the steps.'

'Almost done,' says Baz, making another deft cut. Tap tap tap. The strips smell sweet and resinous and it is all Tom can do not to reach down, seize hatchet and log and do it himself in the proper place.

'All set,' says Baz, standing with his kindling and returning to the fireplace to start work on the teepee. Crumpling a newspaper with a photo of sports fans in woolly hats and scarves, cheering on the team after months of confinement. He remembers that game. They'd won, 22–18. He and Tom had been there. It felt like more than just a game. It felt momentous, as if they had defeated something far greater than just a visiting team. They had defeated a malevolent force that had held the world in thrall, an invisible legion that killed and maimed. But they had united in defence. They had played a cautious, strategic game, countered its every move, anticipated every incursion, and they had won and here they were: 30,000 fans, arms raised in jubilation. They'd got the ball over the line. A short-lived triumph.

Baz arranges a lattice of kindling strips but Tom is bustling in with a bundle of tī kōuka leaves, tightly furled.

'Here you are,' he says. 'We find these burn better.' He shoves the bundles onto the grate and all Baz's careful symmetry is ruined. Then, as Baz searches for his matches, Tom flicks a firelighter he keeps hung by the hearth for just this purpose.

The fire leaps to life. The room becomes soft and warm.

The fog is a white blanket around the house as they gather at

The Fourth Night

the table. Didi has roasted Ani's fillet perfectly à point. E has dressed potatoes with lemon zest, oil and herbs, and has made a salad of fresh green leaves, rocket and parsley, and the tiny scarlet tomatoes that self-seed every year all over the remains of Bimmi's garden. Safe within their wooden box, the people eat and drink, and when they are finished they sigh, replete, and someone says,

'Where did you learn to cook like this?'

Didi says, 'It's a long story.'

'We have time,' they say. So e tells them a version of this tale.

The cook, the magnate and the pirate chief

A sixth tale of one who, after divers misadventures, at last attains a goal of unexpected felicity.

When Didi was still pupating, still inhabiting the chrysalis skin into which e had been born, still Danny DeCicco, still he, still him, he had a job on a yacht.

It was dark and sleek, the property of a magnate with interests in Saudi oil, American real estate and selling armaments to anyone who wanted them, with a fine indifference to national frontiers. Powerful businessmen and the corrupt leaders of several nation states were among his closest friends. He assisted them in pillaging their countries and concealing their immense wealth. There were stories of thuggery, bribery, racketeering and double dealing, but his parties were legendary. His public face was smooth and mellow, the owner of mansions in Mayfair

The Deck

and Paris and New York, racehorses, jets, a private island and this yacht, *Sirena*.

Two hundred and twenty foot, helipad, cinema, twelve suites decked out in chamois leather and birdseye maple, and forty on the crew, including Danny DeCicco, who joined as a galley hand in Monaco. He had been wandering the world, seeing what lay beyond Lygon Street. He had worked in clubs and hotels, restaurants and bars, but he had begun to wonder if a yacht might be more glamorous. Summers, they would cruise the Med and up into the Black Sea, winters they would cross to the Bahamas. He imagined celebrities, movie stars, sports stars, A-list celebrities, willowy Russian models, a lot of business types freed of the suit and the thobe kicking back and partying beyond the reach of the paps and their probing telephoto lenses.

Fazil's guest list was indeed stellar, though Danny DeCicco knew it only by report from others on the crew when they gathered in the cramped staff quarters below deck. He never saw the stars himself, being kept busy washing pots, wiping down the grill, chopping mountains of shallots, stripping the skins from tomatoes as the temperature in the galley nudged 40 degrees and the floor beneath his feet heaved and rolled while he wielded a sharp knife. The head chef, Walter, was an irascible Austrian with no patience for error, but Danny DeCicco was keen to get things right. He was methodical and he persevered, and Walter took a liking. He showed Danny DeCicco useful techniques and permitted him, when the galley was not too busy, to observe and learn.

Up on deck, Fazil and his guests reclined while below deck the crew in the galley sweated it out. In the brief intervals between guests, they took their chance to visit the places where *Sirena*

The Fourth Night

was docked. Beautiful places, exotic places. Danny DeCicco sent photos to his nonna back in Brunswick. It was not a bad gig.

But in Danny's second season on board, Fazil got into trouble. Word was that he had defaulted on a massive loan and suddenly he was being pursued by authorities in several nations for fraud, theft, money laundering, manslaughter, murder and a raft of other crimes. It was decided it would be best if one of his most valuable assets, *Sirena*, took herself off to the Maldives for a spell beyond the reach of the official assignees and requisition. The yacht was dispatched with a skeleton crew down through Suez into the Indian Ocean.

Three days out of Aden, they were attacked by pirates.

The crew on *Sirena* watched them come. Two boats, lean and purposeful as sharks, sliced a wake through the surface of the blue sea. There were many like them along this stretch of the coast, and they were becoming increasingly effective. There had been some king hits. Profitable container ships, a highly exploitable cruise ship, a couple of tankers, and cargo ships flying the flags of several nations. The pirates had traded up their old rusty craft for fast boats equipped with some serious weaponry.

Normally, *Sirena* would not have ventured into these waters unaccompanied. She would have waited for a convoy with naval security, but there had been an element of haste in her departure. The Americans had been on their way with warrants and summonses, so Fazil, who had always been a gambling man, had ordered *Sirena* to leave with only the usual security detail on board. They would make a run for it, shoot the gulf and get into safe equatorial waters.

The Deck

The pirates had another plan. *Sirena* was fast, but they were faster. *Sirena* had guards and guns, but the pirates' guns were bigger and their crews were young and reckless. They hit the bridge, wounding the captain, they swarmed aboard, shooting on sight. They killed one of the guards outright, and the chief engineer.

Danny DeCicco and Walter the chef had locked themselves in the chiller, each armed with a Wüsthof eight-inch kitchen blade, but they were dragged forth and herded with the rest of the crew onto the bridge, where they were handcuffed and forced to their knees. Trapped in the grip of a gang of manic, doped-up kids slinging some pretty sophisticated weaponry. Danny was no expert on guns but these did not look like old AK-47s, ex-Russian army. These weapons looked new and sleek and deadly in the hands of skinny youths. It was not a comfortable situation.

Hour after hour, they knelt on the floor as the temperature climbed. Forty degrees. Forty-two. The pirates were demanding millions. They seemed to know what they were doing. An older guy was handling the negotiation, a tall man, handsome, distinguished. He was calm, he was in control. He spoke a little English, and when one of the crew tried whispering to another in German, it turned out he spoke that too, for he had spent some years drudging in the hotels of Europe. With a statesman's gravitas he presented the pirates' demands, and when they reached an impasse he turned to the men kneeling on the floor, selected one, had someone lift a phone to record and shot the man between the eyes. The chef, Walter, slumped heavily to one side, gurgled, and lay still.

There was a moment of disbelief.

The Fourth Night

'You see, we are serious,' the negotiator said to Fazil's representatives. 'Consider our offer.'

Then he turned to his captives, looking a little bored: the CEO after a tiring meeting, stretching his arms above his head, sighing. 'So, who is the chef?' And then in English and German, 'I would like some lunch. Ich möchte etwas zu Mittag essen.'

There was a pause. Danny put up his hand. He was led under guard down to the galley, where he commenced to make lunch.

He was no chef but he had watched very carefully. Nor did he have any idea what the pirate chief might eat. Fazil had been a plump man with a particular fondness for French food, the classical menu. Pâtés and sauces and delicate desserts. Such had been their haste to leave that *Sirena*'s chiller and freezer were still stocked with the necessary ingredients. Danny decided to play it safe. Steak frites.

A good ribeye, medium rare, with a buttery hollandaise and a pile of twice-cooked frites. A cheeseboard to follow: the rich creamy cheeses Fazil adored. Coffee and a chocolate truffle. Danny was fairly certain the pirates would not touch alcohol, but Fazil had a fine cellar stretching the whole length of a corridor. Bottles of the finest crus, carefully curated to the correct temperature. Danny selected the most rare, the most expensive and, accompanied by the kid with the machine-gun, carried the meal to the bridge.

It was silent when Danny entered, bearing the tray. The chief must have had a name but no one used it. It would probably have been akin to invoking the wrath of God. He was watching a screen. Football. A replay, an old game, a World Cup played before a massive crowd, thousands chanting. Looked like Germany versus Argentina. A repetition of ancient history, the

The Deck

result foregone, but the pirate watched anyway. The chef's body had been dragged away, a trail of blood leading to the doorway.

The chief received his tray. He regarded the bottle closely, read the label. He nodded appreciatively. He poured a little into a glass. He handed it to Danny, who took a sip. The chief took up his knife and fork, cut a delicate slice from the steak and speared a chip.

'You! Taste!' he said to Danny, who obliged, and when he remained well, he was permitted to stand by while the chief filled the glass, swirled the wine and examined its colour against the light. He began to eat. He switched off the football.

The bridge went quiet, every eye fixed on his jaw as it moved rhythmically. He ate deliberately with full attention, devoured steak and chips, then turned to the cheeseboard. The room looked on until he laid down his knife, belched long and loud and waved to Danny DeCicco.

'For them, too. Something.' So, Danny made pirates and prisoners steak also and frites. And because god knew if it might be their last meal on this planet so it might as well be a good one, he poured them all wine from the collection.

When all had eaten, the pirate chief beckoned Danny DeCicco to collect the plates and clear away, like a banker issuing orders in a downtown restaurant.

'Not bad, little man,' he said to Danny. 'But next time you try harder, no? Understand? Versuche es beim nächsten Mal mehr, kleiner Mann.' And to a background chorus of belching, he turned back to negotiation.

From then on, as the yacht circled aimlessly under the command of its wounded captain, Danny tried harder. The negotiations progressed at a glacial pace. Day after day, the

The Fourth Night

chief made his demands. One by one the members of the crew were dragged from the room, never to return, while down in the galley Danny did his best, consulting Walter's recipe file and his memory of his lessons with the master.

He prepared tournedos Rossini, the filet fried in duck fat, a slice of foie gras, a shaving of white truffle, a rich Madeira sauce. A fine Medoc, Château Beaulieu. A chocolate tart for dessert.

He prepared Veal Prince Orloff, with a soubise of onion and duxelles with cream, coated in a thick Gruyère-laced Mornay. He made terrines and elaborate desserts. He produced a bœuf en croûte, the filet wrapped in pâté, mushrooms and crêpes, all encased in puff pastry, and served with a buttery sauce Béarnaise.

The pirate chief chewed and swallowed. Between glasses of the finest vintages he argued for ransom with the yacht's distant owner and when he was disappointed, dispatched another prisoner to their watery fate until only the wounded captain and Danny remained. And all the while, day after day, Danny DeCicco sweated in the galley, producing a succession of the richest, most opulent recipes he could muster, each of which he tasted before the chief would pick up his knife and fork and begin to dine.

The pirate chief was a greedy man. He consumed, unaided, quantities designed to feed an entire dinner table. After a couple of days he became lethargic and the whites of his eyes turned the colour of egg yolks, but, still, when Danny DeCicco arrived on the bridge with his tray, he reached for the knife and fork, took up his wine glass and proceeded to dine mightily.

Danny sensed gathering impatience among the other pirates.

The Deck

Their plan had been a resolute seizure of the yacht, some determined and ruthless negotiation, a swift capitulation by the owners, a sizeable cash payout for them all and a triumphant return to whatever rust-bucket port it was that had spawned them.

But the chief seemed in no hurry to finalise a deal. After lunch each day he was sleepy, swept by the benevolence that succeeds a good meal. He sat before the screen in the warm room, his yellow eyes closing against his will, like the eyes of a sleepy hawk. The men muttered and their fingers twitched at their shiny new weapons.

One afternoon, midway through a particularly fine lunch — Confit de canard, the duck legs gleaming, the Sarladaise potatoes fried to a crisp turn in duck fat — the pirate chief paused. He laid down his knife and fork. And then he groaned, an agonised cry, and clutched at his breastbone.

'Ahh, ahh!' he howled, his face running with sweat. His face was the colour of fine butter. He stumbled to his feet and then collapsed to the floor, writhing, unable to issue a single order.

His men milled about uncertainly before one of them assumed control. He took charge of the negotiations, and within a few hours he had reached an agreement. The owners offered an amount that met with the pirates' unanimous acceptance while the chief groaned in his luxurious suite, liver and gallbladder in excruciating revolt.

The pirates abandoned the yacht. They re-boarded their sleek shark boats, bearing their enfeebled chief with them. And Danny DeCicco came too, at the chief's insistence and at gunpoint. He climbed aboard the pirates' craft, bringing only his kitchen knives, for no chef will leave a ship, even at

The Fourth Night

gunpoint, without his favoured knives. That at least the pirates understood: the love one can feel for a good knife. The captain they left on board, to nurse his wounds and make his way alone as best he could, south-east towards safe haven.

Danny sat without speaking as the craft cut its way towards shore. His role he assumed to be that of hostage, a final guarantee that the money promised would be paid and that there would be no recriminations. He assumed that, once the money had been deposited, he would be of no further use to the pirates and their chief and it would be his turn for the bullet to the head.

But as they approached the settlement that was the pirates' base, the chief roused himself from his stupor, lurched to sit at Danny's side and put his arm about his shoulders.

'Over there,' he said. And he nodded to a cluster of concrete high-rises, half built, overlooking the beach. 'Paradise Club,' he said. 'Beach resort. My friend Mr Chou build a hotel. Luxury hotel. Top hotel! You work there. You cook my lunch.'

Which is how Danny came to be a chef, valued employee at the Paradise Club, a complex that in time received a five-star rating in *Destinations* magazine.

'And that,' says Didi, gathering up their empty plates, 'is how I learned to cook.'

'I always rather liked pirates,' said Pete, 'when I was a kid. They had great clothes — cloaks and boots and the hat and the parrot. They had dress sense. I liked their style.'

'All that swash and buckle,' says Philippa. 'Unless you were the one being swashed.'

'Hamid wasn't so bad,' says Didi. 'We got along.'

The Deck

The fire crackles in the grate and the fog is grey rags and tags at the window. They sit and talk. Maria frames the scene. It's automatic, this business of taking notes, planning the shot, considering the dialogue. How much each character should say, how they would direct that comment to the length of the table or to camera, would it be sufficient to establish the tension between the people gathered in this room?

There's Philippa presiding from the head of the table, overseeing the direction of discussion, doing that annoying thing she has always done of taking responsibility for everyone's happiness, keeping everything calm and sweet by batting away unpleasantness.

And Tom, poor desperate Tom, reduced from the star he used to be and now acting it instead, the jovial host, but no one can keep that up for ever and every so often the jolly old mask slips and there it is: despair. His eyes falter. He has no idea how to live this bit when he is no longer his job, when he is no longer the handsome prince, but portly and balding and frightened.

And Ani who is sweet and kind and glad to be alive, and Pete. And Didi, who is interesting, there's a savagery in Didi. And her beautiful Zoe, in whom the future has yet to take shape. And right at the bottom of the table, on the edge and even quieter than usual, is Baz. His guitar has been laid aside, he seems restless and he refuses to meet her eye. And when she sees him glance over at her then look away, she feels, for the first time in her life, shame.

For she too has a story, as everyone does, of how she stumbled into her life and tonight perhaps as the fog drifts in rags at the window it is the time to tell it. Some elements are well rehearsed, told many times before in profiles on television and in magazines with photos of herself holding some film industry award, or seated in her Point Chev apartment, or peering through a lens, checking an angle. The lifelong documentarian, the Companion of an Order of Merit, the Arts Icon. People like her story with its predictable narrative arc from naïve ingénue to polished professional. It is the way such stories are supposed to go. But there is more to tell and tonight is the time, and this is the place, and this is the audience to whom she should tell it.

The traveller, the crossroads and Death on his bicycle

A seventh tale of one who, after divers misadventures, at last attains a goal of unexpected felicity.

This tale begins with felicity. The giddy joy a young traveller feels as she lifts the little window shade from time to time and looks down from 35,000 feet at the same immense stretch of blue.

She was journeying to a far country. She could speak its language and she knew all about it, having seen its silver shadow over and over on screens large and small. She anticipated clusters of towers reaching up into an arc of blue sky. And roads laid down flat and for ever across deserts. And small towns with Main Streets and diners and drugstores, and cities whose names were the words of songs.

She already knew the names of its filmstars and singers and astronauts and presidents. She had seen one slump in the rear

The Deck

seat of a limousine by a grassy knoll. She had seen one walk on the dusty moon and say it was a giant leap for mankind.

When the ocean came to an end she stepped out onto dry land, all her worldly goods on her back in a bulging backpack. In her pocket was the address of a cousin of a girl she had worked with at the temping agency back home where she had made the money to pay her fare. Other than that crumpled name, she knew not a soul in this whole wide land and nobody knew her. Among the milling crowd on the concourse, no one was likely to have lived next door to her auntie or gone to school with her brother. For the first time in her life she was alone and she was free.

The cousin lived across the city in a canyon. The traveller got off the bus, shouldered her pack and walked up a road. There was dry scrub at the top of the hills on either side, but down here at street level there were palm trees with a flutter of leaf at the top of a tall skinny stem. There were apartment blocks and buildings plastered white or pink with swathes of red flowers falling from little metal balconies, and the air smelled of car exhaust and dry earth and eucalyptus.

Her friend's cousin waved vaguely in the direction of a sofa.

'You can crash there,' she said, and turned back to work on her script. It was a long process, she said, getting a script to screen. Years. Her typewriter stood in a corner of this room on a table covered with piles of paper and a long narrow strip of timeline was pinned across two walls. Its interlocking lives looked like a barbed-wire perimeter.

The cousin took her that night to a party at a house further up the canyon. The house was big and brightly lit, and the people at the party had beautiful teeth and amazing clothes.

The Fourth Night

They talked and laughed and knew one another and she passed among them, weightless. She drank white wine. Then red. Then white again. She saw a person do that thing she had seen on the screen with the powder on the glass-topped coffee table and the rolled-up twenty-dollar bill and whoosh it was gone.

She stepped out onto the terrace where there was of course a pool, a blue rectangle, flipping reflected light. She looked up at the hillside ahead and saw it, printed in white capitals. HULLYWO D.

'Wow!' she said, spilling white wine on her T-shirt in her excitement, because the sign meant she had truly arrived. She had stepped through the silver screen and stood in the presence of a sign she had seen before, though not like this, broken and misspelt. But there it was, just ahead and undeniably real, tinted palest pink in the reflected glow of a VistaVision Cinerama sunset.

Someone was standing nearby. Short, stocky, dark hair, glasses, cigarette.

'Yeah,' he said. 'They're gonna fix it.'

As if the sign were of no more significance than a sign reading GIVE WAY or NO EXIT.

'New in town?' he said, as she dabbed wine from her front. He might have been a couple of years older, maybe more. She was never good at ages. 'You want another one of those? Or would you like a real drink?'

She said, 'A real drink,' and he vanished into the crowd and she thought, well, that's the last I'll see of him. She was feeling the wine and the jet lag. Her head floated free of her shoulders, so she sat down on the edge of the pool and dangled bare feet in the water. And then he was back, and he had brought with him

The Deck

a couple of glasses with orange juice, a strip of peel and tequila so they sat side by side dangling their feet and drinking the sunrise as the water bounced bubble light across their faces and the sky overhead turned purple. The sound of voices and music grew and they had to lean closer to talk, he in a quick, explosive staccato, she in an accent. She had never realised she had an accent, but it seemed she did. A cute accent. A Limey accent.

'I'm not English,' she said, and she said the name of her country, and he repeated it as if it were exotic, like Bali or Morocco. He pronounced it with a Noo, not a Nyoo, which was interesting, and he asked her what she was doing here.

'I'm an actress,' she said, the first time that she had ever said the word. It felt exciting and also a little awkward in her mouth, like a new filling, something she'd have to run her tongue over and over until it was familiar. 'I want to work in movies.'

'Doesn't everyone?' he said. Then he asked, 'Can you type?'

As a matter of fact she could. Fifty words per minute. It was her great skill. Her mother had insisted she learn when she said she wanted to be an actress after her success as Puck in the school production in a silver foil suit.

'You'll need a backup,' her mother said, so she had done typing in form five instead of French. She was fast and sometimes accurate, and it did indeed pay the rent when she moved to the city and needed the money to travel to America and become an actress. It was not impossible. Olivia Newton John in the black spandex and red heels had done it and she was Australian, which was close. You didn't have to be American. She had spent several months temping, typing invoices and Final Notices and Dear Sir, and Yours faithfully.

'You got a Green Card? Visa?' he said. And when she said no,

The Fourth Night

he said well, there were ways and means, and by the end of that night she had a job offer, assistant to the Producer's Assistant in a small independent studio founded by the young, creative and ambitious, working in a cramped office off Virgil Avenue.

She typed her 50 wpm, answered the phone in her cute accent, attended to the filing, fetched the coffee, rolled the joints required by the Producer's Assistant and on occasion slept with him. Her pay, in folded bills, was slipped into her bag each week.

She went to one audition but found herself in a room filled with young women like herself only more glossy and self-assured with the beautiful teeth and she knew she was all wrong, the way she'd known she was all wrong in that stupid pink bridesmaid frock.

She actually preferred the office where the phone rang off the hook and people yelled at one another with an amazing lack of restraint. She preferred the constant buzz of gossip, who was on their way up, who was on their way down, who was an arsehole, who was a sweetheart. She observed the way scripts were chosen, actors recruited, movies constructed piece by piece, money raised, money spent, money made. She didn't want to be out in front of the cameras with the frocks and the red carpet, but around the back of the silver screen where it was all machinery and rough canvas and unvarnished scaffolding. She liked finding out how the illusion was created. The messy business that lay behind the smooth façade. It was like becoming party to a secret.

She saw one of the Beach Boys scratching his bum while he examined the LPs one afternoon at Rockaway. She saw Al Pacino coming out of a downtown bar. She saw Olivia Newton

The Deck

John in jeans and sneakers crossing the street with a dog on a leash. She felt as if she were at the centre of the known world.

The interviewers decades later always liked the story of how with her typing skills and expert joints she had contributed to the making of movies: a biopic set in Vegas about a famous singer of the 1940s who came back from addiction, a comedy set in Anaheim about a couple in the throes of midlife upheaval. She stayed on, she married the Producer's Assistant when it seemed expedient for residency, she helped make movies in the decade when the big downtown movie palaces with their velvet seating and starry desert skies and plaster fantasies of distant Araby were closing or being chopped into tiny boutique pieces. It was the decade when downtowns were becoming desolate and dangerous and the audience preferred their fantasy delivered by new video technologies, viewed on a small personal screen from the safety of the living-room sofa.

Some years later, a child and several relationships distant from the Producer's Assistant, she was watching rushes of a new movie, a thinly veiled fiction based on the experience of a farmer in Wisconsin whose dairy herd had been poisoned by contaminated feed marketed by a major company. The company was duplicitous, defending its massive profits. Its managers were brutish, aggressive, fiercely defending their immense profits. The farmer was persistent, a heroic everyman played by a popular actor, risking everything — his marriage, friendships, mental stability, the farm — in a struggle against injustice. It was the decade of the movie in which everyman in his baseball cap, everywoman in her short skirt took on negligent big business.

She had sat in the dark looking up at the screen and found herself thinking, quite suddenly and without any prelude, 'This

The Fourth Night

is not my place.' This farmer in his cap with his pickup truck and his big red barn belonged here. He had been magnified many times and translated by film into a hero. She found herself thinking of farmers like the ones she had known as a child back home, farmers who wore woolly beanies and tartan Swanndris, who rode muddy farm bikes with their dogs racing away to bring in the bleating flock. When had she ever seen them on a screen?

She was overcome with longing for her own country, where she did not have a cute accent and where she knew how the whole place worked from the inside without having to be instructed.

And that, as the interviewers always said, was the start. This was the prologue to the career in which she would create the documentaries that helped define her country, identified its heroes and villains, held up the mirror to its reality and left, as the media handouts always put it, her enduring legacy. That was the story she had told the interviewers over and over.

Except it was not the start at all. That came earlier, and tonight, looking around the table, she wants to rewind to something she has never told the interviewers or anyone else. She wants to admit to misadventure.

There was that other party.

The night before she left for America.

An old house out on the edge of town where the roads were laid down by set-square across the plains. Music pumping from every window. She drove out there with the boy whose room she had been sharing. His bed, his flat in the city, while she put together her travel fund. She was going to be an actress in the movies or, if that didn't work out, she would buy a horse

The Deck

and ride across Spain. Something like that.

The boy paid the rent. She had sex with him. It seemed like a fair deal. The boy also had a van, an elderly Kombi with uncertain brakes but a vehicle nevertheless, and the two of them drove in it together to the party along those straight empty roads. He was quiet, quieter than usual. She was excited, voluble. She was leaving in the morning. He was staying.

She sat in the passenger seat in her party dress, a pre-war silk petticoat she had found in a second-hand shop and dyed in the washing machine, inadvertently splattering purple all over one of his flatmate's work shirts, new and white with a pointed collar.

'Get her out of here,' the flatmate said to the boy, and she'd said, 'Don't worry. I'm going anyway. I'm leaving next week.'

She could hardly wait. She had tried on the petticoat once it dried. It slid over her body, clinging to her breasts and the curve of her bottom. It looked great. She laced up her boots and sat in the van as they drove, swigging rum and Coke she had mixed up in a bottle.

She wandered off when they got to the party but she could feel him watching her and it was really irritating, like being watched by a collie dog. He seemed reproachful, as if she were abandoning him, when he had known all along that that was the deal. She could not possibly spend another year in this city, in this country.

'I mean,' she said, surveying the room when they first arrived at the party, 'just look at them! New Zealanders are so ugly. No sense of style.' The boy had looked around at his mates in their sagging woollen jerseys, wrinkled jeans, sandals. 'And uggh . . . Socks! Can you believe it? Socks and sandals!' One even had a

The Fourth Night

mullet and another a snaky ponytail. As for the girls with their sturdy thighs . . .

She downed her rum and Coke, said she needed a pee, disappeared into the crowd. He glimpsed her from time to time, dancing with a drink in her hand in a detached, ironic kind of way. Or leaning in a doorway, glowering as someone tried their luck.

She could feel him, mopey, watching her. It made her cruel, his evident attachment, the sticky cling of him. It made her dance more wildly, flinging her arms around people she didn't know, dancing close with the mullet, his hard nothing of a body, dragging her out into the dark, but she pushed him off so he stumbled back into some hydrangeas, looking stupid. 'Cocktease!' he said. 'Bitch!' And she said, 'Yeah, yeah,' and walked off back into the party, hoping he hadn't left stains on her tie-dyed petticoat.

She looked around for the mopey boy just as things were warming up. Cars were arriving, people were packing into the rooms, the noise level was rising, someone had made a start on demolishing the old dunny out the back and the mopey boy was using the wood to build a fire. It would not be long before the guitars came out.

She grabbed his arm. 'Let's go,' she said. 'I've got to pack.'

And because he had drunk a lot and smoked to the point of easy floating calm, she said she'd drive. She hadn't had much, just her rum and some godawful punch, she was fine. She climbed into the driver's seat and he lit up another joint, and they set off back towards the glow on the horizon that was the city.

She drove fast. She couldn't wait to get away from that party, from this place, from the boy's heavy arm draped around her

The Deck

shoulders. He said, whoahh, slow down, but she knew what she was doing, she'd been driving for ever, since she was six, when her dad let her drive the truck around the paddock while he fed out from the tray. She drove with the window down, one arm crooked on the sill. The van charged along the centre line, faster than it had gone in years, everything rattling and shifting.

They approached an intersection and flew across.

'We need some music,' she said, and she reached over to turn on the radio when out of nowhere there was a thing ahead, a thing without a light, a thing that was a bike and something in a dark coat, and she swung the wheel but not far enough, not soon enough, so the thing thumped into their door and scraped the side, but she kept on driving into the dark while the boy yelled, 'Stop! Stop! You've got to stop. Christ, you can't just keep going!'

And he reached down and pulled hard on the handbrake, dragged at it so that the van veered and spun but stayed upright, facing back the way they had come. She sat with her hands on the wheel, looking straight ahead, then very slowly she drove back till the headlights picked out the tangle of tyres and handlebars and the hump that was a body in the long grass by the side of the road.

She switched off the engine. The night air poured in and the stillness. Cows were munching on the other side of the hedge. There was no moaning, no movement. They knelt beside him.

An old man, his head tipped at a sharp angle, his legs splayed, broken glass glittering on the road, whisky from the smell of it. No pulse.

Old Wattie Todd, on his way back from the village, his regular Friday visit to the Four Square to pick up a sliced white, some

The Fourth Night

golden syrup and a pack of sausages for the week, then a few drinks at the pub until the landlord threw them out. All those years since he got back from Egypt, and those poor buggers in the trench looking up as the 19th charged down on them screaming, mad with terror and rage and the flames rising, his bayonet slicing into flesh, the startlement in their eyes as Wattie Todd, young and beautiful, came out of the dark, like vengeance, like the wrath of God.

But still, those startled boys. Poor bastards. Old Wattie Todd slowly pedalled the long dark road towards his hut by the river.

They knelt beside him on wet grass.

'Oh fuck oh fuck oh fuck,' said the boy. 'We have to find a house and ring the police. What is it? 111? 999? What is it?!' He was babbling. 'Oh fuck . . .'

The girl was shaking, trembling in her thin petticoat.

'I can't,' she said.

'What do you mean?' he said, scrambling to his feet. 'We've got to. You stay here. I'll go and find a house.'

'I can't,' she said.

'Well, I'll stay and you go and find a phone. There'll be a house back up there, behind those trees. It's not far. You go. I'll stay.'

'I can't,' she said.

'Well, we can't both go,' he said. 'One of us should stay in case a car comes along. Oh, fuck. Oh, Christ.'

'I can't go,' she said. 'To America. My visa . . .'

'What?' he said.

'I can't have any convictions,' she said. 'I've killed someone. I didn't mean to kill him. But it'll count just the same. I won't be able to go.'

The Deck

Away down the road there was a tiny glow. Headlights approaching. He began walking towards the glow, waving his arms while she sat in the long grass beside the old man.

It was weird, she thought, looking down at him, how motionless dead was. She had seen plenty of dead animals before. Sheep destined for dog tucker, clasped between her father's legs, the head dragged back, the quick stab of the knife and the blood gush as the animal kicked, its glassy eye panicking, and then the slump, the acceptance. She had been sent out each spring to pick up the dead lambs in their curly yellow jackets beside the crimson flop of afterbirth. She had seen dead rabbits, hares and possums, one that gave a little wriggle and a joey climbed from the pouch and became a pet. She had seen dead kittens in a wet clump in the sack. Her father insisted they drown their own kittens, it was part of farming and they had better get used to it.

But never a person, not in real life. She had seen dead people on the silver screen. They died shot clean through the chest outside the saloon. They spun and fell. They were drowned in their chariots as the sea closed over while the Israelites made it safely to the other side.

But never like this. She looked down at old Wattie Todd lying on the grass, all smashed and bloody. The headlights cast everything in extremes of light and dark. His face was deeply shadowed, his cheeks sunken beneath high bones, his mouth dragged open on gappy teeth, blood trickled from a wound on his scalp. She reached out and touched him and he was still warm, but he was dead, and people were walking towards her and she heard the boy saying, 'I was driving, and suddenly this guy was right in front of me, in the middle of the road, no lights or anything, and I hit him.'

The Fourth Night

Then he started to cry, and someone was putting a jacket around her shoulders and a blanket around the boy's shoulders and he stood there, lit by the headlights like some old chief, his head up, not meeting her eye. If she were filming him, she thought, she'd film from just this angle, down low on the grass. He was the image of the old-time hero.

Careless driving causing death. Possession of an illegal substance. Driving under the influence, though there could be some concession on account of Wattie Todd who was well known in the district for his late-night cycle rides. No lights. No luminous vest. There had been many near misses.

She left as planned. Flew away next morning from the city.

It had been a long winter. Fog had blotted out the streets and left halos around streetlights and people felt their way home along walls and fences. The flat had been icy, green moss around the window frames, and she had huddled with him under all their coats and sleeping bags and they wore woolly hats to bed. Their hands had felt their way through all those layers of bedding and clothing to the warm bare body beneath.

But that night they barely spoke. They made their statements to the police, then drove back to the flat in silence, she observing the speed limit, taking care on every corner. They climbed into bed, and she lay beside him watching the car lights on the street outside crisscrossing the ceiling. They felt like strangers.

And because he was a stranger it was possible for her to slip out of bed in the early morning, grey light sapping all colour, their room reduced to shapes in black and white. It was possible for her to dress quickly. The stranger had fallen into a restless sleep and lay on his back, one arm flung back as if warding off something. He could have been a fallen soldier, a young

The Deck

knight killed in combat. He lay still, the tuft of hair at his armpit exposed, the sound of his breathing like small waves breaking as birds woke in the kowhai outside and the world began to switch to full colour.

It was possible for her to take the Kodak Super 8 from the mantelpiece and to film him, a long slow take. And then it was equally possible to tuck the camera into her backpack, open the door and leave. No sticky goodbyes, no pathetic thank yous. She couldn't bear them.

She flew away to the back of the east wind, looking down as the vast ocean spread itself between them, and on the farther shore she found felicity.

'And that's how it happened,' says Maria when she has finished a version of this tale. 'That's the whole story. That's the truth. And I'm really sorry.'

Baz gets to his feet. He picks up his guitar and goes out into the fog. The others are silent.

'Right,' says Philippa as the pause lengthens. 'Drink? Cup of tea? Anyone?'

No one is quite in the mood for tea or talk.

'Think we'll call it a night . . .' they say.

They drift away.

The fog closes behind them like a curtain.

THE FIFTH DAY

Early morning. Dawn on a white day, sun, moon and stars invisible. But they are up there in their customary alignment as the Earth rolls over to face the sun.

Ani takes Raffi down through fog to the beach. He'd been restless all night, standing at the door growling, hackles up, at some night creature, a rat, a possum lumbering across the deck towards the ngaio.

'Shut up, Raffi,' she'd said, but he would not be quietened, even when she let him sleep on the bed. He barked and jumped down to paw at the glass. He would waken everyone, so as soon as it was light enough she took him out.

The fog closes about them, ice-cool after the heat of the previous days. She likes its strangeness, the way it closes off every possibility, only a metre visible in any direction. Raffi stays close, too close, growling at her heels. She has to be careful not to trip over him as she sets out to walk to the far end where the

The Deck

cliff face is composed of black rectangular slabs framed by ribs of pale stone, like paintings in a gallery, canvases of black matte or gleaming enamel.

It was one of her perfections, walking to see them each morning, stopping midway by the log that has been smoothed to burnished silver where she can hang her towel as she goes for a swim. She likes establishing such routines in new places. The towel on the silver log, the early swim. The coffee shop in a strange city where the bad-tempered barista slams down the cups and the waitress with the manga tattoos flirts with the tradies. She likes singling out the one perfect artwork in a gallery filled with paintings by famous artists, yet she goes back over and over to the one drawing of the little bird. The one perfect pencil on her desk at home that is the perfect diameter in her hand and produces the perfect line. The brand of paper that is the perfect degree of whiteness and porosity. Her life is made up of such singular things: the perfect route to the centre of town, the one cup with the little chip on the rim, the one friend, the one dog. The one man.

The log emerges like the femur of some long-extinct gigantosaur. Twenty paces further on there is the skeleton of the little blue kororā with its dried skin and its head turned side on, resting on a pillow of kelp and white barnacles. And forty paces beyond that is the place where delicate gulls in red stockings and black eyeliner stand about in a crowd maintaining an orderly distance from one another. Usually they would rise up shrieking at her approach, leaving white dot dot dots of guano at regular intervals across the sand, but today they do not stir.

'Weird, eh?' she says to Leo, who is of course walking beside her, but a little way off, a shadow in the fog.

The Fifth Day

'They're confused,' he says. 'Like us that time we took the wrong turn coming back from the lake? Remember?'

Of course she remembers. The road narrowing as they drove further into whiteness, steep drop-offs on either side and fences slung with the pelts of dead goats, her with her head out the window watching for the edge, him with his hands clenched at the wheel, swearing. And the pub when they emerged at last where they spent the night on a saggy wirewove bed while the toilet through the wall played a jazzy little drop drippety drop number but it didn't matter. It was funny and they were warm and safe and wrapped about each other.

At last the black rocks loom and she has reached The End. She turns to walk back. As she turns there's a puff of air and the fog rips a little and in the gap out in the bay she sees a light. A small white light. It dips and sways, and now that she thinks about it, there is a sound that has been there all along at the very edges of her consciousness, a rhythmic metallic rattle. She walks more quickly back along the beach, Raffi waddling and wheezing to keep up as the fog begins to tear apart and the sun inches through. She finds the track among the marram grass that leads up to the house. Every leaf, every stem is threaded with drops of water. The fog shreds and the house rises before her, a solid black box.

Tom is out on the deck with the binoculars trained on the bay.

'Did you see it?' he says. 'The masthead light?'

It had surprised them all. Sound travels readily here, magnified between the cliffs, but no one had heard the boat arrive, the unravelling of an anchor chain, an engine reversing seeking purchase on the bottom among sand and rocks. No one

The Deck

had heard voices, yet a boat hangs out there in the luminous space between water and sky, halfway to the heads.

'It looks a bit rough,' says Tom, adjusting the focus.

Forty foot maybe? Forty-five? Two-masted ketch, white fibreglass with a faded sea-worn look, the waterline stained bright green with algae. There's no sign of activity on board, sails roughly furled, lines left on deck in tangled grey heaps. There's no flag, nor can he make out any name or hailing port. There's a dinghy on board, tied down on the cabin roof.

All that morning as the fog lifts and brightness resumes no one sees anyone emerge from the cabin though the hatches are wide open. No one makes an attempt to tidy away those lines, nor swim, nor launch the dinghy. Just stillness.

All that long day, while up on the hillside Tom finished fencing the spring. When they leave tomorrow it will be with the knowledge of a neat job done and clear water trickling as it should through the pipes. He had walked up with Zoe, who had asked him about reception here. Yes, he'd said. It's not one hundred per cent reliable, but somewhere up by the old barn you might be in luck. He pointed out the way.

Zoe had been so bored. Bored right through to her bones, so bored her head hurt. She knew of course why she had to be here, hiding out till her crazy parents had gone off to their stupid volcano and she could safely return to her real life. She knew she had to do this if she was to realise her plan.

It is going well so far. She has it all organised: her grandmother is set up to care for her. She'll move down, they'll get a flat. She'll cook meals and stuff and satisfy the school that Zoe is being properly looked after, not sleeping on the street or under

The Fifth Day

a bridge. She'll be able to go back to school, hang out with her friends just as she did before. She'll be able to work on the song they were practising for this year's RockIt!. She'll get to go to the Year 9 camp. She will probably qualify for the swim squad this year and maybe even the football under-15s. Beyond the hilltop lies the future in all its gleaming possibility.

Meanwhile she's stuck with all these old people who are okay, though they smoke. She's definitely smelled dope. And they talk all the time about nothing and they drink way too much wine, which isn't really that nice though everyone makes such a fuss about it. She's tried it, and it's sour and not as good as that raspberry vodka mix in the can or the peach stuff Yani had found in his parents' drink cabinet and brought to a party. She is never going to smoke and she is never going to drink wine.

And that's another thing: her birthday! She'll have an ordinary birthday, with a party and burgers and a trip to the climbing wall or the corn maze. Something fun. So, on balance, everything is planned and everything should work out just fine. The old people may be boring, but at least it's better to be here with them than looking forward to a birthday on a volcano with no friends at all, only the crazy parents waiting for giant lizards to hatch. When she thinks about that — that it might perhaps be true because why else would her parents go to so much trouble? — the thought makes her feel giddy and sick. Better to be here, plodding up a hill, the sun back in force after its retreat behind the curtain of fog and hammering down.

'Just another hundred metres or so,' Tom had said as he loaded some leftover scraps of timber onto the quad-bike trailer. 'Stick to the track and you'll find a spot.'

The track winds up in big loose curves. There are macrocarpas on either side with enormous complicated trunks and cargoes of magpies gargling. The sun is directly overhead and the trees cast little shade. Zoe plods along on rutted clay, climbing steadily and checking her phone at every turn, but the screen stays stubbornly blank. It seems so much effort just to use a phone, but all she wants right now is to know what they are doing, her friends, Rakaia and Mia and Yani and Noah and the others. She wants to talk to them. She wants to explain, to tell them at last about Más a Tierra.

'You mustn't breathe a word,' her mother had said.

The little kids had not been told they were leaving. They were too young to understand, but Zoe was old enough to be aware, and with that came responsibilities. She must not give any hint of their plans. Massive forces were ranged against them. People who looked quite ordinary were their enemies. They might even be old friends, people you had known for years, but they were not what they seemed. Not any longer.

They had been contaminated. A micro-particle had been injected into their bodies when they were immunised against one of the viral waves, and via this particle they could be manipulated by the Cabal to do terrible things: kill people who didn't agree with them, kidnap their children and keep them in cellars and do disgusting things to them, rape them, suck out their blood, cut out their kidneys and sell them on the internet.

On the surface they could seem kind. They might say they just wanted to protect people and keep them safe, but Sophie had heard about this family who had been arrested as they tried to board a flight in Auckland on their way to the Metanoia. They'd been dragged off the plane and taken into custody and the children had not been seen since. They were most likely in

The Fifth Day

some government bunker being reprogrammed, injected with the particle and co-opted into the Cabal's worldwide force.

Zoe had sat on her bed, listening to the jagged whisper, her mother's eyes wide and frightened.

'So, you mustn't say anything to your friends,' she said. She had Zoe's hand in a fierce grip. 'It's really important. The most important thing I've ever asked of you. Do you understand? Don't tell anyone you're leaving. Don't say goodbye. Just carry on as normal, pretend you'll be at school on Monday, you'll be going to camp, all that.'

'But can't I ever tell them what happened?' said Zoe. 'Why I left? They'll be worried if I just vanish.'

Her mother shrugged, 'Once we're in Valparaíso maybe. But, really, they're going to forget you soon anyway. Everyone is going to forget everything and everyone. You'll forget them too. You'll forget everything about this life. But, if you like, you can send a text from Chile.'

That had been the hardest thing. Pretending to people who knew her really well that everything was normal, that she'd be going to camp.

They'll be at school at this moment, she thinks, hanging out in the music room till some teacher throws them out, or off in the corner by the netball courts that was theirs, the kids she's known for ever, laughing and talking and shooting a few ironic, carelessly competent hoops. More than anything she wants to be with them.

She keeps climbing up the track, counting the steps between patches of shade, pausing to drink from her water bottle, sweating and checking her phone, which stays frustratingly blank.

The Deck

She plods uphill as the world folds in on itself and turns into a horrible scary place. What if it was true? That the volcano really could emit the energy field that would cause the Universal Forgetting? Her mother was so happy at the thought of that, the new start, the planet beginning all over again and so much better than before. And, yes, it is a mess with the ice melting and the polar bears swimming for ever and the dead fish and the floods and hurricanes, but would forgetting be better? Would it be better that everyone forgets, the planet rolls back and starts over with just The Chosen Ones in a lush green world filled again with birds and animals?

Would it be better if everyone forgets the people who have been their friends for ever? What if what her parents said was true and they are living far away on Más a Tierra and they forget all about her? Forget she was their child and that she had been born? Forget that Zoe had ever existed? Would everyone forget their brothers and sisters? Would they forget maps and how to get to places?

Qué mundo tan horrible! They had been learning Spanish for Valparaíso, though her mother said it was just to begin with, because in the Metanoia all languages will be one, national borders will fade away, and everyone will automatically understand one another. In the meantime, they learned a bit of Spanish. Her mother had learned to speak it when she was a little girl in America, and she said it was quite easy because mostly you could just say an English word and put 'ah' or 'oh' or 'ay' at the end. Zoe liked the sound of it, the clatter and rush of it, and she liked the dancing. She had downloaded videos of the dancing, the slow glide, the flick of high heels, the flashing eyes. You wouldn't mess with those girls.

The Fifth Day

She had thought she'd like to learn to dance like that when she was older. There was this studio in Buenos Aires where they taught tango properly. She wondered if it was anywhere near Valparaíso, but when she looked up Buenos Aires, all she saw was photos of crosses in city parks and big trenches lined with coffins and people rioting with their arms reaching up.

And if the Metanoia were true, would dances be forgotten too? Would everyone have to start again with new steps? New music?

She plods on. It's all so depressing. She probably isn't even going to get much older. She'll probably die, like that girl Rue in *The Hunger Games*, when she's still young. *Una niña.* She needs so much to talk to Rakaia because Rakaia simply doesn't worry about this stuff.

'They'll sort it,' she said. 'All these scientists are working on cleaning up the oceans, all that stuff. Ms Trott told us about this boy in Ireland who invented a liquid that removes plastic particles from seawater. It's like a magnetic fluid. It was amazing.'

Rakaia is the Year 9 Rep on the enviro-group and does beach cleanups. And Mia doesn't care about anything except her pony and her baby brother. When Zoe begins to fret, Mia looks puzzled and says, 'What are you going on about? Come on. We've got to feed Crunchy.' And in the business of splitting a bale, peeling off some hay, making sure the trough is filled with water, Zoe could forget about the ice shelf and the polar bears and feel happy again.

But now her friends are far away and she might as well be on Mars in one of those horrible space capsules that makes her feel sick just to think about. Astronauts wear nappies. Great big maximum-absorption nappies inside their space suits, to fly for days so they can walk around on a rock. Yuk.

The track rises to a flat area on a spur overlooking the bay. There's a tumbledown shed and an ancient truck through which poroporo grows, with its witchy leaves and orange berries that must never be eaten. There's broken glass and rusty wire and the shed is covered in old man's beard, which is a noxious weed, of course, like blackberries, and must be destroyed. She went on an expedition once with the enviro-group to hack at old man's beard in a patch of regenerating bush behind the school. It was horrible work, hot and grubby, and she decided that afternoon that she would always wrap her sandwiches in paper rather than plastic, and she would avoid buying balloons and other stuff that was non-biodegradable, but she might leave the noxious weed removal to Rakaia and people who liked that kind of thing.

An apple tree grows beside a big rock on the far side where the track winds further uphill. Its trunk is hairy with lichen and its branches are laden with tiny red-striped apples. And, as she nears it, a ping!

A single bar. A flicker of connection, but maybe enough to find her friends, who she does not want to forget, not ever. Nor does she want them to forget her. She does not want that, even to become one of the chosen who will marry a lizard.

'Ezra says you are very special, sweetie,' her mother had said.

Zoe does not want to be special. She has never wanted to be special, not even captain of the B volleyball team or class rep on the student council. She just wants to go to camp with everyone else and do the Night Challenge where you stay out in the bush for an hour by yourself, no phone, no one in earshot, and it's

The Fifth Day

scary but amazing and sometimes people saw glowworms. And there was a Mud Run, it was a tradition every year, where you had to wade across a river, then wriggle under this net through mud and everyone got totally soaked and mucky and their photos, grinning and hilarious, arms around one another, were put up on the school web page. Last year, and two years before that, the camp was cancelled, but this year it could happen and she'll be there. While her mother and Jason and the creepiest man in the world are off greeting the lizards.

The grass under the apple tree is soft and green and studded with daisies. The little striped apples hang heavy on the branches, and some have fallen. Zoe sits in its soft leafy shade and flicks open the screen, hoping to find Rakaia, who is always incredibly loud. Always VERY VERY LOUD, messaging in capital letters: WR R U?????!!!

The screen is blank but the single bar still shows, so she types a message to her friend, who would never in a million years deceive her or cause her to be arrested, injected, trapped in a cellar. For weeks Zoe has done as she was told and not breathed a word, but now she can tell her friend that she's in this place miles from anywhere, with her gran, and she'll be back next week, in time to go to camp, smiley face thumbs up firework explosion. She presses Send and off the words go, flittery into the wide blue sky.

Then she waits.

Down in the bay she can see the little boat swinging slowly at anchor. She picks an apple and lies back in the soft grass chewing every mouthful thirty-two times, which is the correct amount of time to get all the goodness. The juice is sweet and sticky in her mouth. Above her head the sky is scraps of blue

The Deck

through green leaf. Her eyes flutter. And close.

She wakens to something cool touching her hand. Something damp and rubbery. She lies very still and slowly opens her eyes. Two big brown eyes look deeply into her own. Long black eyelashes. A soft pointed head. A deer, a doe with velvety ears that flick back and forth as it nibbles the apple that has fallen from Zoe's hand. The deer scoops up the core with its long rubbery tongue, so close that she can see every hair, every fine whisker. The animal lifts its head from time to time, then eats another windfall and another, its teeth crunching like the sound of footsteps on a gravel path, juice and foam dripping from its mouth.

Unhurried.

Unworried.

Zoe can hardly breathe. After a time the deer folds its long legs and it's like watching the skinny poles of a tent being collapsed as it sinks to its knees beside her. She can feel it breathing, warm and steady against her own body. She can smell the dry, wild smell of its coat. She can feel the movement of bone and muscle as the deer settles to chewing its cud. She lies with the deer under the apple tree and for the first time in weeks she feels completely calm, completely safe.

They lie together for a long time till a sudden sound, a bird rising in a cackle from a tree, startles the deer and it scrambles to its feet, one hoof scraping Zoe's bare arm, and it leaps away up the track.

Zoe sits up then. Her T-shirt sticks to her skin. The imprints of the deer's body and her own are clear among the daisies. Her phone screen is still blank, but maybe they're in science now with Ms Trott, who is old school and makes everyone drop their phones in a box on their way into class. She sends another message anyway. She tells Rakaia about the deer and how amazing it was that it just sat beside her like it trusted her. She taps at the keys, but the words confined to the screen are nowhere close to saying the beauty, the astonishment, the quiet reassuring warmth of what has happened here. To tell that, she will have to wait until she is right beside Rakaia in the corner of the netball court while the others goof around, shooting hoops. Then, face to face, she will be able to tell her story properly. It will be a version of this story:

The maiden, the deer and the apple tree

An eighth tale of one who, after divers misadventures, at last attains a goal of unexpected felicity.

But for now all she can manage is the abbreviation on the screen, no more than 100 letters about a deer and an apple tree. She sends it off, then she leans back, picks up another apple, and waits for a reply.

On the far side of the bay, down by the beach, Baz lies on his back looking up at rust and ragged steel. The exhaust dangles, snapped in two as he crossed the ford on that first day. A steep lip, the rocky bed scoured in summer storm, and his van had been heavily laden. Tools, gardening gear, boards, bed, stuff he had picked up here and there on the offchance it might come in handy: bits of wire and timber, jars and cans, nails, washers, who knew . . .

He likes having it all to hand, hearing it rattle behind him as he drives down the rutted gravel roads to the breaks he loves the best, the ones that are difficult to access and known only to the locals and a few like himself who value isolation, rarity, the unimpeded wave. The van rides low under the accumulated weight. It catches on potholes and cattlestops and now it's hit the edge of a ford. It is probably time for a bit of a dung-out. He should toss out what he no longer needs.

And not just the stuff in the van.

He had thought she was long gone. What was it? Over forty years since he opened the door to find her on the step like some stray cat, newly arrived in the city, wanting somewhere to stay. Just a couple of days till she found a place.

He knew as he stood holding the door half closed that this was not a good idea. Tom had moved out some months before to a cottage by the river where he and Philippa spent their weekends happily painting and stripping fireplace surrounds, and his new flatmates were not keen on people occupying the sofa in the sitting room for days, weeks on end. One, who had a job working in planning for the city council, had called a flat meeting and moved — he actually used the word 'moved' — that the sofa, as communal property, was not to be used as a spare bed for longer than one night at a time and that a surcharge of five dollars should be levied to cover toilet paper, soap and other incidental expenses. But here she was with an enormous backpack, far too bulky for hitchhiking.

'What have you got in there?' he said, playing for time.

'Nothing,' she said. 'Just stuff.' A couple of pairs of sandals and some clunky boots, as it turned out, a sleeping bag, a tangle of clothes, a leather jacket, a Kodak Instamatic, a transistor radio, a world atlas, a school copy of Shakespeare's plays, a book of photos of Marilyn Monroe, a folder into which she had copied the words of songs (Mitchell, Cohen, Collins, Dylan) and poems (Plath, Eliot) along with some of her own about autumn and loneliness.

He let her in, and everything turned out exactly as he had known it would.

The flatmate said, 'I thought we had a consensus on this?' But it was late so she stayed, just for one night, mind, and Baz gave her a blanket, then lay in his bed, waiting. Hearing, though she was three rooms away, every sound. The rustling of her sleeping bag, the creak of the sofa as she rolled over, the padding of bare feet down the hall towards him.

And it was as he had known it would be: intense, and not her first time. That had been with one of the shearers back on the farm and it had been pretty messy with blood and that and she didn't think he had a clue what he was doing, but this here, with Baz, was heaps better, and did he think being circumcised made a difference? What did it feel like, rubbing away inside her? And do people always do it like this, face to face, and why not like the sheep and the cattle back home, her on hands and knees, him entering from behind?

She stayed several months, and she was always like that: curling in close, then drawing back and asking questions, observing him with a detached curiosity as if he were an object of interest and she was taking notes. Sometimes he woke in the morning to the click of the Kodak Instamatic.

'Stop that,' he said. He didn't like it, this scrutiny when he was unaware and probably drooling into the pillow. But on that first morning when he had woken to find her gone, there was a snap of regret. He checked and her pack was still by the sofa, its contents spilled all over the carpet. She came back just as he was getting dressed for work, his Job in Television, pushing a broom around in his white techie's coat, shifting the furniture and adjusting the lighting booms.

He didn't like to ask where she'd been, it felt too soon for that. She walked in, put her arms around him, and she smelled of the morning, cool and clean. She was tall, almost as tall as him, and she laid her head against his shoulder, and that day for the first time he was late for work. Completely missed the setup for *Garden Time*.

Under the van, scraps of rusted metal and dry mud rain down on his head as he pulls at the broken section and tugs it free. He's got everything down here close to hand: snips, a couple of ring clamps, wrench, a beer can he's trimmed and cut along the seam to cuff the join. He likes this, using things that would normally be discarded to effect repairs. He likes keeping something old but functional alive: this van, for instance, is way past its use-by date. It's not handsome enough to be retro, it's not old enough to qualify as vintage, its engineering is primeval, failing every test for emissions and efficiency. It scrapes through the warrant each year thanks to a mate who is renovating an old house and for whom Baz does some carpentry gratis. But not for ever, says the mate. You're gonna have to toss her in, and soon. The recycling yard looms.

But the van still goes. It revs into life when he turns the key. It holds everything he needs in its rattling interior. Though perhaps now it is time to lighten the load.

The Fifth Day

And not just in the van, he thinks, lying there on his back on a bit of old carpet, sliding ring clamps on either side of the gap in the exhaust.

His life. Her. That rusty old attachment.

He does not hear her approach though he has been aware of her since the moment she walked out unannounced onto the deck with that granddaughter of hers. From then on he has known, without looking, exactly where she is in the room, who she is talking to, hearing her voice through all the others. That husky rasp that sounds as if she's spent years in a bar, breathing in the smoke from twenty a day, crooning into a mic about some man who done her wrong.

He has been waiting for her, ever since she slid down the bank in that pink bridesmaid's dress. Ever since he opened the door to find her standing on the doorstep with her backpack asking for a place to stay, just for a night or two . . .

'Hey,' she says now. He cannot see her of course, not from down here under the van, rust peppering his face. All he can see are her legs, slender and tanned, and her bare feet with their long narrow toes. They are exactly as he remembers them. Legs and feet do not age as dramatically as other parts of a human body.

'Sorry about the camera,' she says. Rasps.

He's aware of his own legs in old shorts protruding from under the van and it makes him feel vulnerable, a bit ridiculous. She often made him feel like that. As if she found him curious and amusing when he was just doing things as he had always done them. Doing his sit-ups every morning with his feet tucked under the bed-end in time to 'Honky Tonk Woman'; always 'Honky Tonk Woman' on the stereo. His one and a half cups of coffee. No more, no less. The way he insisted on precise numbers, no approximations. No 'in about 1943', or 'around 150km away', no 'See you later: say, sixish?'

He grips ring clamp and beer can tightly around the break in the pipe, fumbles for the wrench and begins to tighten the bolt.

'That was a horrible thing to do.' Her feet shuffle in the sand. 'I mean, you'd been incredible that night. You took it all on, you rescued me. You did more for me than anyone ever has, before or since, and I was such a little bitch, and I'm so sorry.'

One ring clamp is firm. He fits the other in place and reaches again for the wrench. The dust rains down. His goggles are fogging.

'I was just focused on getting out, you know?'

He twists the bolt. Holds the beer can steady. Careless driving causing death. Driving under the influence of a prohibited drug. Possession of cannabis. His Worship Mr McLachlan, Stipendary Magistrate, took a dim view of such matters. Wallace Todd had served his country. He had risked his life for his fellows, only to be killed by the negligence of this young man. A fine of $150, plus court costs. Two hundred hours of periodic detention. Disqualification of driving licence for two years. Name suppression denied.

So the wave swept in and carried Baz, the particle subject to essential forces — *gravity G, buoyancy B, drag D* — to an unexpected shore. Not towards a career in medicine or science or television or any one of a number of alternatives he had fleetingly considered, but to a hillside in the high country and a work gang of young guys like himself, funny, easy going for the most part, cutting a track up through the bush on government land to the tussock tops. He had been dropped into his life.

The Fifth Day

Above his head, the clamp takes hold. The can fits tight and snug.

'I feel terrible,' she says.

And so she should. Leaving the next morning without a word. She'd made a statement at the police station that tallied with his own. They returned to the flat. She did not once say thank you. And when he woke in the morning after a restless sleep, it was to find her gone. The backpack was no longer in the corner of the room. She'd gone off to the airport exactly as she had planned. She had not bothered to say goodbye, and she had taken his bloody camera. The Super 8.

'Bit late for sorry,' he says.

'I can buy you a new one,' she says. 'There's a new Panasonic just out. It's fantastic.'

'I do not want a fucking camera,' says Baz, giving the bolt a savage twist. The beer can buckles and threatens to split and wreck all his careful mending. 'I haven't wanted a camera in fucking decades. That's your department. Okay?'

'So, what can I do to make it right?' says Maria.

'You can piss off,' says Baz.

She crouches down and peers under the van.

'Come out,' she says. 'I want to talk to you. I can't talk to just your legs.'

He looks up at his repair. It looks good. There's nothing more to do down here.

'Baz?' she says. And there's his name in her mouth.

He grasps the bumper and slides out, awkwardly, dusting rust and metal flakes from his hair, gathering up the wrench and the snips, the broken piece of pipe, tossing them in his old metal toolbox. He stands at the open side door, putting everything

The Deck

back in its place, his back to her, saying nothing.

And then, as he knew she would, she steps in closer. He can feel the warmth of her at his back, though she has not touched him.

'Baz?' she says again. 'Look, I don't know how to say how sorry I am. I've done stupid, horrible things to all sorts of people in my life, but that with you, that was one of the worst. And I can't say anything except I'm sorry and it happened so long ago, last century, and now I don't want to die not being your friend.'

He pauses. He can hear her breathing.

'Are you?' he says.

'Am I what?' she says.

He turns and looks at her, and she looks straight back, the way she always did. Straight between the eyes.

'Going to die?' he says.

''Course,' she says. 'We all are.'

And for the first time he thinks, that's true. Not even thinking it, but recognising it the way you recognise an old friend and their reality. His bones, his body are going to stop. His heart will cease to beat. And all this day, its sunlight and wind and the sea rolling in will carry on, but me with my bare feet in warm sand, my hands stained with oil and rust, I won't be alive to feel it. I'll be a little pile of ashes. His ending comes roaring up on him, and what matters now is how he rides it into the wipe-out, the white foam of his own annihilation.

'Baz?' she says again.

Her hair catches in the wind. A strand blows across her face, over her eyes, and she leaves it there. He brushes it aside, and there she is because the eyes don't age either. She reaches up,

The Fifth Day

takes his hand in hers and they stand there by his old van, which should go for a bit longer with his makeshift bodged tin-can repair. It'll last maybe only for a day or so, maybe just the trip back into town, maybe much longer. Who knew? Nothing lasts for ever.

Later that day, mid-afternoon, Philippa suggested the cave. It would distract Zoe, who seemed depressed and quieter than ever. Maria had disappeared of course. Typical. Absolutely no sense of responsibility.

Poor kid, thought Philippa as she made Zoe a sandwich then watched her earnestly chewing a tiny mouthful. What a choice she'd been offered: crazy parents, or negligent, self-absorbed grandmother. Philippa knew from long professional experience what that kind of choice could mean for a child. Sometimes it was no choice at all.

'We'll take out the boat,' she says. 'It's not very often conditions are so perfect. We wanted to do it every time we came out here when we were kids, but the weather generally prevented us. We managed it only once and it was amazing. So today we're specially lucky.'

Zoe cracks a small polite smile. Delicately removes a slice of pickle from her sandwich. 'It sounds very nice,' she says. 'Thank you.'

The three children, Philippa, Maria and their brother with not a life-jacket between them and Bimmi pulling mightily on the oars of a wooden dinghy, sturdy legs spread wide and grunting with each stroke in a way that gave them all the giggles. The boat skimmed the base of the cliff, then turned and glided through the narrow gap. She remembers the high arch of the cavern

The Deck

overhead, sunlight piercing the shadows, like the Hall of the Troll King in an old book. She remembers the sound of their three voices, calling to make the echo ring, and how on the way back they had taken turns to row while Bimmi sat at her ease in the prow, taking no notice whatever as they traced a zigzag course for shore on an incoming tide. Philippa had crabbed horribly to begin with, pulling fiercely on the oars, scarlet and on the verge of tears, determined to get it right while the others laughed. At last Bimmi broke her silence.

'Don't try so hard, Pippi,' she said. 'Now. Deep breath, take it easy, nice and steady and pull . . . Pull . . . Pull . . .' until Philippa got the knack. They flew back across the water, and she held them all straight.

Now Philippa has her hand on the tiller of the runabout. Philippa, Ani and Zoe. Pete said he'd stay and keep an eye on Raffi. Tom was off up the hill, turning a fence into a masterpiece of constructivist art, and Maria? Well, she'd be following up on that story from last night, reeling Baz back in. Philippa had seen the look on his face when her sister walked out onto the deck. The way for a split-second his face lit up. Here we go again, she thought.

Here we go, as she gives the starter a savage tug and the runabout leaps into life. Here we go a-bloody-gain. She holds the tiller steady as they hum along the base of the cliffs, leaving a long wake that made it look as if the bay were being unzipped and laid open.

Zoe sits in the prow, liking the flick of spray over bare skin. Seals, caramel-coloured kekeno with their pups tucked in close, roll over to watch them pass, waving a desultory flipper. The

The Fifth Day

boat rocks a little, a gentle motion as they near the headland where a slit opens at the base of the cliff. They turn towards it head on, then Philippa guns the engine before cutting out so that they glide through the gap, keeping their heads down, into the body of the hill. In sudden silence Zoe looks up.

It takes a moment for her eyes to adjust to the light in here. The cavern reaches up into darkness, pierced by holes in the rock where sunlight falls through at sharp angles so that as they drift, they pass from spotlight to spotlight. The walls of the cavern, arched and moulded by fire and water, glitter where the sunlight bounces across their surface and the sound of the sea is muted, together with the cries of gulls. The water breathes beneath them, long and deep, and great hanks of bull kelp swing this way and that just below the surface.

There had been no reply to her message this morning, even though she had waited up the hill for over an hour. Her call had flown away into empty space and she was not sure why. Maybe Rakaia has lost her phone. Or maybe Ms Trott confiscated it. Or maybe it's not charged. Rakaia would definitely have replied if she'd read Zoe's messages, especially the one about the deer and how it came and lay down beside her. She loved that kind of stuff: nature being amazing. Birds that did elaborate dances, worms that lined their tunnels underground with pear pips, trees that lived for a thousand years. Now Zoe has another thing to tell her, about this mega cavern that you can hardly ever get into and how she is here, drifting on the slow breath of the sea.

Ani also looks up. She thinks of the person with her toes, her hair, her ears who might have ventured through the gap, because when you are descended from no one in particular, not from someone whose name is remembered and recited over and over by generations, then you could be descended from anyone. They could have been anywhere. Right here, for example, in this cavern. That person could have slid through the gap and drifted, hearing the high-pitched call amplified within the void, the cries of sea creatures that could also be the voices of women calling, bringing together those past, those present and those still to come.

Philippa keeps her hand on the tiller and an eye on the time, because the tide will turn and the wind will shift and it would not do to be trapped in here. She steers for the gap and back they go through the slit in the rock, reborn into the light. Out in the dazzle of the bay, the yacht rocks from side to side, a row of seagulls lined up on the cabin roof.

'How about we go and say hello?' she says. It is what she had been planning all morning as she stood on the deck, twiddling with the focus on the binoculars, wondering if there might be another pair of binoculars out here, trained right back at her. Or maybe not. The stillness disturbed her.

There was not a lot of flour in the cupboard but she had used some to make muffins. One dozen cheese muffins to mask curiosity with some semblance of being neighbourly. They are there beside her in a plastic container as she turns the boat in the direction of the intruder.

'Good idea,' says Ani because it feels like the right thing to do, to welcome newcomers on their arrival in a bay.

The runabout bats across the water. Ahead, the yacht hovers on silk. Sails still roughly furled, cabin ports veiled, no sound except the clatter of halyard on aluminium mast, the squawk of

The Fifth Day

gulls. The birds along the cabin top watch their approach with glassy eyes, then rise as a flock as they come alongside. Flap and wheel and cark cark cark.

No face at a porthole, no one emerging out onto the deck. Up close, the yacht seems even rougher than it had seemed from shore. The paint is blistered and peeling like flaking skin, stanchions are bent and buckled and trails of rust stain the sides. She steers around to the stern. The name is faded and illegible. Just a shadow of an L perhaps, an A, a K. No hailing port, no serial number, no suggestion of origin. It feels forlorn in its shabby anonymity. No hint whatever of obsessive marine neatness, no hint of the freedom-loving gypsy spirit roaming the oceans of the world.

'Hello?' she calls. And then, trying for something more nautical, 'Ahoy?'

She feels faintly silly, puttering around with her container of muffins and her feeble 'ahoy'. But they're here now, so she ties on to the swim ladder, says, 'Wait here,' to the others and clambers aboard.

The companionway is wide open, and from its mouth there is a breath that is at once sweet, like hyacinths or some heady spring flower, and sour too. Blue-vein cheese. Meat that has stood too long in the sun. Dog shit.

She breathes through her mouth and climbs down into the cabin. It's filthy. Stained and crumpled, food scraps rotting in a pot and the birds have been in, scavenging among plates and empty bottles. There's sewage in the head and vomit on the floor. And in the forepeak, a tousled bed.

Two people are lying side by side and face to face. They are young. A young man in T-shirt and jeans, a young woman

The Deck

whose long blonde hair spreads over the pillow. Their legs are intertwined and her hand rests on his hip. And over them, over everything, the bed, the floor, a crimson lacquer of dried blood.

So it's here. The organism, making its way to this green corner.

Neither woman nor man can see her. Their eyes are glued shut. His breath is an intermittent dry rattle. She moans, a kitten mew, and her hand flutters. *Help me! Help me!*

Too late for help. Too late for comfort. Philippa stands at the foot of the crimson bed, knowing it would be inadvisable to reach out and touch. Contact of any kind is inadvisable. Hugging a friend for comfort is inadvisable. Cuddling a small child is inadvisable. Sitting companionably beside a stranger on a bus or at a concert is inadvisable. That is how this one spreads. By touch: skin to skin. The tiny burr sticks to the body, its sole purpose to locate a new host, dig in, replicate, consume, survive.

'You okay in there?' calls Ani from the runabout.

Philippa backs away, trying not to breathe, trying not to touch. The muffins in their container she leaves at the foot of the bed.

'Yes!' she calls. 'All good!'

She emerges into sunlight.

'Bit of a mess in there,' she says as she tugs at the sliding hatch but it is stiff and swollen and cannot be closed completely. She climbs back into the runabout, rinses her hands in the sea, then starts the outboard. 'No idea where they've gone. Maybe there was a second boat. Anyway, they've obviously decided to leave this one moored here. Hope not for too long. It's a bit of an eyesore.'

Ani regards her curiously. They have known one another too long for successful concealment. But Zoe sits happily looking ahead to shore and planning a surreptitious escape once they

The Fifth Day

return, up the hill to the hot spot by the apple tree where she can check again for a reply and send another message.

Before they have gone a few metres the gulls have circled. They are back on the cabin top, lined up and hopeful, watching them leave with their round bright eyes.

THE FIFTH NIGHT

The night is still and warm, though tall columns of cloud have formed ranks out to sea and there is a crackle to the air that promises thunder. The sun has set in glory, the moon and stars have taken their customary places in the firmament and a silver halo rings the moon. On Earth, there's the usual skitter of people doing this and that, going here and there, and in this corner a few are seated around a table on a deck overlooking the sea. Their last night in the bay.

They are eating mussels gathered that morning. The low tide had exposed rocks that were normally underwater. The mussels there had lived their seventy years firmly anchored to this singular place, a sweet uneventful life of ingestion, procreation and release. They were big and bearded and full of flesh.

The people eat them steamed with wine and garlic. Moules marinière, says Didi, presenting the platter, and fresh bread rolls made with the last of the flour. The people toss the empty

The Fifth Night

shells into a large bowl. They drink the last of the wine. Didi has used the last of the eggs and sugar for crème caramel.

Delicious, say the people, as the warm evening air ruffles their grey hair.

While out in the bay at the edge of vision, that pinpoint of light.

It's distracting.

'So they've just left it here and buggered off?' says Tom.

'Looks like it,' says Philippa.

'Was it even a "they"?' says Maria. 'Did anyone actually see whoever was on board?'

No, they all said. Not a soul.

They sit on the deck looking down at a solitary boat, and in a split-second each person invents an account of its origin and purpose for being there. Their accounts are based upon their own experience of the world and their assumptions of what people might or might not do. Their scenarios pay heed to the state of the world and how it drives people to behave in certain ways determined by time and place. Their scenarios are formed in accordance with patterns learned long since in the deepest recesses of babyhood, of narrative sequence, consequence, and the operations of chance.

They drink the last of the whisky, look down at the masthead light, that little lamp twinkling out in the bay, and they each, in that split-second, make up a story.

Zoe sits surreptitiously feeding titbits to Raffi, who is pressed against her leg under the table, loving her. She feels Raffi's wet tongue scooping a bit of mussel from her fingers. Maybe the people on the boat were refugees, escaping from a famine like the one Ms Trott told them about. She had shown them footage of cracked earth and withered stems and a long line of people walking along a road. One of the girls was wearing a woolly hat exactly like the one Zoe herself wears in winter, with a pompom on top, and she was pulling a suitcase on wheels over the potholes and the suitcase was practically the same as hers too. It contained everything the girl would need because behind the long line of people smoke rose from a burning city. Some of the people were pushing shopping trolleys with bundles on top, and some carried the smallest children in their arms, and all their faces when they turned towards the camera had a look that was like a closed door.

Perhaps the people on the boat had been able to escape and sail away from starvation? Or maybe it wasn't that at all. Maybe they were just having an adventure, like that kid in her class at primary school whose family had spent a year living on a boat, visiting places where there were monkeys sitting in hot springs with little snow caps on their heads, or a theme park with the world's third-most terrifying rollercoaster, or the place in Iceland where Khutulun in the movie marshalled her army before leading them into battle against the Spiderfolk. Zoe had seen the pictures on the kid's blog and photos of life on board, the family sitting around the table in the cabin playing cards, or diving off the boat into impossibly blue water, or holding up a fish, and in every photo they were laughing.

Maybe a family like that could have arrived in this bay after many months at sea and maybe they decided to stay. They have had enough of adventuring. They have abandoned their boat and are already ashore where they plan to find a house and the grownups will get jobs and the kids will go to school. They will

The Fifth Night

play cards around a table and live quietly and happily ever after.

She breaks off a piece of bread. Raffi gulps. And probably, she thinks, they will also get a dog.

Didi also thinks of refugees, but not in flight from natural forces. E's protagonists are fleeing horrors that are entirely within human control: some legal process endorsed by ideas of a deity that orders who a person must be and how their body should look and function, and how they must conduct their lives and who they are permitted to love. The people on e's boat are in flight from words on a page, written in the most exquisite calligraphy. Words that look like tendrils and sweet natural growing things upon a trellis but imply brutal penalty for those who transgress their edicts. There is one penalty for the man and another penalty for the woman, for this distinction — simple, binary, of male and female — must be rigidly enforced. It is the deity's will and there must be no confusion.

There is no place for ambiguity, for the person who chooses to be neither. A transgressor can be male, condemned therefore in an orderly, legal, entirely human process of statement and judgement to be buried up to his waist in a hole in the ground. Or a transgressor can be a woman, whose penalty is to be buried even deeper, up to the neck, her arms pinned to her sides. Then stones are dropped upon their skulls by people who have been persuaded by words on a page that this is the will of a harsh god and that they are right to kill. They fling the stones that litter the ground of this bare rocky place.

But Didi's story has a happier ending. In e's story the accused managed to escape before arrest. They made their way somehow from the interior to the coast, where they found this shabby craft and took their chances on the open sea. They set out to find a place where gods are as big and wide and beautiful as the sky arching over the curve of a warm receptive Earth, and everything between their two divine bodies is love.

Pete stretches out, hands behind his head. He could easily imagine a story about escape from plague, for the silence of those empty corridors is still fresh in his mind. The rattle of the food trolley, the muffled voices from behind closed doors, Ernesto's cheerful 'Hey, man! Zup?' Until the day he didn't arrive, and Pete did the deliveries alone.

All that is still there under the present joy, like a layer of ash and bone and burned homes under metres of rich earth.

But no. He opts for beautiful. He chooses instead two honeymooners, suntanned, windblown, who have sailed off into the blue at last alone, while over their heads the angel takes a break from smiting and pestilence and, with nothing to do, brings them love. Love for ever true. Pete hums along with Bing and Grace. He reaches out his arm. Pulls the beautiful creature beside him in close. Thinks of the two who could perhaps be out there at this very moment, lovers who are male, or female, or some other definition of their choosing, and the rocking they make as their bodies intertwine. However they are constructed, they move over and under and about each other, skin touching skin.

Uncontaminated. Suntanned, windblown. True love. He hums along with Bing. Oh, how lucky they are.

Ani also assumes love. She assumes a man and a woman who built a boat. Practical people who spent evenings and weekends

The Fifth Night

companionably at work in a shed in their yard, following a pattern they had found in a book. Ani is a little vague on the intricacies of such a design, but she can imagine his contented whistling as he planes the teak for the starboard settee. He is a man who loves timber, the grain of it, the smell of it. He strokes it when he has sanded it smooth as if it were a breathing body. The woman, too, hums contentedly to the radio as she applies varnish to a wooden handrail.

They planned to sail their boat around the world. They spread nautical maps and charts over the dining table. They studied manuals and attended classes in seamanship. They learned about the patterns of currents and air that would carry them across oceans. They traced the trade winds and read guides to the wonders of the world and planned the routes and acquired the skills to reach them.

But the boat took many years to build, and the time for departure kept receding until they were both due to retire from the jobs they had done over many years. Ani is vague about exactly what those jobs might have been: nurse? Bus driver? Sales assistant? Systems analyst? Busy jobs, at any rate, that took up far too much of both their lives. And always there was this mirage of the boat they were building in their yard, freed at last from its cradle and swaying at liberty across a warm tropical sea.

The woman and the man were getting old. Some people they knew, people not much older than themselves, began to tremble uncontrollably, or wheeze, or stagger. Some people they knew died. Clearly life was not infinite, and if the woman and the man were ever to see whales migrating off Tonga or watch the sun set from Mauna Kea, they must do it now.

The day dawned. They set sail, their friends waving to them

The Deck

from the shore, and it was exactly as they had imagined. The slap of the mighty tail as the animals breached only metres away, the scent of islands, the brush of something against the hull late one night, the sense of another creature only millimetres away through the skin they had so carefully applied over all those months as their boat took shape within their yard. They experienced storm and contrary winds and a snapped mast and nothing for it but to keep firm hold of the wheel, keep her straight and look ahead. Their boat was strong and held them safe.

They became older. He began to wheeze. All those years breathing in wood dust. His chest heaved as he tried to pull in a sail. He coughed, and there was no escaping the sound of it in their small boat, though he brushed off all her suggestions that they call it quits. Sell the boat. Go home. Get medical treatment.

Until there came a day when they dropped anchor as fog rolled into a bay.

Ani had seen Philippa's face when she re-emerged from that cabin. She knows there is something grim in there, but really, in her story, would death itself be so grim? Would it not be one of those endings that people say is to be desired?

'She died doing the thing she loved.'

'At least he died doing the thing he loved.'

That's what they always say. And really, thinks Ani, would not the shabby boat be preferable to the immaculate room in the dementia unit? Better the lull of water under the hull than the orderly bustle of the ward. Better to go out hand in hand before withering to a husk between clean sheets. The ending is inevitable, but some endings are to be preferred over others. Some could almost be called happy.

The Fifth Night

Baz's story is of a man who has spent his life on a boat, all his needs stowed around him. A bony, dishevelled man who has spent his time seeking out the breaks. Not the well-known breaks with the surf schools and the tours and the competitions with the brash young dudes looking for corporate sponsorship, wearing the gear, promoting the product.

This man has sought out breaks that are as yet unnamed, unclaimed and difficult to access except by boat. Their number has been dwindling every year but still it is possible to find them: the secret curve of warm tropical water breaking on a long reef, a stretch of white sand, a break that hasn't yet been tamed and diminished by being given some cute name. Water has not been tied down by words nor measured for level of difficulty. It is its pure, uncontaminated self. Once there, the man has discovered the easy vibe among a handful of others like himself who live for the moment, for the day. Sometimes there has been another person on board with him, and that has been good for a while, but he's been content also to sail on his own.

The man's boat definitely looks pretty rough. Maybe he's found his way here into the shelter of the bay to do some minor repairs before he heads back up north, like those birds he sees when he is far out to sea, beyond sight of land. Season after season he has looked up and seen their tiny wings beating, following the path of sun and moon and stars.

Peeyoo peeyoo peeyoo they call now from the bush in this bay, and then the dying fall. The man can hear them. Another few weeks and they will fly north for the winter to the scattering of islands, the atolls and tips of old volcanoes clad in forest and surrounded by waves breaking in all their infinite variety, and he will follow them. The Earth will circle the sun and after a

The Deck

time he will follow them back again on their return to the south.

In the meantime, he doesn't seem to be in any hurry, this man Baz imagines living a life that has not been so very different to his own. The life of the solitary wanderer in all those songs Baz and his generation learned in youth, where the singer heads off down the road, no use in calling his name, babe, he'd go with those four strong winds, the ones that blew lonely. It's a life, thinks Baz, and it's been a good one, the one that rolled in and picked him up all those years ago as old Wattie Todd lay lifeless on the side of the road.

The lifetime succession of temporary jobs that left time for the bright morning and the moods of the sea. The subtle satisfactions of clearing a bit of ground for revegetation and seeing the trees grow tall. Or filling a bin with apricots or grapes, some plump ripe fruit. Or riding a mower back and forth across some suburban park, leaving an even sequence of parallel lines in his wake. It's not much of a legacy, and the pay has been crap, but what a life. What a fine life.

And wasn't it good, he thinks, taking up his guitar out there on the deck as they all compose their little narratives, to see her naked in his bed again? And if he has begun to shake — and he has, though no one else is aware of it yet — well, isn't it good that she's turned up out of the wide blue? Maybe she'll stay a little longer this time.

Maria's story begins with the boat in a long shot framed by the twinned headlands. A shabby ketch in a remote bay. Could be a drug drop, she thinks, the boat coming in under fog, loaded with millions of dollars' worth of complex chemicals designed to alter the brain and deliver a massive profit when released onto the streets. There seems to be little activity out there, so perhaps the stock has already been transferred to smaller, faster boats and the crew are in some bar in port, toasting the success of their enterprise, avoiding coastguard, air surveillance, police.

Could be illegals, finding their way here driven by war or drought or flood or economic collapse or because they want a job, a home, an opportunity for their kids. Another little craft making its way from one place to another laden with people hoping for something better. Like her grandparents escaping the aftermath of war, like her great-grandparents escaping famine and starvation, and her great-great-grandparents who were forced into motion by eviction and land enclosure.

There have always been the little boats laden with their cargoes of hopeful travellers. But now there are so many. The rusted fishing boats and overladen inflatables stocked by exploitative criminals who take the money of the desperate and abandon them to the open sea, the border patrols that await them, and the detention centres, the camps, the repatriation flights.

Maybe there is something out there that would be worth following up? Maybe she should check it out before they leave tomorrow, see if there's someone on board? She'll take her camera, because she always carries a little camera from long habit. She could get a few shots, see if the people on board might be willing to talk, to be interviewed. She sometimes feels she no longer quite understands the intricacies of the world, but perhaps she could begin here and see if it turns into something that opens up the possibility of narrative, something that might be a way into a wider theme: homelessness, for instance.

The notion of home in an era when great tides of migration

sweep over the planet as humanity shifts about restlessly on its blue globe. She sits on the deck, feeling that lovely little jitter that is always the start, the bubble of curiosity, the 'why', the 'what if', the 'who' and the 'how' rising within her. The beginning of a story.

Philippa hands around the coffee. She has been doing her best to be convivial but she alone has seen the lacquered bed. She alone has seen the young woman, the young man, lying side by side. *Help me! Help me!* A story has taken shape in the crevices of her crumpled brain. A version of a story that might have been told by the young woman with her long fair hair.

The fair-haired girl, her sweetheart and the green isle
A ninth tale of one, who after divers misadventures, at last attains a goal of unexpected felicity.

She was born in a city by the sea on an auspicious day. The woman who attended her birth, a rotund creature in apron and headscarf, blessed the baby with a flick of her bloodied hand, muttering some words that would bestow health, wealth, beauty, love, happiness and a long life.

Over many years these things came to pass. The fair-haired girl was the daughter of a man who owned an engineering firm and had close contacts in the Party from whom he received many favours. He thrived. Her mother had studied navigation and taught at a naval college. Her grandmother had commanded a

The Fifth Night

Liberty ship during the Great Patriotic War, conveying supplies, munitions and the wounded in the Baltic. She went down with her ship when it was hit by an enemy torpedo, despite flying the hospital flag. She received many posthumous honours and her portrait hung, framed in laurel leaf, in the vestibule of the tall white house where the girl grew up. A tall white house behind a high wall, overlooking the harbour.

The girl learned to sail as a child, skimming in a little Optimist across the water in summer, and over ice under the dragon sail, four times faster than the wind, in the hard winters. Her long hair flew. She was strong and beautiful and fiercely determined. She received medals of bronze and silver and gold.

One day she was racing against a young man, also tall and strong, also determined. Their iceboats flew, finding the fastest route in a brisk breeze, minus 10 degrees and sunny, out to a little island and return, mere seconds between them. She won by a hair's breadth, though he said, when he stood to speak at their wedding a few months later, that he had been too distracted by her beauty to compete properly. The wedding was an elaborate affair attended by all the dignitaries of the town.

Not long after, however, there was a change in the weather. Her father fell out of favour with a powerful man. Contracts were cancelled. His company faltered and was seized in forfeit. He died. Her mother lost her position at the naval college. The sea rose and storms swamped the bottom floor of the white house. It became unliveable. Drought sapped the land and plague made its appearance on its white horse. And war too, an old enmity breaking into new life. The town and its port were destroyed in three days of fierce fighting.

The young woman and the young man tried to escape.

The Deck

They spent all their money on a ticket westward, but the train managed only a short distance before it was destroyed by a bomb released many thousands of kilometres away by another young man nearing the end of his shift and keen to get back home to watch the game. He had identified the target: the long black snake of wagons winding across scorched earth. He got sign-off from his superior and hit the button. Done. He filed a successful engagement, put on his jacket and left the building.

The young woman and the young man were unharmed and undeterred. They made their way from the wreckage back to the coast, where they found a yacht, not large, but still miraculously intact at its mooring. They stocked it with what they could scavenge, and under cover of darkness they sailed away. Charting a course southward between islands and the toes of continents. Their screens remained blank, all systems out, so they were forced to rely on the old ways she had been taught: calculating direction and distance from stars and manual measurement.

Their journey took many months. They suffered many vicissitudes. Storms and strong winds. Near wreck on a long reef bleached to bone. The smell of ash hung over a burned land as they filled their containers with a trickle of fresh water. They suffered the constant fear of interception at sea and arrest. But at last, on the horizon, they saw mountain tops, snow clad.

They found a green isle and sailed south along its coast, seeking an anchorage. Fog drew in as they came upon a bay between headlands. Its waters were still and the air smelled of damp green leaf. They dropped anchor, rejoicing in their safe arrival. They ate and drank and lay side by side on their bed, smiling into each other's eyes, hands clasped, unable to believe their luck.

The Fifth Night

The young woman's tale ends there, but Philippa, busily handing around the coffee, could add the ending. She could add the putter of the runabout, late afternoon when no one was especially paying attention. Philippa was alone. The gun lay on the seat beside her and warm summer air brushed her arm as she held the tiller in the direction of the yacht suspended on a glassy sea. She could add the swaying as she tied up to the swim ladder, the soft footfall across the deck, her entry into the lacquered cabin. She could add the snap of a bullet fitted into its cradle and the cool metal nose of an old .22 nuzzling at matted hair.

Help me! Help me!

There you go. Keep breathing. Nice and steady.

The crack as she squeezed, so gently, so kindly, putting poor sick creatures out of their misery.

Breathe.

One shot. Then another shot. Youth and beauty startled and fell back. They lay quiet, ruined face to ruined face upon their bloodied bed. Then Philippa could add the rocking of the yacht as she left them there, and the way she tugged at the companionway hatch though it was stiff from age and neglect and had to remain slightly ajar. She could add how she clambered back into the runabout and returned to shore and how behind her the gulls circled, came into land on the cabin roof, lined up, waiting.

She could have added the true ending to the young woman's tale, but she won't. No one will ever hear it. Philippa will never take it down from the high shelf.

The Deck

'Milk?' she says. A liqueur? A chocolate? They eat the last of the chocolates and talk as night falls, and out at sea the cloudland darkens, lightning playing about its towers and mountain tops. The warm air crackles.

And then, a little breeze. The merest rattling among the leaves of the ngaio beside the deck.

The storm falls upon them with sudden fury. It rises over the headland, bruising sea and sky purple and black, and roars up the bay, tossing leaves and branches over its shoulder.

The people scurry before it. They run about, anchoring the table, the barbecue. They carry the deckchairs inside. They close the doors and watch from behind glass that buckles in the blast and threatens to crack and let it all come in.

And then a thunderclap almost overhead. It rings in their ears. They feel the vibration in the breastbone. And the lightning flash sees them all frozen, mouths open, as it comes to earth through the apple tree up the hill near the spring, breaking its heart in two and leaving a charred hollow.

Raffi howls, though Ani is cradling him close. Thunderclaps roll from cliff edge to cliff edge across the bay, like some old god veering about on a chariot with iron wheels. A river bursts over their heads and hailstones the size of golf balls drum on the roof so loudly that when the people turn to talk to one another they can hear nothing. Just the mouth, opening and closing, trying to say something.

Water streams over the glass. Another lightning flash, closer still, and this time the power goes out. All the ingenuity of conductor and transformer is defeated at one blow and the people are left in the dark, fumbling for a torch, a phone, for a lighter or matches, and where are the candles? The darkness

The Fifth Night

is absolute. When they do light some candles — the last of the candles — their flames are tentative.

The house that had seemed so solid, commanding the view, feels flimsy now, cruelly exposed up there on its ridge. It shudders as the gusts hit, and a bough breaks on the ngaio tree and falls with a crash over the deck. They look out through shattered leaf at this storm and think of others they have seen or heard about: news photos of hillsides that melted to mud and slid over villages. In Bolivia. In China. In America. Cars upended in the mud like toys abandoned in a sandpit. Cows huddled on scraps of land as the waters rose. People wading along roads in Bangladesh. In Germany. Suburban streets where motorboats churn, gathering up people who have waited for rescue on the topmost peak of the roof. In Australia. In Holland. Mountainsides where cables have snapped and refuges have tumbled and all the people inside them have fallen into a chasm. In Italy. In Nepal. Rivers surging over cities built in their deltas, people crammed on boats and canoes seeking higher ground, coasts where waves chew into insubstantial settlements set on shingle banks, sheets of lightning arcing over hundreds of kilometres. Don't stand under a tree for shelter. Don't touch water or stand in the vicinity of an electrical device. Don't stand by a window. Yet here they are, standing by a window.

The crib has become a drum, beating retreat. It is Baz who is first to say, well, might as well call it a day. They dash through the rain to their beds.

'I hate the thunder,' says Zoe, the duvet pulled up tightly around her chin, counting elephants: flash, one elephant, two elephants, three . . . boom.

The Deck

'You'll be fine,' says Maria, stroking her hair the way she should have done more often with Sophie when she was small and afraid of thunder. Her daughter was afraid of so many things: thunder, the dark, snakes even when they moved here where there weren't any snakes.

'But they could easily get here,' Sophie had said, clutching at her arm. 'In someone's luggage. They could get out and be everywhere, except no one's noticed.'

She was afraid of choking on lumpy food and crossing the road and being left alone, even when she was perfectly safe. She was old enough to manage on her own. She had Maria's phone number. Zoe's head is smooth under her grandmother's hand. A lightning flash. One elephant, two . . . The thunder crashes over them with such force that Maria, despite herself, flinches.

'You'll be fine,' she says, because that's what you say to people when they are frightened, even when you know it's not necessarily true.

Sometimes there is a snake in the bananas.

People do get hit by lightning, sometimes more than once.

And the cat can run out onto the road and be knocked over by a car, and you can be home on your own in a dismal flat and there is no one there to help.

But still we insist that all will be well.

'You'll be fine,' we say. Everything will be fine. In the end, justice will be done, right will prevail. The good and honourable will be rewarded, if not on this Earth then in some fiction of everlasting life. And none of it is true. The serial killer goes on to enjoy a contented old age, playing bowls and tending his lilies while the girls he killed with such pleasure have long since rotted underground.

The Fifth Night

The genocidal dictator dozes in the sun on the Côte d'Azur.

The commandant of the death camp plays with his grandchildren and has a permanent seat at the opera.

And she, Maria, has been complicit in the fiction. She has fancied herself with her camera recording the obfuscation of some dubious CEO, dodgy scientist, corrupt politician, as the recording angel, the agent of retribution. She has dragged them out into the open, placed them magnified many times on the screen, zeroed in on the telltale comment, the shifty expression, the little tics that betray lies and deviousness.

She has spent her life creating stories in which the wicked are hunted down and exposed to public censure, and when the lights go up and the audience leaves the theatre or switches off the screen, it is with the comforting sensation that goodness will triumph in the end. And if it hasn't triumphed, then it isn't really the end. She has fancied herself a disciple of reality and fact, when really she has just been composing fictions, entertainments with colour and music, around the theme of a correctible world.

'You'll be fine,' says Maria, stroking the child's hair till her breathing steadies and she slides into sleep. Maria sits watching the strobe of flash and roar, the world turned to black and white, and all she wants is a drink. She yearns for the cool bottle in her hand, its contents pouring into the glass, the sweet oblivion in an empty room.

It would be so easy, wouldn't it, to cross the deck, open the glass door and take one of those bottles from the cupboard. The wine's all gone but there will still be some liquor no one likes, some crème de menthe, some saffron-flavoured gin, some retsina brought back from holiday. She could finish it off then

The Deck

head down in the storm to Baz, who will be waiting for her, she knows that. She'd tap at the side of the van and slide open the door. Then she'd slip in beside him, into that warm doggy bed of his, while the hail rattles away on his old van and it would be as if they've skipped the past few decades and picked up from the moment just before Wattie Todd at the crossroads and the deadness of him on the damp grass beside her knees.

She thinks of the way Baz felt when she laid her head against his bare skin this afternoon. She remembered him then. How his skin had always smelled salty, of seawater and sweat and smoke, and how his hair when she touched it curled tightly at the nape. She remembered too the sound of him. The steady thwup thwup of his heart, the kitchen gurgle from gut and stomach.

This afternoon she had lain beside him as sunlight fell on their bare bodies and it was just as it always was.

It was just as it always is, when two creatures locate each other in the muddle. Two sacs of skin containing blood and bone, old sacs now with maybe only a decade, maybe two, maybe less, to register sensation. Two sacs of organs that have evolved over an unimaginable number of days and nights from planetary dust to tiny microbe, to worm, to fish, to timid little shrew, through all the twists and coincidence and U-turns of evolution, blundering through time towards this moment.

And somehow the heart keeps up its cadence, two billion beats or so since the first excited ticking in the womb. The lungs inflate, deflate, inflate. The stomach and the gut and the bowel still clutch and squeeze. The nerves still jitter and the brain still arranges what is happening into meaning. Though perhaps not for much longer, because all that will stop.

They will falter and fail and then there's death and rot.

The Fifth Night

But for now, the sacs are sentient and they are feeling a set of impulses that may have been designed for the purpose of procreation but that's long past. Egg and sperm might once have oozed from the sac to further the species, but now the impulses have another purpose entirely. What has been left are responses that could be identified and labelled as Guilt, and Anger, and Resentment. And what is released in that moment of conjoining is Forgiveness, and Delight, and Love.

So, Maria does not go off to find the gin, nor does she go down to join Baz in his van. What if Zoe woke and she wasn't there? This time she mustn't stuff it up. She must make the kind of choices people make in the final frames. The choice where the bride abandons the wedding and runs off with the young man in the back seat of the bus. Or the boy escapes from the brutal institution and makes his way to see the sea for the first time. And in the final frame he turns and regards the camera and it is clear that he has made the right decision.

She stays where she is, stroking her granddaughter's hair, trying to get this bit right.

In the pod next door, Leo has hold of Ani's hand. She can feel his big calloused palm, his strong fingers holding her own, and she feels happy as rain and hail pound.

Whaiāipo.

The word arrives unbidden. It's one of the words she has learned in class as she has tried painstakingly to assemble a language.

Whaiāipo.

The one whom you follow into the dark.

The beloved.

The Deck

It's hard to learn a new language at her age. She should have picked up the words when she was very young, the way a small child picks up shiny things at random: sea shells and bottle caps and flowers. She should have learned the words when everything was being named for the first time, seated on someone's warm knee, not at a desk in a classroom with that empty after-hours feel and the smell of adolescent bodies and orange peel and the cleaner's floor polisher whirring out in the corridor.

She had hoped for some miracle of genetic memory, that somehow the words would have been lodged in the recesses of her brain, like the memories of flight in the brains of migratory birds who find their way across vast oceans by some feat of inheritance. It doesn't seem to work that way for humans, not for her at any rate. She listens and repeats and often as not forgets. But sometimes a word is so perfect, so beautiful, that it flies in and stays.

Whaiāipo.

She loves that word. She had not realised before the classes that words in the mouth are little pictures. This word contains the picture of a person following another person out into the dark. There's a place where everyone is gathered around a fire, there's warmth and shelter and the murmur of voices, but the one you love stands and leaves the group. He ducks his head under the lintel and leaves, and you rise and follow, out into the dark where you can sense him waiting somewhere in the shadows, his arms reaching out to gather you close into his warm embrace.

The wind howls and rain streams against the glass and hailstones hammer on the roof.

It's biblical, she thinks. The plague of hail in the last days,

The Fifth Night

every stone the weight of a talent. And she must have said it aloud because Leo replies. He says, 'Yes, it is in the fact.'

Slam goes the wind, and the pod shudders, threatening to drag free and tumble down the hill. She sits up in her big wide bed and finds her torch, her pad and pencil and begins to draw. She draws a little house surrounded by immense stormclouds. And then she draws the interior, where the pig sits in a warm room, a big soft armchair, a fire in the grate, a book open on her lap. And, yes, there's another pig opposite her, in his own armchair with his book also on his knee, and he is smoking a pipe, one of those curving Meerschaum pipes he likes, because in this version a pipe can do no harm. Some music is playing, and though she can't draw the sound of Miles Davis you know it's there. You can hear it over the engine rumble that is the creek in spate, bearing stones down to the sea.

Philippa, too, hears the creek. It wakes her. They had gone to bed in silence, as had become their habit, she on one side of the bed, he far away across the tundra, a dull huddle under the duvet. Although the world outside the room was full of noises, inside the room there was that silence, the concentrated silence of two people engaged in a kind of arm-wrestling. Do you give in? Will you be the first to speak? The first to reach out and touch the other? And, if you do, will the other shrug you aside?

Or will the other turn towards you? Will you put your old arms around each other, find your way back across the tundra to the place where you lie skin to skin under a single sheet? Will one of you mutter Sorry, and the other say Me too, yes, me too.

Will they say, Should have thought, should have said, should have understood, should have known.

The Deck

Will they perhaps find that good place where they can begin to laugh at the absurdity of themselves, see themselves as figures in the long comedy of marriage, missing their cues over and over, forgetting their lines, overacting, fucking up?

Will they be able to shrug and say, Ah well, we say what we say, we do what we do for reasons that make sense at the time, because that's the kind of humans we are. We're made up of all these bits and pieces, thrown together from the moment we emerged squalling, or even before, back when the tiny platelets that were ourselves first developed the dimple that would become, as good little deuterostomes, our bums and not our mouths, unlike the majority of creatures who choose a nice mouth as their first distinguishing feature. But there you are: you are a human with your little dimple bum, beginning to be.

The rain falls and the wind blows, and she dozes, and when she wakes he is not in the bed next to her. When he sleeps, he whistles very quietly on each out-breath. She has always rather liked that. It's oddly reassuring, like the sound a bird makes in a midnight forest. But there is no sound, and when she reaches out the bed is empty. It is very dark. No moon. No stars. No standby lights or streetlights, just the dense black dark.

'Tom?' she says. And his voice comes back to her from the window where he's fretting at the storm.

'The creek's getting up,' he says. 'Can you hear it?'

Yes, she can. She gets up and fumbles her way towards him.

'Hope we can get across the ford tomorrow,' he says, because they can talk about this. This ordinary thing, the problem that must be solved now. Their shared life has been made up of problems, large and small, that must be solved. They have been good at it, have managed a life of calm organisation, lists

The Fifth Night

attached to the fridge with magnets, calendars on their phones alerting them to conflicts with dates, meetings, appointments. Things to do. Things to collect. Payments due. Subscriptions. Their lives have been lived as clockwork. Their time on Earth ticking by, second by second.

'Have to wait and see,' she says. 'Deal with it in the morning.' And she stands behind him and puts her arms around him. He does not turn towards her but he puts his hand over hers, and that is something. They stand together looking out at the rain.

'Woo hoo!' says Didi as the room lights up, e's body a flare, e's hair a wild halo. E rises with the storm, exhilarated as always by roar and speed and risk and incipient chaos. Pete prefers the calm heart. He has always liked untroubled routine. The blissful Sunday morning ride out of the city to the coast when he has been back onshore, the smooth cadences of a road ride clipped to the machine, human at one with exquisite technology.

Out there on the road after weeks of dealing with dictatorial management, volatile performers, irritable techies, discontented guests. The pampered, entitled, alcoholic, addicted, irritating, unhappy and downright crazy individuals who for whatever reason decide it would be a good idea to climb aboard a ship with 4000 other individuals who might simply be intent on having a good time, but could, just as easily, prove to be as discontented, irritating and downright crazy as themselves. Out there on the road after weeks of that, how Pete has loved the Sunday morning ride, alone or with a few mates in an easy peloton.

Out there in his sleek black Lycra skin, hair concealed beneath his helmet, the wrinkles he has tried for years to smooth away with expensive potions promising eternal youth, invisible beneath blue reflective shades, he could easily pass for fifty-five. Maybe fifty. He could shed the years, hitting that sweet spot where the tarmac appears to flow without effort beneath the wheels.

Didi has come out with him once or twice, and it has been good, spinning along in e's wake, watching the flex of muscle and sinew, the curve of that perfect ambiguous bum lifting from the saddle on some gentle rise. But Didi really prefers the gnarly trail, the swift reflexes and rush of a steep unfamiliar descent, pumping over rock and tree root, airborne over steep drops, riding at speed into tight corners.

This storm, too, sets em alight. Pete's wild angel, who has him pinned down in a strong grip, and all Pete can hear, deadened by thunder, rain and roar, is the groan of their coupling.

Meanwhile, out in the bay, youth and beauty lie side by side, unmoving on their shabby catafalque as it is dragged from its mooring, smashed onto the reef, and sinks till only the tip of a mast is visible, a crossed stick above water.

THE SIXTH DAY

After tumult, a sweet morning. Sun, moon and stars restored to their accustomed places in calm, indifferent alignment. On Earth, the people emerge from their pods like small animals from their burrows, blurry from lack of sleep. They look about.

Slips have scarred the hills up and down the valley, leaving long finger-scrapes of raw clay, torn trees and fallen rock. Leaf and branch litter the deck. But the creek is already falling as rapidly as it rose, and the stones it carried downstream overnight can be removed from the ford. It will be possible to leave as planned.

The people clear away the stones. They inspect the solar panels. They are cracked and dented by hail and will need proper professional attention. The power is out but there is enough gas in the bottle to fire up the barbecue one last time for coffee with the last of the beans, the last of the milk, the last of the bread and marmalade. The taps gurgle ominously and

The Deck

the water runs sepia, but there's enough in the tank for showers and washing dishes.

The people store the runabout in its shed and the barbecue in its appointed place under the deck. They strip their beds and pack their suitcases. They load their cars and prepare to leave.

Philippa stands on the deck while Tom does the final inspection, securing the place as best he can without power to operate the shutters that enclose each pod.

'I don't like leaving it like this,' he says. It makes him edgy. The glass doors gleam in the sunlight after their drenching overnight. They look out to sea, wide eyed and vulnerable.

Philippa shrugs. 'We've no option,' she says.

She has the binoculars out and is scanning the bay. The yacht has disappeared and it has left a strange gap. It might not have been there at all, with its flaking paint, its stink, its gulls and its bloodied bed. The weird beauty of those two young bodies, lying face to face.

'I don't even know if we'll be able to repair the solar panels,' Tom is saying. 'I don't know if we'll be able to get the parts, let alone find a tradie who can come out here and do it.' He frets and fiddles. Maybe repair will not even be possible. Maybe the entire system is fucked. Maybe all the wiring will have to be replaced. The size of that task, the prospect of unravelling what has been installed with such care, the unbearable act of demolition and removal and the vast expense of reconstruction. It overwhelms him.

Philippa still has her eyes glued to the binoculars. She does not seem to understand the scope of what might be required. She is raking the bay, back and forth, and . . .

The Sixth Day

'Ah ha!' she says. She has found it. A shadow under the water, a stain of oil glistening, the tip of a mast like two crossed sticks by the rocks at the cavern's mouth. Such a relief. Burial at sea. A clean internment, washed by the ocean, the fish probably already finding their way in through the open hatch. 'There they are!'

'Who?' says Tom. 'You mean the yacht?'

He feels no satisfaction whatever. The sinking of a single boat is of no consequence. The fact is that there are hundreds, thousands, more of them out there. Flotillas of the desperate are in movement around the planet on small boats and large. On rubber rafts and speedboats, dinghies and yachts, fishing boats and trawlers, requisitioned livestock transports and cruise ships. The barbarians in their grubby craft are circling this coast, and his crib looks so unbearably vulnerable.

He wonders for a moment about defence. What could he do? He has a brief fantasy of a bearpit at the foot of the deck, dug deep into the earth with sharpened sticks set in the base and a surface camouflage of sand and scrub, but he knows as the image flashes between the synapses that it is just that: a fantasy. Pointless. There is no time for bearpits and sharpened stakes. He locks the glass doors, pulls the curtains over. Pointless.

Zoe wheels her suitcase down the steps to her grandmother's car. She is so happy to be leaving, going back over the hilltop. She cannot wait another day without that little ping signalling some silly post they've made of them all with orange-peel teeth or adding funny voices to a clip of Mia's pony nuzzling their cat. Or just words on a screen saying anything at all so she knows they are there, and she can reply and say, Me too, I'm here. Her gran has said they should wait a little longer before going back, just to be certain. Enough time for her family to be well clear of the country. She and Zoe will spend those extra few days at that old guy Baz's place. He has a house up the coast somewhere north of the city.

'It's a bit basic,' he had said as he made the offer. 'But you'll be safe there. Not too many neighbours and they pretty much keep to themselves. It'll do for a while.'

He looked weirdly excited by the idea, and her gran, too, was way more enthusiastic than seemed necessary, especially for a person who never bothered with hugs or compliments or birthday presents, never bothered to say 'thank you' or 'excuse me', never made herself small and sweet. Her mother said their gran was totally monomaniacal and obsessional and lacking in social skills, and whenever Zoe misbehaved she was told she was just like her. Uncooperative and difficult.

But here was her gran saying thank you to the old guy's offer, all smiles.

'Thank you,' she said. 'That sounds great. Doesn't it sound great, Zoe?'

So Zoe also had to say, 'Yeah. Great.'

And when they didn't think she was paying attention, just listening to her playlist with her earbuds in, she noticed they were all giggly as they helped each other load up her gran's car and that disgusting van. If his house was anything like the van, it would be a dump. But here they were giggling, though they were practically dead, and it was like being around Mia and Yanni when they were getting together, play-fighting over a basketball.

But 'Yeah,' she had said when her gran asked if she'd like to stay at the old dude's house. 'Does it have internet?' And when he said yes, there was excellent coverage, she had said, 'Sounds good. Thanks.' She was happy to go wherever the words could fly and settle on the screen.

They set off late morning, leaving the pods to fate. The cars form a convoy, Tom and Philippa leading the way, with Ani, Didi and Pete behind, minus Raffi. He has chosen instead to ride with Zoe, standing on her lap with his paws up on the windowsill, nose pressed to the gap.

Baz follows, driving slowly. The chassis scrapes crossing the ford but his tin-can fix holds and the van roars off along the flat.

Maria is last, Zoe curled up in the passenger seat with Raffi on her lap. The old dude's actually got a rainbow sticker on the back window of the van, and a faded sign saying 'THERE IS NO PLANET B'.

For real? thinks Zoe.

Tom drives cautiously because the road is littered with small slips where banks have collapsed overnight. The chilly bin occupies the back seat, filled with his miraculous catch. There was no point in leaving that behind in the freezer to melt and rot. When he looks back in the rear-vision mirror he catches glimpses of the bay and the scattering of black boxes that are his creation. They become smaller and smaller, dwarfed by steep hillsides and the long blue reaches of the Southern Ocean that emerge into view beyond the headlands as they climb higher. He navigates the car around the slips. At one point they have to stop to push aside a boulder that has crashed down from the tops, all of them together giving it a good old heave-ho till it

The Deck

rolls over the lip of the road and lumbers off, smashing trees on its path to the valley beneath.

'Whoooo!' they whoop, watching it go, and when they get back into their cars they put on some music. They hum along. They are on their way out, on their way home.

The hilltop swings into view around a steep corner, only a few hundred metres ahead. Not far now. The bay is no more than a blue crinkle on the coastline far below. Another tight corner, and the convoy comes to a sudden stop.

A stretch of hillside has fallen away. A huge scoop has been carved from the road, leaving only a strip a metre wide along its innermost edge. The rest has slid hundreds of metres down into the valley in an avalanche of clay and stone and broken trees. Where the road used to be is a chasm fifty metres across, bare clay still trickling with water and stones. The narrow remnant strip of road borders a void.

They get out of their cars and stand looking down. A sheer drop. A morass of mud and tangled branches.

'What do we do now?' says Pete.

No one answers immediately. They stand looking at the gap.

Phone for help? says someone.

The emergency line?

911.

That's America. It's 111.

Phone 111.

Phone Civil Defence.

Phone the council. What's their number?

Phone road works.

There's no connection.

The Sixth Day

There'll be a connection somewhere close. We're nearly at the top.

Phone a helicopter company.

That'd cost a fortune.

Well, what do you suggest? How are we going to get out of here?

Go back down to the crib? Get out the runabout? Send someone along the coast to port, charter a boat big enough to hold us all, take us out?

It's a long way to port.

It's a rough stretch of coast for a little runabout.

Doubt we've got enough fuel.

And what about the cars?

We'd have to leave them. Deal with them later.

If we can charter a big enough boat, we could take them too.

That'd cost a fortune!

Well, have you got any better ideas?

A helicopter could lift them out.

A helicopter would cost a fortune.

Look, it's going to cost a fortune whatever we decide! Get used to it!

What a fucking mess.

What a nuisance.

What a pain in the arse.

Cazzo!

I've got work tomorrow night.

I've got a plane to catch in the morning.

I've got a meeting on Friday.

I've got all that fish in the chilly bin . . .

There's a rattling of wheels. Zoe walks past them, dragging

The Deck

her suitcase over the gravel. She is wearing her woolly hat because it's cold up here, the first whiff of autumn and the cold season to come, and she is walking purposefully towards the tiny strip of road above the chasm. Before anyone can stop her she has stepped out onto it and Raffi trots obediently after, both of them seemingly oblivious to the drop under their feet.

'Zoe!' calls Maria. 'What are you doing? Stop . . . Come back!'

But Zoe is not listening. She is walking quickly and not looking down because she learned long ago at Tiny Tumblers that if you look down when crossing the beam you could lose your nerve. You must just keep looking straight ahead and walk steadily towards the safe bit, where the coach is waiting to lift you down onto the floor.

She picks her way through the rubble that has fallen with the slip, and it's nice having Raffi there, panting a bit and pattering along at her heels. Her phone is in her pocket, and as soon as she gets to the top she knows there will be a ping and they will all come hurtling towards her, the words and the video clips, her friends' voices and their faces grinning back at her. So she just keeps right on walking towards them.

And Maria says, 'Well, I guess that's one solution.' She fetches her suitcase from the car and a warm jacket because who knew how long they'd have to walk? Maybe they'd get a lift? Then she sets off after her granddaughter, whom she has put in this position so must keep close.

And Ani follows because that's her little dog running ahead, though she hesitates. Who knew how long that strip of road would last, barely supported beneath their feet? It looks fragile, and the earth is still unsettled, a trickle of mud still falling. But she can feel that warm, calloused hand holding her own. She takes a firm grip and steps out.

And Baz grabs his bag and board and follows because that's Maria over there on the other side and he does not want to risk losing sight of her again. The rubble slips under his big feet but he has found his balance many times before on more slippery surfaces.

Then Didi, who goes first because Pete really does not like heights.

'Don't think about it,' says Didi. 'You think too much. Think of a song. I'll be right ahead. Just sing and follow.'

So Pete does that. He sings through clenched teeth about dancing down a street on a cloud rather than a strip of clay and gravel and it is most definitely *amore*, and he keeps his eyes firmly fixed on Didi's sleek back. Didi walks ahead, balancing e's suitcase and forcing emself to focus on work: on e's mates on the line at the lodge, waiting for em to get back so they can begin planning the autumn menu. Kahawai, wood-roasted. Venison. A fig compôte. A salad of heirloom tomatoes . . .

Tom insists on taking the chilly bin as well as the suitcase, though it's awkward and unwieldy.

'It's too much,' says Philippa. 'Too heavy. That bit of road doesn't look very stable.'

Tom says nothing in reply, just wraps his arm around the bin and sets out onto the narrow strip of gravel. Midway across he stumbles, unable to see exactly where he is putting his feet. He grabs for a tree root and, against the odds, finds one that holds fast, but the bin slips from his grasp. It tumbles down into the void. The lid comes loose and all those little silvery fish, the last of their kind, spin and fall in the sunlight and land in mud as

The Deck

Tom releases his hold on the tree root and scrambles as fast as he is able for solid ground on the other side. He reaches it and stands there with the others, unable to look back as his wife follows.

Philippa has taken her time, sorting the clothes they will most need into a single suitcase and locking the car carefully because who knew when they'd return? The suitcase bumps over uneven ground. Trickles of clay and pebbles fall away under her feet as she steps onto the narrow strip, but it holds until she is across. And then behind her, as in all the stories, the bridge to safety judders. A gap opens in its surface midway, and all traces of the road crumble completely and fall away.

There is no option now but to carry on. The road winds upwards, a couple more bends before the hilltop. Zoe is already well ahead, walking determinedly, head down, dragging her suitcase, and Raffi is right behind her, panting to keep up on his stocky little legs. The others follow more slowly. Their bags are heavily laden and catch on the gravel. They fear the little wheels might break on such rough ground.

Because then what would they do? With all their stuff? How would they carry it all?

Up here the bush gives way to tussock. The people climb slowly in sunlight. There is a cool wind as they arrive at the hilltop. It catches the tussocks and they toss their golden hair. To and fro. In the distance, the mountains of the Main Divide are just visible. Only their very tips are clad in snow and the hills between are scorched golden brown. They have their own beauty that is not quite yet the barren beauty of other rocky planets.

The road back to the city winds downhill, devoid of traffic.

The Sixth Day

There is the ping of connection up here, but when the people look down at their screens, it is to see the news they had been expecting vanishing in a glittering flood. Before they can be read, words disintegrate into a random hail of letters. Fact and information vanish, as do lies and propaganda, communication and commercial endorsement, games and movies and music and the recorded literatures of the world, the comedian entertaining thousands, the porno star spread-eagled for penetration, the person jumping over a high bar, the baker icing the cake, the politician attempting to turn the tide of history, the whole panoply of civilisation disappears. In the blink of an eye.

The people stand on the hilltop watching it go, falling back before the inexorable rise of a black line that advances from the bottom to the top of every screen, ruling out every possibility. The cacophony of voices in all the languages of the world goes silent.

Their screens are dark.

They tap hopefully at the surface but it remains smooth and glassy as the ice that forms over a muddy puddle.

Zoe, however, has left already. She is walking on down the road, moving quickly because somewhere, sometime soon, there will be the ping and flicker of response. She just has to keep moving and it will happen. The others can see her and her bobble hat flickering in and out of view around the corners. Raffi is a small white dot at her heels.

They have no option but to follow.

So they take a firm grasp of their suitcases and set out.

Just another of those lines of people walking along a road, hoping for home.

THE AUTHOR'S CONCLUSION

The novelist leaves them there, her paper dolls, walking along in their imaginary land.

She leans back in her chair to stretch her spine, stiff after so much time spent sitting at a screen, a year and a half since the first summer day.

A lot has happened.

Winter, spring, another summer, another winter and now another blowsy, technicolor spring. The kōwhai by the gate is busy being yellow, the magnolia in the garden is being pink, old trees with ancient lineage. Kōwhai that can live 1800 years. Magnolias that evolved when dinosaurs plodded about the planet in all their feathered, clawed and horned variety, back in that fluoro-bright, comic-book era when the novelist's hands, cramped now after working on the keyboard, were just tiny pink paws, scratching in the undergrowth.

A flock of waxeyes is at work this morning, shredding the

The Deck

flowers from both trees. Tauhou, 'the newcomers', who made their way unaided across the ocean only a couple of hundred years ago. They flit about, sweet and funny, dropping a confetti of pink and yellow on damp grass.

The world outside the window is busy. The city hums to itself in the spring sunlight. The children in the day-care centre are out playing in the sun with their xylophone bing bang bong. A plane flies overhead, gaining altitude as it lifts off from the airport. The borders are wide open again and the tourists are flying in and out. A rubbish truck rolls along the street, the young men hopping on and off to gather bins full of bottles from the student flats for recycling. The air is filled with birdsong, engine drone and the sound of smashing glass.

A lot has happened while the novelist has been making up alternative reality.

The virus has blown about the planet, its tally recorded with that weird contemporary exactness: today the figure for total infections worldwide since the first mention of Wuhan and the pangolins, stands at 620,978,064. Six million, five hundred and forty-two people have died. The media is bored. Already the virus is being reported as if it belongs to the past tense, though it is still present, evolving, mutating, adapting.

It is here this morning, making its way around the sunlit city, having breached the borders long since. Months ago it flew in on the body of a traveller and set out across the country, its progress recorded on screen in red dots like a spreading rash. The novelist's daughter is a doctor. She was issued with guidelines in advance of the virus's arrival: ten pages of diagnostic procedure, lists, timelines and tickboxes. *Hypertension Yes/No. Epilepsy Yes/No . . .*

The Author's Conclusion

Once the initial assessment is completed and you have determined the patient should be Covid Care 2, immediately create a task to send a pulse oximeter . . .

The novelist liked that adverb 'immediately', that noun 'task'. A pandemic had been reduced to directives and plain speech. A few hundred years of methodical inquiry were at work here to counter the chaos of bodies piled in a street, the rootling of pigs, the breakdown of civil order.

There has been, too, a welter of analysis, commentary, graphs and studies attempting to ascertain the exact impact of this virus. A feature in this month's *Economist*, for example, compares the number of deaths in individual countries with normal rates of mortality between January 2020, when Covid made its presence felt worldwide, and October 2022.

The tally of 'excess deaths' is another of those league tables where the novelist looks by reflex for countries comparable to her own, small places with a population of around 5 million.

Denmark (population 5.8 million) has suffered 4900 excess deaths, Ireland (5 million) records 6000 excess deaths. Wealthy Norway (population 5.4 million) has lost 5500 people. Singapore (5.7 million) adopted a strong public-health policy with strict border controls but failed to vaccinate universally and when Covid broke through in October 2021, they went on to record 3700 excess deaths. Bulgaria (7 million) did very little to control the virus and has lost 72,000 people so far

And this country? The sunlit place outside her window? Its 'excess deaths' tally for the past two years stands at zero.

Precisely zero. The lowest figure in the world.

The public-health measures adopted to stop Covid also stopped the annual incursions of flu. The country experienced

The Deck

2000 fewer deaths than normal between January 2020 and October 2022. Two thousand people have died here from Covid-related illness but that has dialled the running total of 'excess deaths' back to zero.

Figures can be cold things, and comparison can seem callous, but for the novelist that 'zero' offers some reassurance. The hastily assembled army of workers, those decisive laws, mandates and regulations, the whole barricade of protection held the border, delayed the arrival of the virus in the first crucial months of the pandemic and allowed time for mass vaccination. The barricade prevented the deaths of thousands. She has been enabled to sit at her desk playing with her paper dolls while outside her window, the world was busy.

She watched from a distance as the young and strong flung themselves at obstacles. They paddled tiny canoes through choppy waters and leapt over a bar set higher than the ceiling of her room. They swam and cycled and walked along a road with that weird rolling gait that looks nothing like actual walking and must be hell on the spine and the hips. They poured with sweat in searing heat, the kind of heat that caused seasoned athletes to faint, collapse, risk death in a record-breaking 'hottest Olympics ever'.

They twisted and turned and spun and went for gold, until they stood at last on the podium holding aloft a posy of flowers: green eustomas grown by farmers in Fukushima, who were no longer able to grow vegetables in soil radiated by the collapse of a nuclear-power plant during the earthquake of 2011. They grew flowers instead. Frilly green eustomas, and yellow sunflowers from Miyagi, where the parents planted them around a school from which their children had been swept away in the tsunami that accompanied the quake. Eustomas and sunflowers and a little mascot, a little chibi samurai in blue called Miraitowa, whose name combines 'past' and 'future'.

The athletes drove their perfect bodies to perform extraordinary feats before the silence of empty stadia. Their audience was invisible, concealed from the virus behind the television screens. The athletes waved their posies to them nevertheless. They held their hands to the camera to make a love heart, they blew kisses. And it all felt poignant and sad. And far too hot.

From a distance, the novelist also watched a war. A city street was reduced to rubble for reasons that seemed vague. A revisiting of a complex history, some business of territorial reclamation, the vile initiative of an egoistic leader. A family huddled in a basement, an apartment block was blown open on chairs and tables and the shatter of ordinary lives, a girl knelt, holding a heavy gun, an old lady retrieved her cat from the ruins of her home. Lines of people formed at the borders. The images the novelist had thought belonged in black and white to the distant past, to the catastrophic wars of the last century, reappeared in full colour as the present and a terrible future.

The novelist has watched rivers of rain falling on cities and villages. The thin layer of topsoil on which life depends melted to liquid and flowed down a hillside. A house was upended like a toy in the sludge. An apartment block bobbed out to sea. More lines of people waded up to the waist through filthy water. Hurricanes spun like Catherine wheels on the face of a small globe viewed from space. There was lightning and thunder and drought and cracked earth and fishing boats slumped in dust, and rivers shrunken to channels narrow enough to walk across. She has watched flames and dense black smoke and people

The Deck

sitting on picnic chairs on a beach surrounded by burning bush awaiting rescue.

In the eighteen months since the novelist began making things up at her computer, the smooth handfish has become extinct, with its puffy red lipstick and its little splayed hands walking about on the ocean floor off the coast of Tasmania. And the European hamster also, with its worried little face framed in white sideburn whiskers and its sweet clasped paws. The Indus River dolphin, rendered blind in the murk, has blundered its way to extinction in the mucky puddles that are all that is left of its once wide primeval sea.

One afternoon the novelist walked along a beach near her home. The sand glittered with fish. Shining bodies flapped in the sunlight, a species not normally found this far south, but here they were in their hundreds, gills flickering in the choking light of cruel day. A few people were out with buckets, but it felt weird. Too weird for foraging.

One summer morning some people stormed a library. They were angry because the council had insisted that staff and visitors to public places must be vaccinated and wear masks. They yelled and spat on the windows and wrote slogans about freedom in their own saliva. There were more angry people one afternoon driving in the northbound lane as the novelist was driving south. A truck, lights blazing, horn blaring, advanced, followed by vans and cars daubed with slogans. They were making their way towards the tip of the island where they anticipated a Dunkirk-style fleet of little boats would gather to carry them over the strait to Parliament, where they would protest about the masks and the vaccinations. They carried banners and a muddle of flags including Old Glory, as if the country had somehow

The Author's Conclusion

become, without anyone noticing, a fifty-first state. And nooses, because this was not so much a protest as a lynch mob, intent on executing the prime minister. As one enthusiast put it, they would 'hang her by her heels' from a parliamentary balcony, along with other ministers of the Crown, health officials and maybe a journalist or two.

They erected their tents on the parliamentary lawn. They danced to Twisted Sister, they were not going to take it, NO! Not any more! They put up a bouncy castle to entertain their children and posted images of themselves, their faces filled with the same vacuous manic glee you see in old photos from the American South, where the mob surrounds a tree from which dangle the strange fruit of black bodies.

They had been undone by fiction, by words and imaginings of doomsday scenarios featuring vicious cabals and grotesque evil. Hillary Clinton had killed a child, drunk her blood and wore her flayed skin as a mask. Princess Diana had been murdered as she was attempting to stop the attack on the Twin Towers. Lizard people walked the Earth and occupied the halls of power. Real, living people and news clips were mashed up with child sacrifice, Jewish blood libel and the pervasive fantasies of movies and online gaming in which heroes equipped with a range of ingenious weapons and augmented body parts take on the forces of evil. They face them down and bam bam bam defeat them in the name of big words like Liberty and Individual Freedom. And threaded through this confusion of fact and fiction was a deep mistrust of vaccination.

They were 'antivaxxers'.

The miracle that had spared the novelist, her generation and the generations that followed, the creeping death of tuberculosis,

The Deck

the horrors of polio, measles, scarlet fever and other yellow flag diseases of the quarantine islands had become an object of suspicion.

Here were people crazed with fear, threatening to execute the government ministers and health officials who were offering them protection from a new and dangerous disease.

There were never many of them. Their protest was small. Nothing to compare with the 15,000 who marched along Lambton Quay and the 50,000 who marched up Queen Street in May 1981 opposing an apartheid-based rugby tour. Nothing to compare with the 35,000 who marched in towns across the country in 1971 to protest against the country's involvement in Vietnam. Not as many as accompanied Whina Cooper on the hīkoi of 1975.

But the 2022 protestors were amplified, recorded and very loud. They yelled and threatened and pissed on the parliamentary lawn until after 23 days they were dispersed, setting fire on their way out to tents and trees and a playground slide.

The slide had been erected on the parliamentary lawn in 2019 to mark International Children's Day. It was beautiful, a sculpture as much as a piece of playground equipment, built of the very finest materials, of chrome and red beech. It was loved and played on, and it was also a symbol, as every object, every statue, every tree placed on a lawn in front of the seat of government must be. It symbolised the government's commitment to the wellbeing of the children within its jurisdiction. Its destruction also seemed symbolic. This was a visual representation of the alternative to democratic debate and good government. Mud and piss and charred wood.

The protestors trashing the parliamentary lawn, the people

The Author's Conclusion

in the convoy of trucks and Old Glory, the people spitting on the library windows, had been undone by fiction. Or rather, by a confusion of fact and fiction in which what was true and what was fantasy had become obscured.

It was a distinction that had once been clear. When the novelist was four and taken to a library for the first time, her father had pointed to the difference. The library was imposing, a stone-built Athenaeum on the main street constructed in the nineteenth century to deliver knowledge freely to the citizens of a properly functioning democracy. The ceilings were high, the big room was hushed, just the rustling of pages turning at the newspaper table and the thwump thwump of the heavy swing doors closing behind them.

'Now,' her father said, pointing to the shelves in the children's section to the right of the entrance, 'every week you can borrow two books from this side.' He pointed to books that had numbers in white ink on their spines. 'And two books from this side.'

Those books did not have numbers. The distinction was evident. The numbers meant those books were true. You could believe them. You could learn things from them. You could *know*. The books without numbers, on the other hand, were stories. They were made up, even when they featured real places like Paris or real people like the Queen. The important thing about those books was the way they made you *feel*.

The distinction held good for years until, as the world approached the millennium, it began to blur. It was the decade of the hybrid, when technological wizardry permitted Forrest Gump to turn up alongside Hitler or John Lennon and no one could spot that it was not real. Dinosaurs walked the Earth in what looked for all the world like a wildlife documentary. And when the onscreen hero entered the dark tower knowing danger lurked at every corner, the player held the gun in his own hand, shooting with devastating accuracy and feeling the sensation of destroying evil from the actual comfort of the living-room sofa.

It was the decade of the 'faction': a story that hybridised fact and fiction in the same way that chefs were creating fusions from the elements of separate traditional cuisines. Books were published that purported to be fact, marketed as autobiography, biography, history and travelogue, unless critical objection demanded their rebranding as fiction, their heroes not true but 'fictive metaphors'.

The novelist played with faction herself, in a short story that proposed with footnotes and great seriousness, that a former premier, Richard Seddon, celebrated as the epitome of the 'strong leader', had been a woman. The novelist was trying to make a feminist point about the notion of strength in leadership at a time when there had never been a woman prime minister in her country. When someone told her that her story had been held up at a public meeting as evidence of actual political chicanery and the concealment of truth, she thought it was amusing.

Not any more. Not when the mashup of fact and fantasy persuades people to threaten to hang an actual living, breathing woman prime minister with one of their nooses from a parliamentary balcony.

Fact itself is under fire. In 1921 the great CP Scott, editor of the *Manchester Guardian* for over 50 formative years, had famously stated that in news reportage, 'comment is free but facts are sacred'. A journalist's fact could be tested for its veracity, just as modern science depended upon the provable

The Author's Conclusion

hypothesis that distinguished it from magic or religious belief.

The distinction was useful. It offered certainty, a solid platform of objective detail in the midst of the flood of experience and sensation that is ordinary human existence. It was an ideal, of course, and not always achieved. Those sacred facts were always subject to personal prejudice, party political affiliation and editorial bias. But Scott's dictum remained a journalistic aspiration, until it ran slap bang into the Trumpian alternative where no fact is reliable, let alone sacred, and every report can be doubted as fake, spin or propaganda.

In this decade when the deliberate confusion of fact and fantasy is all-pervasive, what is the point of sitting in a room making things up? What can be the point of fiction, imagining an alternative reality, as the world outside the window is relentlessly destroying itself, one hamster, one fire, one war, one flood, one playground slide at a time?

Stories have always offered insights into other lives, the minutiae of private delight, private shame, the curiosity of strangeness or the comfort of recognition and a sense of shared humanity. They have offered a narrative structure that suggests that there is order in chaos. They have confirmed the reality of redemption and justice. They have delivered the satisfactions of style and language. They have entertained, amused, dealt that frisson of horror, in the game of 'let's pretend' and 'what if?' that is played in the private space between storyteller and audience.

But what can fiction offer now?

There is that story — a true story, fact not fiction — about a plane, British Airways flight 009, on its way from Heathrow to Melbourne in June 1982. Thousands of metres above

The Deck

Indonesia it encountered a cloud of volcanic ash. Far below, a volcano had erupted. A high plume of molten glass rose and entered the jet engines, and all four clogged and stopped. Flight 009, with 256 passengers on board, began its inexorable glide down towards the ocean. Flames trailed from its engines, choking, sulphurous smoke filled the cabin and the pilot made an address to the passengers that has become legendary for its calm understatement.

> *Ladies and gentlemen, this is your captain speaking. We have a small problem. All four engines have stopped. We are doing our damndest to get it under control. I trust you are not in too much distress.*

Then he and his crew set about doing just that: their damndest, commencing the restart drill, over and over, alerting Jakarta Airport of their predicament and finally, when the oxygen masks threatened to fail, taking the plane into a steep 6000-foot dive in the hope that they would find sufficient oxygen at a lower altitude to keep them all alive. The dive had an unexpected and felicitous effect. As the plane dropped past 13,000 feet, the ash plugs were dislodged, the engines roared back into life and the plane was brought safely in to land.

It's an extraordinary story, told in interviews, a documentary film and in a book written by one of the passengers, Betty Tootell, who was travelling back to New Zealand with her 81-year-old mother. Together, as their plane fell from the sky and the eerie quiet of extreme terror filled the cabin, she writes that the two of them read fiction.

The Author's Conclusion

'Mother picked up *Northanger Abbey* and I delved again into *Mansfield Park*.'

Side by side they entered a world imagined long before by a young woman, of houses and the people who inhabit them, and the task that never leaves us, of finding love.

The novelist thinks about this as she tidies her desk and puts away her paper dolls, her novel done. Disasters even greater than a volcanic eruption loom beyond the window, though that, too, is always part of the mix in these quivery islands. Twenty-eight earthquakes recorded on Geonet since yesterday morning, slight shimmerings detected beneath the placid waters of a caldera that last exploded 1800 years ago with a roar that was audible around the world.

On the wall by her desk there's a poem. It's printed carefully in felt tip with all the letters in different colours. Her granddaughter wrote it at school when she was seven and the teacher kept it. She pinned it to the wall among the lovingly detailed drawings of futuristic spacecraft and wonky ponies with crossed legs.

THE FUTURE

I go to sleep each night
thinking of the future
even though we may not have one
because of Climate Change
wondering what will happen,
when it will happen, where it
will happen. Sometimes I feel
like a boat on a stormy sea,
torn between then, there,
now, here.

The Deck

The poem is there because it makes the novelist consider what she is doing, sitting at her desk making things up when small children are imagining such things. When the littlest ones play in the sunlight across the road in a dwindling world. Where can be the comfort of fiction when all the facts are pointing downward to annihilation?

Bing bang bong . . .

There was a moment, though, back when she was starting on her novel. The pandemic was still unfamiliar. The country had gone into lockdown for several weeks and a sudden silence had fallen, not just over the world outside the novelist's window, but all across the globe. Only a few months earlier, 19.09 million tourists had been flying into Paris each year, 8 million visited Barcelona, 11 million flew to India, 4.8 million clogged Venice. And 3.8 million came in to land on the novelist's small islands for a few days of feverish activity. They drove in buses to see a lake, they flew in helicopters to see a glacier, they rode in jet boats through a canyon.

Then suddenly the fever and agitation stopped. The planes were parked up in the desert bone-yards, countries withdrew behind their borders and the world went quiet. Boulevards and plazas emptied and the air cleared. The snowy peaks of the Himalayas floated into view from cities many kilometres distant. More birds sang.

It felt like a glimpse of the past, like something remembered from furthest childhood.

The novelist remembers scarlet fever. It was a blur of heat and nightmare, blood soaking the pillow, the chill of a cold facecloth on hot skin, a confusion of day and night. Until one day she woke up.

The Author's Conclusion

Sunlight was dappling the bedroom wall through the leaves of the tree outside her window. The sound of the kids playing in the school grounds beyond the back fence was distant and peaceful. Her skin felt cool and new, and her dad gathered her up in her new skin and carried her because her legs were too wobbly to stand, out into the garden where the flowering currant by the dunny was in full pink blossom.

Last time she had seen it, it had been bare twig and shreds of damp black leaf.

Bees wriggled in the flowers, and her father held her in close so she could look properly. Each bumblebee had tiny wiry legs with little yellow rompers of pollen. Heads down, they squirmed in the flowers, and the air was filled with their buzzing and the smell of blossom, and everything dazzled and wriggled with life.

The pause at the start of the pandemic felt like that. A glimpse of the past, but also a glimpse of a possible future.

We can pause. We can stop. We have a choice. We can imagine another story.

The pandemic is not over, yet there are cries on all sides to revert to the way the world was before the virus, to return to something called 'normal', no matter how compromised or destructive. There are great forces, too, ranged against optimism.

But there was that glimpse of the mountains, wasn't there? That quiet, kind moment?

Maybe a new mode of thinking and being was setting seed among the lockdowns and masks and global tallies?

Maybe a new world is taking shape at the end of the road being walked by the novelist's paper dolls?

It's as valid to imagine that as it is to imagine desolation and destruction as the outcome of a plague. It's possible to imagine a renaissance of beauty and creativity, a reformation that chooses a new god with a new ending, or maybe no ending at all, no apocalypse, just a gentle continuity.

    The novelist would settle for that.

    A life lived beneath sun and moon and stars in their customary alignment, as light as a bubble.

Confesso nondimeno le cose di questo mondo non avere stabilita alcuna, ma sempre essere in mutamento e così potrebbe della mia lingua esser intervenuto . . .

Conclusione dell'Autore
Decameron di Giovanni Boccaccio

I acknowledge that the things of this world have no stability, but are ever undergoing change; and this may have befallen my tongue . . .

The Author's Conclusion
The Decameron by Giovanni Boccaccio

ACKNOWLEDGEMENTS

There are many people who have contributed to this book through their writing or in conversations and interviews. The author owes special thanks to:

Mike Atkinson
Nicholas Bollen
Kathryn Bosi Monteath
Danny Buchanan
Chris Crowe
Caroline Davies
Nigel Dunlop
David Elliot
Michelle Elvy
Wendy Harrex
James Harris

Jocelyn Harris
Doug Hood
John Kaiser
Eleni Grace May
Philip May
Moira McCourt
Patrick O'Neill
Huia Parker
Steve Parker
Susannah Poole
Ursula Poole
Duncan Sarkies

Thank you to Rachel Scott for her meticulous editing.

And thank you above all to Harriet Allan and the team at Penguin Random House New Zealand, especially Olivia Win-Ricketts, Gemma Parmentier and, in memoriam, Juliet McGhie.

For more information about our titles,
go to www.penguin.co.nz